PARTICLES IN THE AIR

JENNA PODJASEK, MD

bancroft
press

Cover Design: Alex Kirby
Interior Design: TracyCopesCreative.com
Author Photo: Megan Drane, fireflynightsphotography.com

Particles in the Air Title Info
978-1-61088-537-9 (HC)
978-1-61088-538-6 (PB)
978-1-61088-539-3 (Ebook)
978-1-61088-540-9 (PDF)
978-1-61088-541-6 (Audiobook)

Published by Bancroft Press
"Books that Enlighten"
410-358-0658
P.O. Box 65360,
Baltimore, MD 21209
www.bancroftpress.com

Printed in the United States of America

To Rebecca Petschke, 1954-2012

Prologue:
Mission Beach, San Diego, CA

Emily Williams, prone and relaxing on her beach towel, closed her eyes, her floral cover-up flapping in the breeze. Her book, momentarily forgotten, lay spine-up on the sand. The nearly deserted beach was quiet except for the waves lapping the shore. Her reverie was broken by the low voice of her boyfriend Matt.

"It's too cold," he complained. "Let's go." They had been there more than an hour and his cheeks were flushed from the cool, salty air.

She raised an eyebrow without opening her eyes. "You just want to go to my house because my parents aren't home."

"Get your mind out of the gutter, Williams," he said with mock innocence. "Maybe I just want to warm up. You have me out here freezing my ass off."

Emily sat up and hit him playfully on the arm. "I told you to grab a sweatshirt before we left." Purposely changing the subject, she asked, "So, what do you think? A 4.1, 4.2?"

"Hmm…I'm going to say a 4.5," Matt said absently, gazing out at the navy-blue water. He leaned forward, pulling his towel out from beneath him, half-heartedly shook out the sand, and draped it around his shoulders while sitting back down on the damp sand.

Born and raised in southern California, both Emily and Matt had grown accustomed to the occasional low-magnitude earthquake. So when they felt the mild trembling shortly after their arrival at the beach that morning, they acknowledged it with a shared, knowing look.

As Emily propped herself up, she vaguely registered that there was something different about the water today. It had receded farther out than she had ever seen it. Pieces of kelp and driftwood dotted the wet sand, broken by the occasional glint of a shell. She felt an unexplained spark of unease.

Emily picked up her paperback and tossed Matt his waterproof tablet. "Just a few more minutes," she said, "then we can head back. It's so… peaceful out here today."

Typically, nearby Mission Boulevard was cluttered with tourists, but the day's chilly, gray weather had kept many off the beach. Emily imagined the warm oceanside restaurants and shops, including Sammie's Creamery, bustling today. She was grateful to have a day off from the chaos there. These days, it seemed like all of her free time was spent scooping ice cream into waffle cones for whiny kids with sticky money.

She heard it before she saw it, a roaring that swelled in intensity, reminding her of an approaching train. She looked over her shoulder toward the road, her eyes scanning for the source of the unfamiliar sound. When she turned back, the blood drained from her face. The world around her shrank, and all she could hear was the furious pumping of her own heart.

An enormous roiling wall of white water barreled toward them. For a moment, she sat frozen, uncomprehending. Then, as if one, she and Matt were both up and running.

As she ran, the sound became deafening and Emily fought the urge to cover her ears. Her eyes locked on the elevated boardwalk ahead, she pushed herself as hard as she could toward it. Suddenly, a freezing hammer slammed into her, knocking the air from her lungs. Her teeth clacked together violently, slicing open her tongue. Her mouth immediately filled with a mix of coppery blood, silt, and saltwater. A crushing pain enveloped her as darkness overtook her.

Chapter 1
The Centers for Disease Control and Prevention, Atlanta, GA
Day -50

D r. Mallory Hayes focused intently on the micropipette in her hand, dimly aware that inside her bulky positive-pressure suit, she was sweating profusely. A single drop of perspiration escaped the moisture gathering on her forehead, stinging her right eye. She paused briefly to blink it away. Her movements were controlled and precise. She knew rushing could mean mistakes, and mistakes could be deadly in the CDC's biosafety level-4 lab.

Mallory carefully depressed the white button on the micropipette, dispensing the Marburg virus into the waiting open tube.

Marburg causes a devastating infection in humans with a clinical picture similar to Ebola. Contrary to popular belief, Marburg and Ebola cause hemorrhage in only a subset of patients, and typically only in the final stages of severe illness. Patients with both viruses commonly present with high fever, shaking chills, and malaise. Many also experience severe headaches, crushing muscle pain, vomiting, and voluminous diarrhea. In many infected individuals, this progresses to respiratory distress, hypotension, and multi-organ failure. A staggering three out of five individuals succumb to the disease.

Mallory firmly closed the cap with her left hand and, with a click, popped the clear pipette tip into the biohazard bin. Quietly blowing out a breath, she placed the tube in the centrifuge, selecting the appropriate setting to start the machine.

Mallory now turned her attention to her workspace, methodically placing her materials onto a metal tray. She slid the tray into the autoclave for decontamination. Ensuring her air line was unencumbered behind her, she opened the door to the first of three decontamination chambers and removed the outer pair of shoe covers, placing them in one of a dozen fire-engine red biohazard containers dotting the lab.

Mallory dipped the gloved hands of her positive-pressure suit in the stainless-steel bucket of disinfectant, disconnected the air hose, and draped it over her arm. After keying her code into the airlocked door, it opened with a soft *whoosh*. She stepped into the second chamber and closed the door behind her, double checking that it was firmly latched.

Mallory reattached her air hose and turned on the chemical shower, her breath and heart rate quickening. After several clicks, the shower spurted on and began to coat her with a pink disinfectant.

For a few moments, her vision was completely obscured as foam spattered and ran down her helmet. Mallory immediately took deep, practiced breaths to quell the rising panic she experienced at this point in the decontamination process. *One, two, three…*she silently counted. Pre-programmed to dispense disinfectant for 120 seconds, the shower head clicked loudly, then abruptly stopped. As the mechanism switched to water, there was another loud click. When the soapy film of her mask cleared, her panic eased.

Mallory finished the rest of the decontamination process on autopilot, checking for leaks, removing the suit, and finally proceeding to the last chamber for a personal shower.

Not for the first time, she reflected on the irony that she could work effortlessly with one of the deadliest viruses in the world, where a small tear in her suit might prove fatal, yet experienced debilitating claustrophobia in enclosed spaces. Rationally, she knew there was nothing to fear about the disinfectant process; however, this did nothing to eliminate her anxiety. Mallory donned a fresh set of scrubs and headed back to her shared office in the attached CDC administration building.

She dropped her bag on her desk and sank into her chair, feeling some of the tension leave her body. Her office mate, Rory Wilson, grinned at her over his super-sized Mac computer screen.

"Long morning?" he asked. Rory had the appearance of a scientist straight off Central Casting, with his large glasses and pale, nearly translucent skin. His rail-thin extremities had never graced the inside of a gym.

Shared, often demanding, 30-hour shifts at the hospital had created a fast camaraderie between the two. At the beginning of their friendship, she was surprised to learn he was a passionate classic rock fan and occasionally filled in as a backup guitarist in a local band.

Mallory experienced the same comfort she always felt when in proximity to Rory. He was a genuine person whom she could be herself around.

"A bit long," she said, not wanting to go into detail.

Rory was the only friend she had confided in about her severe case of claustrophobia; however, she still preferred not to talk about it, and somehow managed not to, no matter the circumstances. Rather than take a high-rise elevator, she had once climbed twenty-three flights to visit a friend in her downtown Atlanta condo. To catch her breath before knocking on the door, she was forced to wait several minutes in the stairwell. At work, she told her colleagues she preferred the exercise of the stairs. She had never set foot in the elevator at the CDC.

"So how was the date on Friday? I want details," Mallory said, turning on her computer and straightening her desk. Rory had recently decided to join several dating sites, including, to Mallory's amusement, Tinder.

"Don't think I failed to notice that you're changing the subject," Rory said, "but it was an *interesting* night, to say the least." He took a sip from his coffee cup, the words "Handsome Bastard" visible on the side in blocky script.

Her anxiety forgotten, Mallory listened and laughed as Rory gave her a play-by-play of the evening.

Chapter 2
Paragon Genomics, Malmö, Sweden
Day −50

D r. Erik Lindgren walked quickly on the slick cobblestone street, eager to get to his lab and begin work for the day. It was an unseasonably cool and blustery day in Malmö. The air felt thick with moisture. Any minute, Erik expected another surge from the dark clouds above him. He quickened his pace further, Burberry umbrella clutched in his hand.

The historic buildings he passed were a mixture of Western European brick and wood dwellings with row upon row of small windows. Mossy green cupulas, spires, and chimneys in earthy hues were visible above the roof line. Occasionally, homes painted a muted blue or red served to break up the monochromatic landscape. Previously rare in Malmö, sleek, modern lines of new hotels and shops were becoming more common.

Erik's lab was in one such contemporary building, fourteen floors of smooth metal and glass, the words "Paragon Genomics" embossed in hard-to-miss letters. Erik walked briskly through the double doors, ignoring the polite nod from the security guard. His mind was already in the lab, working on the next phase of his study.

Bypassing his office, Erik headed directly to the lab at the end of the hall, his identification already out and ready for the second security guard stationed at the desk outside the lab. He stepped into a small entry room and entered his 8-digit pin into the keypad, waiting impatiently for the latch to disengage.

Most labs have an air of quiet clutter to them—surfaces packed with glass beakers, lab notebooks, various machines, and boxes of supplies.

Erik insisted his lab be kept in pristine condition, with everything organized in the most efficient manner and tucked out of sight.

His lab was the largest in the building, covering most of an entire floor. Erik was well known in the scientific community for his groundbreaking research in gene therapy. He had been recruited several years ago by the CEO of Paragon himself. The promise of generous stock options and unlimited resources was too intoxicating to pass up.

Wordlessly, Erik handed his coat, umbrella, and briefcase to one of his assistants, then slipped on a crisp white lab coat and blue nitrile gloves, and began to work.

∿∿

That evening, Erik arrived home earlier than usual, wondering to himself what Ada had made for dinner. Ada was 10 years younger than him—he was 42. Her smooth, creamy skin and wavy raven hair made her appear even more youthful than her chronological age.

He swung open the door and was surprised to find the kitchen dark and silent.

"Ada!" he called out. "Where are you?"

He found her in the master bedroom. She was removing items from hangers and placing them into an overflowing suitcase. He watched, stunned, as she threw a few sweaters onto the pile.

She had planned on being gone before I even arrived home. She didn't even have the decency to discuss this with me.

Erik glared at her, his irritation barely concealing his fury. She refused to acknowledge his presence and continued gathering her things, her face impassive.

Without warning, Erik lunged at her. He jerked her violently toward him and grabbed both of her upper arms in a strong, vise-like grip. Her ruby lips dropped open in disbelief. The shock on her face was so exaggerated it was almost comical.

Before this moment, he had never come close to physically harming her. He had rarely even raised his voice to her. He noted with intense satisfaction that her surprise quickly turned to fear as he continued to squeeze tighter. He felt his control returning, dissipating a small portion of his white-hot fury.

How dare Ada, after all I've given her? She is nothing without me. Just an unremarkable artist.

As a single tear slipped down her cheek, he savored the terror in her eyes.

∿

It was at a young age that Erik realized he was different. Always a solitary person, he preferred books and long afternoons in the patch of woods near his tiny Stockholm apartment to the company of others. Part of this was an escape from the reality of his home life, he understood, but it was also how he preferred to spend his time.

It wasn't until age eight that he recognized the necessity of blending in, of showing others what they expected to see. He vividly recalls sitting outside the head teacher's office, squirming uncomfortably in a dark orange chair placed against the wall. He could hear snippets of conversation through the thin walls.

"… said Hanna stole his pencil when he wasn't looking. She apparently refused to give it back… took the time to sharpen another pencil and stabbed her... wasn't seriously hurt but there was a lot of blood… quite a commotion. Many of the children were crying…"

He heard his mom let out a soft, pitiful sob. He felt his mouth turn down in disgust at her weakness.

"… verbal and math scores are off the charts … it's a shame…why we need to expel him…."

He was unable to make out what his mom said in reply. A minute later, the door opened. She stepped out, her eyes red-rimmed, and refused to look at him. He silently followed her to the car, glad to be off the uncomfortable chair and getting back to his book. Plus, he was hungry. He glanced at his mother out of the corner of his eye with barely concealed distaste. He had gone without lunch today because the only food he could find in the cupboards were a few stale crackers. His mother had promised she would go to the store today.

That evening after dinner, he could hear his parents talking in low voices in the kitchen. Margot, his sister, was sitting on the floor close to the TV, the volume low and unobtrusive.

Suddenly, his dad appeared in the doorway. He caught sight of Erik on the couch and staggered over, the scent of alcohol assaulting Eric's nostrils. His father's face was flushed a deep purple, reminding Erik of a ripe plum.

Erik jumped in surprise as the book was unceremoniously ripped from his hands. In the next second, he was slapped—hard—across the face, his bottom lip instantly splitting open. His father regularly hit his mother, especially when he was drinking; however, he had never before raised a fist to either Erik or Margot.

Erik remembers staring down at the bright red droplets falling to the floor. He watched as they merged into the cheap carpet and blossomed into blotches of rich crimson. Curling his small body into a ball on the floor, he instinctively covered his head as he was struck over and over.

After that, Erik carefully studied others around him. At his new school, he learned to mimic his fellow students' behavior.

He practiced at home in the cramped bathroom, rank with the smell of mildew and unwashed towels. Finding a clear spot in the cloudy mirror, he rehearsed: slight frown and down-cast eyes for sadness, open face and hint of a smile for friendly, inclining of the head with a raised eyebrow and cheeky grin for mischievous. He memorized these expressions, refining them over time.

He excelled academically at school, although it was far from challenging. In fact, he was bored much of the time. As he progressed into high school, he managed to fit in and create a few superficial friendships. He knew he was good-looking, tall with chiseled features and an endearing chin dimple.

He learned quickly, adapting and imitating those around him. One of his favorite challenges was ingratiating himself into the lives of insecure teenage girls for the express purpose of taking advantage of them. He found it surprisingly easy if he followed one simple mantra: systematically uncover their weaknesses, then tell them exactly what they wanted to hear. He became a master of subtle, but astonishingly effective, flattery and manipulation.

He showered his targets with compliments and simple, inexpensive flowers from the supermarket. He made them smile with his practiced, self-deprecating humor, something his classmates, regardless of their hormones, would never consider doing.

∿∿∿

The next day, Erik was shaken from his thoughts when a technician asked for clarification on a new protocol. Erik explained the procedure quickly and dismissively. He had little patience for those with less comprehension and intelligence.

"Are you feeling all right, Dr. Lindgren?" the technician asked hesitantly. Erik knew staff members were used to treading carefully around him, so he was startled at this personal question.

"Yes, of course," he replied sharply. He realized that he had been caught staring out the window, deep in thought. This had happened several times that morning, which was uncharacteristic of him. He took a deep breath and resolved to focus.

He turned his attention back to the lab table and the sequencing mechanism humming in front of him. His current study involved the insertion of healthy genes into the cells of guinea pigs with Adenosine Deaminase (ADA) deficiency, an enzyme essential for a functioning immune system. In humans, ADA deficiency causes a devastating disease called Severe Combined Immunodeficiency, also known as SCID. Without this enzyme, certain immune cells, called T and B lymphocytes, are not produced. Without these vital cells, there is virtually no effective defense against the viruses, bacteria, and fungi that the human body encounters every day.

The focus of Erik's work was perfecting the delivery of healthy, functional genes into diseased cells. That is why Paragon had hired him. Since the conception of gene therapy, scientists had encountered a litany of safety hurdles. Scientists hadn't been able to develop a gene insertion that was safe enough for humans. A large part of the problem was the inability to target specific sequences in the genome. If the wrong cells were inadvertently targeted, serious side effects, such as cancer, might occur.

Erik's groundbreaking publication in protein engineering was the catalyst that prompted Paragon to recruit him three years ago. With access to state-of-the-art lab equipment and technology, Erik engineered a novel enzyme, named lutase-2, that facilitates gene insertion exactly where it's needed. Gene therapy has the potential to treat hundreds of diseases, with profits projected in the billions.

Satisfied with his work, Erik finished up for the day, leaving his lab assistant to clean up and complete a few final tasks. His heart rate increased in anticipation of the evening to come. By the time he exited the building, a heavy blanket of darkness had fallen. He raised his arm for a taxi.

"23 Slottsgatan," Erik instructed. The driver pulled away from the curb, merging into the light traffic.

Erik was relieved the trip was over in a matter of minutes; he needed a release from the intensity of his work and his problems with Ada. His Italian leather shoes crunched on the paver stones as he walked toward the oversized wooden doors of The Imperial Club. The building had the appearance of a large, luxurious boutique hotel, complete with lavish grounds and valet parking. Erik felt the familiar surge of adrenaline at the prospect of a long, unencumbered night at the blackjack tables.

Chapter 3
Cynthia and Robert Hayes' Residence, Atlanta, Georgia
Day −47

The sound of tinkling silverware and muted conversation, punctuated by occasional laughter, filled the dining room. Mallory looked around appreciatively at her close-knit family. They were celebrating her parents' thirty-fourth wedding anniversary. Her boyfriend, Marcus, sat next to her, tapping away on his iPhone. Swallowing her irritation, Mallory turned toward her sister.

Mallory was especially close to her younger sister, born just eleven months after her. They had grown up together, sharing everything from crayons and Cabbage Patch Dolls to clothes and books. The two even shared the same bedroom through high school, even though there were enough rooms for each to have her own. They had occasionally argued over boys or school friends, but they always made up and remained fiercely loyal to one and other. Mallory, who had always encouraged Kate to study harder, seemed more disappointed in her substandard grades than her parents.

"How's the new job going?" Mallory asked.

"I've only been there a few days, but it's great so far," Kate answered. "I love the kids, but the parents can be a bit demanding at times."

After high school, Kate had found work as a server in an upscale French restaurant, Canapés et Crème. She stayed there for several years before deciding to go back to school part-time and earn a degree in early childhood education. She had recently started a job teaching in an affluent school in the heart of downtown Atlanta.

"It's pre-school. Shouldn't the kids be there to learn socialization skills and other fundamentals? Yesterday, one parent of a three-year-old asked me if our curriculum included self-esteem exercises." Kate shook her head and smiled. "Learning is different from when we were kids. I remember being introduced to letters in kindergarten. Now kindergarteners are learning to read."

"Things *are* different," Mallory agreed. Mallory noted the renewed energy her sister seemed to have and was glad she had found a career that made her happy.

There was a moment of silence. Trying to draw Marcus into the conversation, Kate asked brightly, "How're you doing, Marcus?"

Marcus was still typing on his phone but glanced up at Kate. Mallory thought she saw the briefest flash of annoyance, but he quickly recovered and flashed them his trademark lopsided smile.

Marcus and Mallory had met more than a year ago, attending a Braves game with mutual friends. Mallory found him charming and witty. He was slightly shorter than her, with penetrating blue eyes and dark hair. Her attraction to him was immediate and intense.

"Things are great," he said amicably. "It's really busy at the firm, but it's a good busy."

Mallory excused herself and let the two continue their conversation, murmuring she would help with dessert. Mallory joined her mother in the kitchen, grabbing the dessert plates and fresh forks. They worked in practiced sync, cutting up the homemade strawberry cheesecake and preparing the after-dinner coffee.

When her mom began talking about her latest book club meeting, Mallory's mind wandered to Marcus.

Marcus worked in a public relations firm founded with two college friends. Although the firm seemed to struggle financially for the first few years, things had picked up recently and Marcus had just signed on some sizeable clients.

He surprised Mallory last week by showing up at her door with a wrapped bottle of Dom Perignon Champagne accompanied by takeout from her favorite Italian restaurant. He flashed her his signature grin and popped the top before the front door was even closed.

"What's the occasion?" she asked, amber liquid bubbling onto the foyer floor. She was already in leggings and a comfortable sweater, ready to settle in for the night with *The Woman in the Window* by A.J. Finn.

"I was able to sign Inspire Intel today. It's going to be an amazing opportunity for the company." He hesitated. "It's also an apology of sorts for having spent so much time at the office lately."

They stayed up far into the night talking and binging Netflix. They polished off the Champagne in the early hours of the morning before stumbling, laughing, to Mallory's bedroom.

Chapter 4
Holdings Condominium Complex, Malmö, Sweden
Day –47

Erik awoke with a start, sucking in a sharp breath. Moonlight filtered through the open curtains of the window. He squinted in confusion, willing his eyes to focus in the gloom.

His head pounded relentlessly, right along with his rapidly beating heart. Images from the last few hours began to flood his brain.

The metallic tang of blood filled his mouth and he began to shiver uncontrollably. His tongue found the empty socket where his molar had been just hours before, the pulpy tissue still oozing. He stumbled over to the sink and vomited. Each heave of his abdomen caused an excruciating spasm of his chest and abdominal muscles. He continued retching even as his stomach emptied.

In a haze of pain, he realized some of his ribs were probably broken. He was able to comprehend little more as the pain became all-encompassing.

After several minutes, Erik caught his breath and slowly slid onto the floor, his back scraping painfully against the brass handle of the cabinet. He looked down to see smears of dark, sticky blood on his bare chest and purple bruises beginning to form on his torso and abdomen.

His eyes were drawn to a faint silver glint from the table. He realized, with increasing dread, that it was his tooth. Shiny and white, it sat there in sharp contrast to the table's espresso color. Erik ran to the sink, making it just before the bile rose again.

᠕᠕᠕

Erik stumbled down the hall and lowered himself gingerly onto his bed. He laid down and closed his eyes, trying to piece together what had happened.

He vaguely recalled inserting his key into the lock and pushing open his front door. As he walked in, he felt a sharp crack to his skull.

He awoke naked on his kitchen table, a pair of strong arms with some type of cord or rope holding him down. He had tried raising his throbbing head, but a hand shot out and grasped his hair with an iron grip, causing him to freeze. What happened next happened so fast he had trouble believing it.

"I'm going to say this once. Niklas wants his money—the one million kronor you owe him." The man spoke slowly, as if to a child, his words heavily accented in Russian. "We will collect the money in exactly two weeks. If it's not all here, the interest will increase ten percent each week. Show me you understand."

Erik didn't answer right away as his pounding head tried desperately to catch up. His eyes struggled to focus on the face looming above him. He was able to make out a black balaclava and a pair of cold, dark eyes. Another man stood by the table, dressed in jeans and a plain navy shirt, with a similar balaclava pulled low over his face.

His head jerked roughly and slammed down, Erik shouted, "I owe Niklas one million kronor. The interest increases each week!"

"Excellent." The man paused, and then added, as if in afterthought, "One more thing. Starting today and continuing each week we're forced to visit, you lose a tooth."

Before he could comprehend what was happening, a rubber ball was stuffed in the back of his throat, causing him to gag. A meaty hand pushed his head back onto the table while the second man pulled out a pair of pliers. He forced them into Erik's mouth, latching firmly onto a molar.

Erik shook his head furiously and the pliers slipped off with a squeak.

His terror was absolute. He couldn't hear anything beyond the whooshing of blood in his ears. His nostrils flared as he noisily pushed air in and out through his nose. He screamed behind the rubber ball, the sound coming out as a muffled screech.

The other man put a forearm on Erik's face and leaned in with all his weight. Erik was momentarily distracted from the pliers by the blazing pain from his head. Suddenly, the pliers were back in his mouth. There was a crack and another explosion of pain. When the pliers were pulled out, he caught sight of a glistening tooth.

The ball was removed, and warm liquid flooded his mouth. He was untied and pushed off the table. Erik rolled onto his side, curling into the fetal position, spitting out blood. He emitted an involuntary, guttural groan.

"If you aren't here next week..." A pause and then he was kicked viciously in the side. "Are you listening to me? Look at me."

The man's dark eyes locked onto Erik's as he forced himself to look up.

"If you aren't here next week, I will visit your mother in Almvik. If she is unavailable, I will go to your sister's flat in Stockholm—Margot, isn't it? Unfortunately..." Another pause. "I'm afraid they will lose more than just a tooth."

The man let the words sink in. "If necessary, I will hunt down every single person you know, one by one."

Erik noted the man's calm, flat tone. He didn't doubt he meant exactly what he said.

∿∿

That evening, Erik lay awake for hours, his mind running furiously through his options. He tossed and turned, unable to find a position that didn't aggravate the stabbing pain in his ribs. Alternating impotence and rage threatened to overwhelm him, making it difficult to concentrate. He finally fell into an uneasy sleep, his sheets damp with sweat and crusted blood.

The next morning, as he pulled on his tailored gray pants, he noted the professional efficiency the two visitors had exhibited. Each breath caused severe pain. His mouth and head were throbbing. Yet, once he was dressed, there was not a single visible mark on him.

Taking a sick day was not an option. He had just completed the last phase of his study and was days away from presenting his findings to Paragon's upper echelon. His mood lifted slightly as he thought of his recent results.

He had unequivocally demonstrated the ability of his novel protein, lutase-2, to target very specific genes. Even more importantly, he was able to avoid activation of the non-target genes. None of the guinea pigs exhibited any of the side effects previously reported. He had the majority of his article already written and ready to submit to *Nature,* one of the best-known and prestigious scientific journals in the world.

He had accomplished what no other scientist had been able to do.

After he showed Corporate what he had achieved, perhaps he could get an advance on his patent royalties. After all, they were slated to make an almost inconceivable amount of money from his work.

Chapter 5
The Centers for Disease Control and Prevention, Atlanta, GA
Day −43

Mallory's feet thumped rhythmically on the pavement between the Global Communication Center and the campus lake. She looked forward to this run before work, when her surroundings were quiet and still. The air was warm and comfortable, with relatively low humidity. Breathing hard, she ended her three-mile run at the gleaming entrance to the main building.

She stretched for a few minutes in the dewy grass, then pulled out her key card and scanned it into the automatic reader. The lobby was bright with sunlight from the enormous wall of windows.

"Hi there, Vernon," she said, warmly greeting the day guard. She handed over her bag and stepped through the security scanner.

"Have a great day, Doc," he replied with a grin.

Mallory went directly to the women's locker room. She peeled off her damp Lululemon running clothes and tossed them in her bag. After a two-minute shower, she dressed and proceeded to the canteen to pick up her usual breakfast of oatmeal and blueberries.

At her desk, she resumed where she had left off on her article for *Virology*. With Rory out in the field this week, she had the office to herself. She planned to take full advantage of the quiet today and get some research and writing done.

Rory had texted her from Nashville last night, where he was investigating a large Salmonella outbreak. Several pet owners and pet shop employees, all exposed to a certain species of small turtle, had been hospitalized with dehydration.

Mallory sighed. She was both dreading and looking forward to her on-call field work next month. She loved the challenge of finding and isolating an outbreak, but she was anxious for the plane flight it inevitably entailed. She didn't sleep much the night before airplane travel and often needed a small dose of diazepam to get through the flight itself. But she refused to let her phobia hinder her as a physician or investigator.

She returned her attention to her writing and, absorbed by her search for supporting papers, barely noticed the rest of the morning fly by. She glanced at her phone and was surprised it was one in the afternoon. She stretched, deciding to grab a sandwich from the café.

She popped her head into the open door of her supervisor, Dr. Nathan Lee, to ask if he wanted anything. Although Dr. Lee was nearing retirement, he was still a dedicated physician and researcher who spent much of his extra time mentoring the younger, less experienced MDs. For her, his guidance had been invaluable.

"No thanks, Mallory. I brought some lunch from home today. How's the paper coming along?" he asked. She forced herself to avoid looking at his unruly eyebrows, which reminded her of two bushy caterpillars.

"It's getting there. I should have a first draft for you to look over in just a few days. Thanks for your input." She smiled appreciatively. "Be back soon."

∿

The café line was blissfully short, the typical crowd having dwindled as the afternoon wore on. The comforting aroma of coffee and bread filled the air. Mallory ordered a garden vegetable soup, half of a chicken salad sandwich, and three large coffees. She knew Dr. Lee and Vernon enjoyed an afternoon coffee—she was going to surprise both with a steaming cup.

Chapter 6
Paragon Institute of Sweden, Malmö
Day −42

Erik glanced at the large digital clock in the lab. In a few minutes, he would present his findings to Paragon Corporate's chieftains. He was feeling confident and well-prepared. He knew his findings were going to fundamentally change medical treatment forever. The only thing bothering him was that he would need to ask the group for an advance on his earnings. It made him slightly uncomfortable, but it couldn't be helped given his situation with Niklas.

He quickly pushed the thought aside as he removed his lab coat and walked to his office. He slipped into his black, tailor-made suit jacket. In the attached bathroom, he straightened his tie and smoothed his hair. Satisfied, he slung his computer bag over his shoulder and headed to the bay of elevators.

Erik checked in with the receptionist and was told to have a seat in the waiting area. Momentarily thrown, Erik hesitated. He had never been told to wait before. He was always whisked into the conference room with a gracious smile amid offers of coffee or tea. He turned slowly and walked to the large couch. He sat, sinking into the buttery soft leather, not bothering to hide his annoyance.

The waiting area was tastefully decorated in warm cream tones and bronze accents. He took out his phone and checked his email. Every few minutes, he looked up and glared at the receptionist. She was studiously avoiding eye contact. He began to feel the first, faint tendrils of apprehension.

After an excruciating twenty minutes, she said, "Dr. Lindgren, if you would follow me."

Erik followed her wordlessly down the corridor and entered the familiar conference room. With a soft click, the door shut behind him. He immediately approached the CEO, Aarav Patel, shifting his expression to appear humble and open.

It was then that he noticed the grim faces around the table. His outstretched hand fell limply to his side. Time slowed as his eyes frantically searched the room, looking for some clue to the somber atmosphere.

Then he saw her—Ada.

His stomach clenched and he forced a breath through his teeth, making an audible hissing sound before he could stop himself.

She was sitting ramrod straight, eyes downcast with a slight frown on her face. Even from across the room, her swollen lips and the yellow-purple bruises covering her delicate features were visible. His dread mounted as he noticed the white cast on her wrist and the wheelchair parked next to her.

A tall, big-boned woman with frizzy shoulder-length hair sat next to her, chair pulled close. Her arm was draped protectively over Ada's shoulder. She looked vaguely familiar to Erik, but he couldn't place her.

"Sit down," Aarav said in a voice that didn't allow room for argument. "We need to talk."

Erik, his face flushed in anger, listened with increasing agitation as the CEO recapped the morning meeting with Ada and her lawyer, Julie Marrow.

Ada was formally accusing Erik of domestic battery. Her lawyer had described Erik's savage attack to the group in great detail.

To his mounting dismay, it became apparent they had already reached an agreement—a settlement. The conditions were laid out succinctly by Aarav. Ada would be provided with an undisclosed financial sum and Erik would be required to resign immediately.

Suddenly, he realized where he had seen the heavy-set woman with the wild red hair—on the news, vocally defending women's rights.

"I wasn't here to—" Erik began desperately.

"Stop!" Aarav said, his own face flushing. "I can barely look at you. How can you even begin to defend what you've done? How could you put the company and all we have worked for in jeopardy? If our investors find out about this, they will pull out before the day is over. You are lucky Ms. Marrow had the idea to come here first, instead of to the press."

One of the other suits interjected. "If we hadn't come to a quick arrangement, Ms. Marrow informed us they would be taking their story to Elsa Karlsson from Svergies Television *tonight*."

Aarav blew out a breath. "Fortunately, they have agreed to avoid the press and have, in fact, signed both a settlement and a non-disclosure agreement. They have also agreed not to pursue criminal charges against you."

He paused and took a deep breath, visibly trying to keep his emotions in check. "You will leave this building and never come back. As per your contract, all work done in our lab, under our employ, is our property. That includes lutase-2. We have reviewed this with our lawyers and they agree. Your personal effects will be sent to your home address. Any further contact with us will be through this firm." He handed Erik a card and then nodded to someone behind him.

Ada must have suspected my funds were dwindling, so the cunning bitch targeted Paragon.

How can they treat me this way? She is nothing compared to what I have created, what I have accomplished. She is obviously exaggerating her injuries. She was able to walk out of the apartment after our argument. Now she has a wheelchair?

Two tall men in security uniforms suddenly materialized. Erik stood there for a moment, a sense of unreality enveloping him for the second time this week. *This can't be happening. This isn't real...*

Chapter 7
Holdings Condominium Complex, Malmö, Sweden
Day –40

The condominium's interior smelled of stale sweat. The pungent odor of alcohol oozed from Erik's pores into the already sour air. He had spent the last two days in a haze of bourbon, playing online poker in a desperate attempt for money. In the end, he had barely come out even.

Seven days until they came back.

He jumped up, grabbing the closest thing to him—a delicate hand-painted vase Ada had left behind. He threw it against the wall with all his strength. He felt a small measure of satisfaction as he watched it shatter. He stood there seething, the whoosh of blood filling his ears. He set to work, systematically obliterating anything he could get his hands on.

It's not fair. I've worked hard for years developing this protein and it's no longer mine. No one else in the world could have done it. I deserve a fortune for what I've created.

It's all the fault of that bitch, that miserable cow. Every bruise and broken bone I gave her was justified.

Dark thoughts clouded his mind. He stared into space, imagining various painful ways he could end Ada's life. First, though, he needed money.

I deserve this money.

Erik grabbed his spare laptop from the back of the closet. After ensuring his VPN was connected, he opened the anonymous web browser, Tor, and clicked on the search box.

He spent the next five hours glued to his computer, stopping only once to make a pot of coffee and take a much-needed bathroom break.

Finally, he sat back on the couch and took a deep breath. He had a plan.

∿∿∿

The next afternoon, Erik showered for the first time in days. He skipped shaving and purposely dressed down in a fitted, plain white T-shirt, ripped jeans, and old running shoes. To complete his ensemble, he found a dark, faded green fleece at the back of his closet. Swallowing the last of his coffee, he turned on his computer.

After removing specifics about lutase-2, his name, and other identifiers, Erik printed out a copy of the paper previously written for *Nature*, complete with several detailed, full-color electron microscope images.

Leaving his wallet and cell phone behind, he locked his apartment and walked several blocks before hailing a taxi. The first taxi refused when Erik told him of his destination—central Rosengard. The second taxi reluctantly agreed when Erik offered to double his rate and add a large tip.

Erik approached his financial crisis as he would a problem encountered in the lab—with a methodical, step-by-step analysis.

He knew Malmö had experienced an upsurge in immigration over the last several years, with the largest population coming from the Middle East. He also knew certain Swedish residents blamed immigrants and the Islamic State for the increase in crime in specific areas. Although controversial and denied by officials, he found an online article discussing specific "no-go" areas in the city—areas where even police and other government services refused to enter.

Erik researched these areas in detail. With his statistics programs, he created a density graph utilizing arrest and crime reports for all the "no-go" neighborhoods. Using a comprehensive map of Malmö, he was able to reasonably narrow down his search to three distinct areas based on the frequency of crimes committed by those from the Middle East—inferred by the name of the person or persons on the crime report.

He cross-referenced his search with recommendations of streets to avoid from multiple travel advisories. He decided to start with the largest neighborhood of the three.

He knew merely entering this area meant risking his life. He also knew he would stand out, no matter how anonymous he tried to appear. But if he did nothing, he reasoned, his life as he knew it would be over.

Surprisingly, he began to feel a familiar rush, which reminded him of winning at the poker table. The taxi driver pulled over, not even bothering to shift to park. As promised, Erik paid the man generously. The instant the door closed, the small car sped away, tires squealing.

Erik stood for a moment, taking in his surroundings.

Much of the area was bathed in an inky blackness due to broken and ·burned-out streetlights. He began to walk.

He walked east, past endless box-like apartment buildings and small Middle Eastern restaurants and groceries. The farther he walked, the more decay he encountered. He passed by small groups of people, who stopped talking and openly stared at him. He saw several people pull out cell phones, their eyes following him.

It won't be long now.

Garbage was piled high along the streets. Dumpsters overflowed and debris littered the ground. Small eyes, presumably from rats, reflected red halos of light from alleyways.

Disgusting.

His rush of adrenaline was now dissipated, and his heart fluttered un-comfortably in his chest. He paused briefly as he heard the crack of gunfire in the distance.

A group of three men stepped out from under a faded green and yellow awning, shoes crunching on broken glass.

"Who are you?" one of the men asked in a thick accent.

Erik became acutely aware of the pounding of his own heart. He was at a momentary loss for words, even though he had rehearsed what he was going to say.

"I'm a scientist," he said, "and I have a proposal for the Islamic leadership." His voice sounded weak, even to himself.

The man spoke rapidly to the others in Arabic. The three men looked at each other incredulously for a few moments and then started laughing.

"Are you fucked in the head?" the first one asked. "Leave right now. You aren't wanted here."

Erik cleared his throat, "Believe me, this is something they'll want to hear—"

"I said leave now…while you still can." The malice in the man's voice was unmistakable.

Erik pulled out several hundred kroner from his pocket, offering it to the men. Before he could say another word, one of the men threw a swift punch to the side of his head. There was an explosion of pain as his head snapped back. He sunk down to his knees. A sharp kick to his bruised ribs followed, and he fell forward, his left cheek pressing against the dirty sidewalk. As he slipped into unconsciousness, he sensed someone roughly going through his pockets.

∿∿∿

Erik awoke surrounded by a large, loose circle of people. A few were looking at him with curiosity or anger; most were ignoring him. As he tried to sit up, a broken piece of glass sliced into his palm.

"Shit!" he shouted.

Several in the group turned to look at him and then commenced talking. He attempted to stand, cradling his bleeding right hand. One of the men came over and roughly pushed him back down to the ground.

"Stay," he ordered, as if to a dog.

Erik remained on the ground, swallowing his humiliation. He did his best to study the crowd around him. He noticed a small group of men looking intently at the now-crumpled article and photographs he had brought.

He began to speak, but suddenly, feeling nauseated and dizzy, he leaned over and vomited on the sidewalk. Several people made sounds of disgust, while others laughed at him contemptuously. Even through the haze of pain, he felt a wave of sizzling, white rage. Heat traveled to his face and neck, causing him to flush a deep red.

They are nothing, worthless—and they don't even realize it.

Erik sat on the ground for what seemed like hours, compressing his hand with the bottom of his shirt to stem the flow of blood. At one point, someone tossed him a dirty shirt to use as a makeshift bandage. He hesitated briefly as he considered the potential contaminants on the soiled fabric. He could worry about that later, he reasoned, if he survived. He tied the shirt tightly around the wound.

Eventually, the crowd parted and let through an older man with a stethoscope around his neck and a shock of bright white hair. Moving with an air of authority, he went directly to the small group of men and began studying the paper and photographs. After several long minutes, he began to give instructions to the group in Arabic.

Two men grabbed Erik under the arms and hoisted him unsteadily to his feet. They walked him into a nearby restaurant and set him down in a chair without a word. The white-haired man sat across from him. He continued to ignore Erik as he studied the material.

"Start talking," he abruptly demanded in Swedish.

Erik did. He talked for several minutes without stopping. The man interrupted only twice for clarification.

After he was finished, the man nodded and stood up, pulling his cell phone out of his pocket. He crossed the room and made a phone call. Erik took a deep breath and leaned back in his chair.

The white-haired man eventually ended the call and looked at the two men standing guard behind Erik. He said something in Arabic to them and, his face impassive, left the room without another word. In halting Swedish, the two men instructed Erik to wait. Someone named Sameer was coming.

More than two hours passed. Erik hated to wait—he wasn't accustomed to it, but he didn't have any choice. He was out of options.

He studied his surroundings. They were in a ground floor café with low ceilings and plain, unadorned walls, excluding the electrical wires. The linoleum floor was scuffed and tinted yellow with age. The tabletop was clean, however, and mismatched chairs were turned neatly upright, legs pointing toward the ceiling.

On the countertop was a dimly lit refrigerator next to an ancient cash register, its soft hum audible in the relative quiet. Its scratched plastic viewing window showcased drinks, fruit, and other snacks. His stomach rumbled.

Finally, the door creaked open. To Erik's surprise, a striking woman with long dark lashes and a black hijab, her hands full of supplies, entered the room. The woman, head tilted down, eyes averted, approached Erik. She seemed to hesitate, unsure of herself.

She pointed to her chest and said, "Aismi hu Fatima." *My name is*

Fatima.

She unpacked her materials, then proceeded to thoroughly clean his wounds. The bleeding on his palm had slowed considerably. She applied a liberal amount of antibiotic ointment and closed the skin tightly with butterfly bandages. Suddenly, the door opened with a bang, causing them both to flinch.

"Hello, I'm Sameer." He proceeded straight to Erik and shook his hand, dropping it almost immediately upon contact. He displayed only a hint of an accent, making Eric think he had been in Sweden for some time. He was clean shaven and dressed smartly in designer jeans and a blue, button-down shirt with expensive black leather shoes. A large, sleek nylon bag was strapped across his chest.

"Let's get you somewhere more comfortable." Sameer gave him a tight smile that didn't reach his eyes. He radiated energy and a subtle excitement, reminding Erik of a wild animal.

Chapter 8
Alexi Place Luxury Apartments, Atlanta, Georgia
Day −39

Mallory was in the kitchen, pouring a bag of Skinny Pop Popcorn into a large glass bowl, when she heard Marcus' phone vibrating on the coffee table. The sound barely registered, though she made a mental note to let him know when he came out of the bathroom. She grabbed some bottled water and settled into the couch, signing into Amazon Prime to start the movie *Life of Pi*.

The phone began to vibrate again, this time making her flinch. Mallory frowned, wondering if something was wrong.

After a moment's hesitation, she grabbed the phone and was surprised to see the name Phoebe. She knew Marcus had an ex-girlfriend named Phoebe, but she was under the impression they were no longer in contact. She set the phone back down as she heard the flush of the toilet and the sound of running water. She took a second to compose her thoughts.

As Marcus sat down, she said simply, "Phoebe called several times."

Marcus seemed to freeze for a fraction of a second, or was it her imagination?

"I'm not surprised. She has a drinking problem—that's part of the reason we broke up. Lately, she has been calling me repeatedly, sometimes leaving incoherent messages. I never pick up." He seemed genuinely frustrated.

"But why were you looking at my phone?" he asked, looking at her intently. "Don't you trust me?"

"Of course I trust you. It just kept vibrating," Mallory explained. "I thought something might be wrong."

He pulled her into a hug. "I would never do anything to hurt you. I love you more than anything in the world."

Comforted by his words, Mallory felt herself relax into him. However, as the night progressed, she couldn't quite shake off a sense of unease.

Chapter 9
Holdings Condominium Complex, Malmö, Sweden
Day –38

In the end, Sameer persuaded Erik to take him back to his apartment, although it turned out to be more of a command than a request. Erik could either follow instructions or he was free to go. It was as if Sameer could sense his desperation and instinctively knew that was not a possibility.

As they entered the suite, Sameer didn't say a word about the broken pieces of furniture and the dishes littering the floor. He went immediately to the kitchen table, ignoring the crunching and cracking underfoot. He sat down, pulled out his cell phone, and made a series of calls. He spoke rapidly in Arabic. After a moment, he was back on his feet, pacing and gesturing as he talked.

Erik sat down on the couch and closed his eyes. He tilted his head back, resting it on the soft suede cushions. Erik knew a few basic Arabic phrases, and he recognized "Allahu akbar." *God is great.*

On the way back to Erik's apartment, Sameer had instructed Erik that he would be his "handler." He was going to stay with Erik until the project was complete. He would help facilitate the transfer of money for online orders of lab equipment, rentals, and supplies.

"I'm working on liquidating the first part of your payment. Five hundred thousand dollars in US currency will probably take a few days to get together. It's coming from multiple sources," he said.

As agreed, the second installment, one million US dollars, was to be handed over upon completion of the project.

Oil money.

Late that evening, Erik pointed Sameer to the well-appointed guest suite and retreated to his room. He swallowed some pain reliever and, though he collapsed on the bed from exhaustion, found himself staring at the ceiling, eyes open wide.

Each time he closed his eyes, he had visions of Sameer standing over him with a knife, ready to ruthlessly stab him the minute he fell asleep. He wasn't sure why he thought this; it didn't make sense logically—they both had something the other very much wanted.

∿∿∿

Erik opened his eyes. The first hint of gray light was beginning to brighten the room. He could hear Sameer in the kitchen, moving around and loudly closing cupboards.

Erik padded out to the kitchen, flicking on the coffee. With bleary eyes, he watched as Sameer pulled a prayer rug and beads from his bag. He set them carefully on the floor, clearing away debris with his shoe. Erik noticed he had already found a large bowl and filled it with water. Sameer took out his phone, tapping quickly with his thumbs. Utilizing the compass feature, he adjusted the rug to face southeast, toward Mecca. It was time for the dawn prayer, Fajr.

Erik ignored him and scrounged around in the mostly empty pantry. He finally settled on a stale bagel and bit into it unenthusiastically.

The prayer done, Sameer stood. As if reading his thoughts, he said, "Fatima is bringing food over for us today. Let's get freshened up and talk about our plans."

Erik grunted in reply.

After shaving and showering, they sat down with Sameer's laptop and began strategizing. The first step was finding a suitable space to lease for a makeshift lab. Given the general lack of rentable space in Malmö, this was no easy feat. It took them the better part of the morning to come up with a few possible addresses.

Their online search was interrupted by a soft knock on the door. Sameer jumped to his feet and ushered Fatima into the room. Her hands were full of grocery bags, and she was forced to awkwardly close the door with her foot.

Erik was surprised to see she was dressed in a high-necked black shirt, dark jeans, and stylish, ankle-high boots. Her head was bare, and her hair was pulled back neatly into a low bun. Gucci sunglasses were perched casually atop her head. Sameer and Fatima were doing their best to stay inconspicuous in this upscale neighborhood.

Without a word, she proceeded directly to the kitchen, unpacked the groceries, and made lunch, then, not eating herself, cleaned the entire apartment. She was quick and efficient, not wasting any energy. Once done, she slipped out unobtrusively with a murmured, "Al-wada." *Good-bye.*

Erik and Sameer spent the rest of the day utilizing new disposable phones and an untraceable computer supplied by Sameer. He worked like a machine, only breaking briefly for food or prayer. Everything was leased, ordered, or purchased under Erik's name. Their cover story, if anyone bothered to ask, was that Erik was branching out and opening his own lab. He was a reputable and well-known scientist—it was doubtful anyone would question him.

Erik made a comprehensive list of what he would need to engineer his protein, clone DNA, and, using his newest gene therapy protocol, create what he needed.

He knew exactly how to do this; his years of research had seen to that. It was now a matter of gathering the necessary materials and not arousing suspicion. By the time the authorities learned of him, he planned on being very far away from Sweden, living under an assumed name, in a country without a US or Swedish extradition treaty.

Unbeknownst to Paragon, Eric had kept a copy of the molecular structure of lutase-2 and all relevant material on a USB thumb drive tucked safely in a drawer at home. This was purely a precautionary measure; he never thought he would have to use it. He shuddered to think what would have happened if he hadn't had the foresight to plan ahead.

He had initially considered selling the information to a competing commercial genetic company. He quickly nixed this idea. When it came down to it, the world of gene therapy was relatively small. Most scientists knew each other or, at the very least, knew of each other. He couldn't imagine a scenario in which he would be able to successfully set up an illegal sale of research material, especially anything patented in Paragon's name. He didn't believe he would be able to escape prison, and more importantly, be able to pay Niklas back in a few short days.

He had ambivalent feelings toward his mother and sister, whom he considered weak and, on many levels, inferior to him, but he wasn't ready to abandon them to unimaginable torture.

It was my years of work that led to the development of lutase-2. I deserve this money.

Chapter 10
Holdings Condominium Complex, Malmö, Sweden
Day −33

There was a sharp rap on the door and Erik looked cautiously through the peephole. He immediately recognized the general build of the two waiting men.

They both had black caps pulled low on their foreheads. One of the men was looking down and one was half-turned away, his face averted. Erik's face heated in anger at the sight of them, his mind traveling back to the pain and humiliation they had inflicted. His throat was suddenly dry, and he swallowed uncomfortably. He took a breath, tried to steady his breathing, and then opened the door.

The men immediately stepped inside, pulling their balaclavas down in one fluid motion. One of the men roughly patted Erik down while the other quickly cleared the apartment. Sameer had left several hours earlier in anticipation of this visit, not wanting to complicate the situation by provoking questions from the two men.

Erik watched as the men counted the money, which was packed tightly in a grocery's paper bag. Sitting in the middle of the otherwise bare kitchen table, it came to a little more than one hundred thousand dollars.

"I have your money—it's all there. The equivalent of 1 million Kroner in US currency. I assume that's acceptable." *US currency was always acceptable.*

The men paused. Smugly, Erik imagined the surprised faces under the mask. They recovered quickly and sprang into action, excited by the prospect of a particularly good pay-day. They undoubtedly received a small percentage of the money.

One man watched Erik closely as the other settled into a chair to count the money. He meticulously separated the hundred-dollar bills into piles of ten. He then layered a second pile, of the same amount, over the first at a crisp ninety-degree angle. In the end, he had a stack of 106. Satisfied, he placed the money back in the original grocery bag.

One of the men, the one who had callously pulled out his tooth just weeks before, spoke. "It was nothing personal." He shrugged. "Just business."

And then they were gone.

∿∿

Sameer and Erik spent the next five days setting up the lab, choosing to lease the closest practical location they could find. For Erik, it was a walkable distance, around eight blocks away from his apartment.

The building was small, with a neglected air to it. A flimsy gray door with a tarnished brass knob separated the front room from a modestly larger room in the back. The space was previously used by an insurance agency. The cheap desks and conference tables were included in the rental agreement for a nominal monthly fee.

The space had poor lighting and a musty, stale smell. The farthest corner of the ceiling harbored a large watermark, the stain sprinkled with black-brown spots of mold. Flakes of paint curled around the edges and dusted the ground underneath. The single bathroom held just enough space to turn around in, with a rust-stained sink and a lone, cracked toilet.

A foul odor greeted Eric when he first entered the bathroom, causing him to breathe through his mouth. He flushed the toilet using his foot and then backed out, using care not to touch anything. Resentment washed over him. He couldn't help but compare this miserable place to his previous state-of-the-art lab at Paragon.

The first thing they did was move the desks and tables into a u-shape against the three bare walls of the back room. They kept a single rickety wooden desk in the front and lined several institutional-appearing chairs against the wall, then added a large, shiny-green artificial plant in the corner and a coffee table stacked with old magazines. Anyone walking by would see a generic waiting room.

Over the next few weeks, the used lab equipment was delivered by expedited shipping: centrifuge, gel electrophoresis chamber, thermal cycler, incubator, industrial refrigerator, and microscope. They were even able to obtain biohazard suits from a survivalist website, no personal information required.

Erik ordered synthetic genes online from thermofisher.com, saving him weeks of tedious work. The commercial lab did the job of molecular cloning and, using PCR technique, or polymerase chain reaction, manipulated the DNA into customized made-to-order gene sequences.

One of the most challenging aspects about setting up the lab was creating an isolation space, complete with a chemical hood and a positive-pressure ventilation system. In the end, they had one of Sameer's friends, a bioengineer, assist with this. He was the only other person to set foot in the lab. It was pieced together using thick plastic sheeting and multiple layers of silver duct tape. A portable ventilation system was connected to the building's antiquated air ducts.

Sameer's friend—Erik never learned his name—extensively tested the system using a gaseous benzoate solution and a large vacuum chamber before announcing it safe for use.

Erik purchased a second-hand autoclave, for equipment sterilization, on eBay. He attached a medical-grade detergent bottle to an aerosolizer and hung it high over a blue plastic paddling pool, complete with brightly colored sea creatures. At the end of each day, the two awkwardly emptied the flimsy pool, maneuvering it into the cramped utility closet and down the drain.

Before Erik could begin work in earnest, one major step remained.

Chapter II
Skane Housing Estate, Malmö, Sweden
Day -19

The room was bright with artificial light and full of worn plastic toys in primary colors. The sofa cushions were stacked on top of one another and covered with blankets, creating a teetering fort. There were four children in total and all appeared to be under the age of five. They filled the flat with noise and energy, making it hard for Erik to concentrate. He struggled to keep his face friendly and not wrinkle his nose when he caught the faint whiff of a dirty diaper.

Johan, who was sitting on his mother's lap, wore a pediatric mask secured tightly over his mouth and nose with a clear face-shield over his eyes. He was dressed in a yellow medical gown and plastic mittens—every inch of skin was protected from the dangerous air.

The gown was made of thick disposable plastic. Johan bunched the material in his tiny hand, enjoying the crinkling sound it made. He was extremely small for his age, which made his large ink-blue eyes appear even more prominent.

Johan had been diagnosed with ADA-deficient Severe Combined Immunodeficiency (SCID) after repeat hospitalizations for failure to thrive. He spent the first five months of his life in and out of the children's hospital for infections and nutritional difficulties. Erik had drawn his blood at Paragon the month prior for research.

The average weight for a typical five-month-old was around sixteen pounds. Johan currently weighed only six pounds and five ounces, just one pound over his birth weight.

One corner of the room was portioned off with red tape and sheeting.

Erik could just make out the edge of a clear plastic crib. There was a single, green rubber ball on the floor and a glider in the corner fit with a transparent cover. Johan's immunologist thought it would be safer to keep him isolated at home rather than isolated in the hospital. Hospital and healthcare settings carried some of the most dangerous, drug-resistant pathogens.

"Thank you for allowing me to draw Johan's blood again. I can't believe the lab lost the original sample. Of course, we will compensate you for your time."

"No problem," Johan's mother replied in a tired voice. She was dressed in an adult version of the gown, complete with sterile white gloves. She looked up, her expression hard to read under the medical mask worn for Johan's protection.

Erik handed her 300 kroner, hoping she didn't question the use of cash instead of the typical check given to research volunteers. He needn't have worried. She simply folded the money in half, pulled up the gown, and tucked it unceremoniously in her bra. Then, squeezing Purell directly on her gloves from a large pump bottle, she grasped Johan's wrist firmly and stretched his tiny forearm out, palm facing up, as she had done countless times before.

Erik had his supplies already set, wanting to draw the serum and leave as quickly as possible. He pulled the elastic band of his mask behind each ear with a soft snap, slid on his gloves, and scrubbed the pale-white skin pink with three separate alcohol wipes. He wasn't particularly concerned about infection but wanted to keep up appearances.

Without a word, he pricked Johan with a small butterfly needle. The baby made a slight squeak of protest, then was quiet. Erik watched as the vial filled with crimson fluid. Once he had two full vials, he removed the tourniquet and pressed a square of gauze over the pinprick mark.

Erik placed the serum securely in a zippered ice pack and gathered his supplies. With a final nod, he was out the door, exhaling a long sigh of relief.

Now I can begin the real work.

∿∿

That evening, Erik browsed online luxury rentals in Montenegro. He closed his eyes, visualizing the shimmering water rolling in against the shore. He imagined lounging outside his private villa, sinking his toes into the sand. Short-term rentals could be arranged online with no identification needed.

After receiving his first installment, Erik spent time depositing the cash in multiple accounts. He visited thirteen different banks, all located randomly around Malmö. He figured if he kept the deposits less than 10,000 per bank, he would remain under the radar—unmemorable. That complete, the money was transferred electronically, first to a bank in Switzerland, then to a Caribbean account, effectively rendering the money untraceable.

On multiple occasions, Sameer offered assistance in acquiring a counterfeit passport. Erik declined; he didn't trust him. Sameer had barely left his side during the previous few weeks, ostensibly under the guise of facilitating the lab set-up.

As soon as the virus was engineered, and when his second payment was in hand, Eric was going to leave the country, without a soul knowing his new name or where he was going— somewhere warm with plenty of gaming tables.

He missed gambling—craved it more than he thought possible. His fingers hovered over the keys. After a long hesitation, he decided there would be time soon enough. He walked to the bar in the living room and poured himself a generous glass of bourbon. Out of the corner of his eye, he saw a brief smirk cross Sameer's face before he turned away.

What a prick.

Without warning, his thoughts turned to Ada. A rush of heat crept slowly over his skin, threatening to overcome him. He sucked in a breath and drained his glass in one long pull, his adrenaline pulsing at the memory of her betrayal. If Sameer wasn't sticking to him so closely, he would have been watching her, learning her routines.

I will kill her. No matter what happens, she will die.

Chapter 12
5 Roslin Street, Malmö, Sweden
Day −6

"Yes!" Sameer said, punching his fist in the air.

For the first time, Erik and Sameer shared a genuine smile, visible through the clear visor of their protective gear.

They looked down at the motionless cat in the cage. Yellow-white pustules covered much of the exposed, pink skin. Some of the lesions oozed a serosanguineous, slightly bloody exudate. Tufts of dark fur dotted the cage floor. The cat's eyes were open and unmoving, conjunctiva bright pink and crusted with a thick, green-tinged mucus.

Although there was a bowl filled with cat food and another filled with water, both appeared relatively untouched. The cat's ribs protruded sharply from its chest, its abdomen concave. Given the circumstances, Erik was glad to have positive-pressure ventilation in the room and a sealed mask; the smell must be horrendous. Infection had a unique, noxious odor.

There were three identical cages to the right of the first cage. Two of the cats hunched nervously in the farthest corner, luminous eyes reflecting the meager light. In the cage closest to the dead cat, a tabby was lying on its side, mewing plaintively but totally still, excluding the rapid rise and fall of its chest. Overnight, it had developed several skin lesions similar to the first cat. Animal waste and animal blood mixed together on the floor of the cage.

Having spent every waking moment of the past few weeks working, Erik and Sameer were exhausted. Although Sameer had no prior experience in biology or lab work, he proved to be a quick learner and helpful assistant.

In gene therapy, a virus is commonly used as a vector, or vehicle, that inserts the gene into the genome of the host. In both research and treatment, the virus is inactivated, so the host will not be exposed to a virus capable of infection. A type of non-infectious adenovirus is used frequently in gene therapy research. Adenovirus is one of several viruses that cause the common cold.

Over the course of several days, Erik spliced the pre-made, synthetic gene sequences with Johan's mutated ADA gene. Using adenovirus as a vector, or delivery mechanism, Erik attached the mutated gene to the target cell with the help of lutase-2.

"What we're doing in the lab has two key differences from my prior research," Erik explained to Sameer. "We're inserting a mutated gene, instead of a healthy one, and we're using a *live* virus capable of causing infection, and, even more importantly for your purposes, transmission to others.

"Adenovirus enters humans through mucosal membranes by either direct contact with a contaminated surface or by inhaling respiratory droplets from contaminated air. Once the virus is in the body, the virus will do what it has been doing for thousands of years—it will replicate.

"The virus inserts its own DNA into the cell and then hijacks the host's own cell machinery to synthesize more virus. The newly made viruses escape by either rupturing the cell or budding out of the cell. Each cell has the ability to infect other cells at an exponential rate."

Sameer interrupted him. "So, how exactly does this wipe out the immune system?"

"I'm getting to that," Erik replied, giving him a dark look. "Okay. In our case, the viral genetic material will also code for ADA mutation genes. Each viral replication will propagate the mutation until it reaches millions, even billions, of cells. The virus really does the hard part for us."

"Does that mean it will spread between people like a typical head cold?" Sameer asked.

Erik suppressed a sigh of frustration. "Not *like* a head cold. Adenovirus actually causes the common cold—the difference here is that a mutated gene attaches. The adenovirus serves two purposes; it allows the spread of the virus, but it also inserts the SCID gene into all those infected. In research, we use inactivated viral vectors, not an actual live virus like the one we're using."

Sameer murmured softly, "Allahu akbar."

"I expected it to take longer," Erik said, deep in thought. "We only injected this cat one week ago. Maybe feline lymphocytes don't last quite as long in the peripheral blood as they do in humans."

He walked over to the second cat and peered into the cage. "This cat is definitely infected. This confirms respiratory droplet transmission—we never injected the other three cats."

"Perfect," Sameer said, already walking to the decontamination shower. He washed off and carefully removed his protective gear as Erik had taught him. Then he stepped to the front room and made a call.

Chapter 13
Central Network Station Headquarters, Los Angeles, CA
Day −3

CNS: BREAKING NEWS

Record breaking tsunami: possibly deadliest natural disaster in US history

Los Angeles (CNS)—The President has declared a national state of emergency in the wake of a devastating tsunami that hit the coast of southern California around 15:35 local time. The city of San Diego, particularly Mission Beach, a popular tourist spot, seems to be among the hardest hit.

Hundreds are confirmed dead, with thousands more missing. The possible death toll could reach as high as twenty-thousand people, with the potential that hundreds of thousands will be without shelter.

Per a brief White House statement, the National Guard and other emergency services are en route to the area. It's unclear at this time how much warning was given to residents and visitors in the evacuation zones and surrounding region.

Authorities are recommending people in the area attempt to reach at least 100 feet above sea level or relocate to areas six miles or more away from the coast.

An underwater tectonic plate shift is capable of producing a series of tsunami waves, even hours after the initial wave impact.

The LAPD recently released these statements on Twitter: "Tsunami in the greater San Diego area IN PROGRESS. Further waves may be forthcoming. Aim for the highest ground possible." Los Angeles @LAPD 32 m.

"If you are currently on a roof or other high structure, shelter in place.

Military and civilian boats and helicopters have been deployed for rescue assistance." Los Angeles @LAPD 43 m.

Authorities warned that evacuation on foot may be necessary as many of the roadways are congested, with traffic on some of them at a standstill.

This is an evolving story. Please check back at CNS.com for important updates.

San Diego Tsunami Update 21:04:

(CNS)—There are preliminary reports of a 9.1 magnitude earthquake thought to have originated from the little-known San Diego Trough Fault Line located in the underwater area identified as the California Border-lands. The fault line is located approximately 25 miles from the coast of San Diego.

There are 2,214 confirmed dead, with tens of thousands unaccounted for, making this the most devastating natural disaster in recent US history.

Many are asking: How could this happen? Experts believe the inciting factor, or epicenter, occurred relatively close to shore.

Dr. Robert Warner, who holds a PhD in seismology and specializes in mapping underwater fault lines, explains, "Powerful seismic activity in close proximity to the shore produces the capacity for tsunami formation in a matter of minutes. In this rare situation, scientists are unable to issue timely warnings."

Prior geologic reports have included this area in their threat assessment; however, based on plate tectonics and previous activity, it was estimated that the maximum magnitude this area could generate would have been on the order of 7.5 or less.

According to experts, a release of energy at a magnitude of 7.5 would have created a much smaller, less devastating tsunami. Evacuation zones based on this prediction included select areas close to the coast, with most of them encompassing areas 25 feet or more below sea level.

Dr. Warner also stated, "Unfortunately, nature is not always predictable. Scientists and researchers do the best they can with the information available to them at the time."

Chapter 14
Alexi Place Luxury Apartments, Atlanta, Georgia
Day −3

Kate hovered close to the TV. Unable to sit down, she alternately paced the room or stood completely still, staring at the screen. Mallory sat on the end of the suede couch with her feet tucked under her, eyes riveted to the news footage.

Kate had shown up at her door an hour earlier, the tip of her nose pink from crying. They had grown up in a small bungalow in Chula Vista, near San Diego. When their dad accepted a position in Atlanta, Kate and Mallory were forced to move cross-country during their notoriously tumultuous teen years. Mallory was fourteen and Kate thirteen.

Mallory refreshed her Facebook page every few minutes. The two sisters had kept in touch with a few close friends from the San Diego area. Relieved, she noticed most of them had marked themselves safe.

"Any word from Brooke?" Mallory asked.

Kate frowned. "Nothing. I just sent her an email; it may be a while before the San Diego area has cell service."

"I'm sure she's fine." Mallory tried to sound reassuring, but her words sounded hollow.

Kate and Brooke had remained especially close, visiting each other on numerous occasions over the years and chatting on the phone regularly. Kate had tried reaching her today but, given the volume of calls, the cell towers were overwhelmed. For the first time, Mallory wished she had heeded Dad's warning to keep a landline for emergencies.

Those poor people. The terror they must have felt as they were crushed by the frigid water. Mallory's eyes pricked with fresh tears. Her stomach knotted, and she felt faintly nauseated, reminding her of how she felt on

9/11.

They stayed up late into the night, Kate eventually settling on the couch next to her. They flipped through channels periodically, hoping for new information. Instead, they encountered an endless loop of the same news, like a song on repeat.

At some point, they both drifted off. Mallory awoke to cheery, golden light spilling in through the open window, making it seem like the previous night had been nothing but a bad dream.

Kate was curled up on the opposite end, snoring softly. Her iPhone lay face-down on the floor and her hand trailed down the side of the couch, as if she were reaching for it in her sleep.

Mallory covered her with a blanket and then checked the phone's screen. It was showing a strong signal; however, there had been no missed calls or texts from Brooke. Grabbing her own phone, she quickly tapped out a text to her parents, letting them know that Kate was with her and they were okay. She sent a message to Marcus and asked him to call when he woke.

She went to the kitchen and flipped on the coffee maker. It was going to be a long day.

Chapter 15
Holdings Condominium Complex, Malmö, Sweden
Day –3

Erik had just drifted off when he was awoken by a sharp rap on his bedroom door. He ignored it and rolled over, swearing under his breath. Sameer pushed open the door, one hand holding a cell phone to his ear and talking excitedly in Arabic. He tapped his leg roughly with two fingers. Erik had to stop himself from kicking him out in irritation. After a few seconds, he reluctantly rose and went out to the living room.

Sameer stared at the TV screen and continued talking in a low voice. Erik followed his gaze.

"Devastating American Tsunami" was displayed in bold type at the top of the screen. Erik sank onto the couch, his fatigue forgotten.

His mind immediately began running through the potential implications. How would this affect his payment and escape from the country? He was desperate to leave and start over. He breathed a sigh of relief as he thought of his counterfeit passport, safely locked away in a file box under his bed.

Using an anonymous email account, he had contacted a high school acquaintance rumored to be into the dark web. Fortunately, his acquaintance knew people who possessed a talent for false documentation. After paying a substantial finder's fee, he was provided an email address.

Morpheus33@protonmail.com instantly replied to his request. Erik sent a passport photograph electronically and paid, as required, with Bitcoin.

Twenty-four hours later, he received the anticipated email. In the northwest corner of Willow Lake Park, near the rocky section of the lakeshore, he would find a brown paper lunch bag under a bench.

Erik had waited until he heard the faint, distinctive sound of the shower from the guest room before quietly slipping out the front door.

He walked briskly to the park, trying not to imagine what would happen if the package wasn't there. What was to stop Morpheus33 from just taking his money? When he spotted the wrinkled bag tucked under the metal bench, he fought the urge to break into a run. After verifying the contents, he slid the passport into his pocket and tossed the bag into a nearby rubbish bin.

When he walked in the door thirty minutes later, he found Sameer fuming, two bright spots of pink coloring his cheeks.

"Where have you been?" he demanded.

"I needed to run an errand. It had nothing to do with our project." He calmly brushed past Sameer and retreated to his room. The sharp click as he locked his bedroom door seemed to reverberate in the quiet space. Sameer didn't follow.

Back in the moment, Erik focused his attention on Sameer, trying to read the man's face as he talked. With his eyes wide and shining, he was intensely absorbed in his conversation and gripped the phone tightly to his ear.

Are those...tears? Erik's lips pulled down in an involuntary frown.

"Mushiiyat allah." *God willing.*

He continued in Arabic for another minute before ending the call and abruptly turning to Erik.

He opened his mouth to speak but Sameer cut him off. "We will strike while the enemy is weak. In forty-eight hours, we are to deliver the virus—sealed in travel-sized soap containers—to an address near the airport. You will receive your final payment then."

Erik felt Sameer's excitement, but for a different reason.

Tomorrow is the day. Once Sameer falls asleep, I can pay Ada the visit I have been waiting so patiently for. Then I will leave this country behind forever.

Chapter 16
Sturup Guesthouse, Malmö, Sweden
Day −2

Barakah Malouf could not believe his good fortune. He opened the curtains and gazed at the sky-blue water of the pool. Stylish, high-end furniture and planters, painted in vibrant colors and overflowing with lush greenery, were placed strategically around the courtyard. It made him feel as if he had been transported to another, better place and time.

A stone fountain was centered in the middle of the pool, the cascading water rippling gently in the breeze. A young woman lounging in a pale-yellow swimsuit, her oiled skin glistening brightly in the sun, was obviously undeterred by the cooler weather. His eyes lingered on her long, trim legs.

His face flushed and he quickly averted his eyes. He sent a hasty prayer to Allah, asking forgiveness for his impure thoughts. He had only ever seen such bare skin on TV, never in person.

He made a slow turn around the room. The colors seemed crisper, brighter somehow, in comparison to the dull, muted hues of Rasmusgatan Street. His family's minuscule apartment on the fifth floor was forever crowded and dirty, no matter how much time his mother and sisters spent cleaning it.

Barakah slept in the tiny second bedroom with four sisters and one brother. His youngest brother, only four years old, spent the night in his mother's room. The two oldest brothers shared the lone twin bed for as long as he could remember, their heads resting on opposite ends. The girls' beds consisted of blankets and old pillows piled on a worn carpet.

He now sprawled out on the oversized bed, arms stretched wide, the duvet and pillows impossibly soft beneath him.

Even though he had been expecting it, the firm knock on the door startled him. He walked quickly to the door and held it open.

"You need to see this," he said eagerly, pulling his two friends, twin brothers Omar and Habib, inside. They tried to remain nonchalant, but Barakah saw their eyes widen at the unfamiliarly lavish surroundings.

The three walked around, marveling at the fresh, crisp linens, tiny bottles of soap, soaking tub and, of course, the luxury swimming pool. Barakah had never been swimming and he was pretty sure Omar and Habib hadn't been either.

"Look what I found," Habib said, pulling out a bag of M&Ms and bottled water from the mini-fridge, tastefully camouflaged as part of the built-in cabinetry. The others quickly came over and selected several items, smiling widely at each other, all pretense at stoicism forgotten.

The three had met through Fakir, their mentor at the mosque. Omar and Habib fled Afghanistan when they were nine years old, eventually making their way to Sweden with their mother. Barakah and his family immigrated from Iran when he was a toddler.

The mosque became a refuge for them all, a temporary escape from the abject poverty of their everyday life. They spent many nights in the community center, hunched over the large wooden table, studying the Quran. Fakir dissected the passages for them and encouraged discussion. He gave them something to look forward to, a purpose.

About one year ago, the foursome stayed out until the early morning hours, enjoying their first hookah lounge experience courtesy of Fakir, the only one of them who could afford the flavored tobacco. They smoked and talked for hours, the camaraderie between them nearly palpable.

At some point, the conversation turned to childhood. Barakah entertained them, detailing the perils of sharing a single bathroom with seven other people. The toilet was separated from the rest of the apartment by a thin curtain, not quite big enough to cover the doorway.

The air was hazy with smoke, and the mixed scents of cinnamon, apple, and mint permeated the air. Barakah began to feel slightly sick to his stomach from the heady tobacco scents.

The conversation paused and Fakir quietly asked, "Are you ever going to share what happened to your family?"

The brothers rarely spoke of the night they escaped Afghanistan.

Habib seemed to consider this for a moment. He glanced at Omar, who gave him a slight nod. After another long moment, Habib began to speak in a low voice, almost a whisper. Barakah had to lean forward to hear him.

"I remember looking up and seeing the stars bright in the sky. The moon was full and helped to illuminate the way. This was good, as the ground was uneven and full of rocks. I was worried my four-year-old brother, Raziq, would fall and hurt his ankle."

Omar spoke, "He was in between us, one minute holding my hand, the next minute running to hold Habib's hand. He was full of excitement because we told him we were on a secret adventure."

"Yes, I remember." Habib paused and took a breath. "We had to leave our village because my father, who was the Pashai tribe leader, had family ties to the Taliban and was sympathetic to their cause. My parents had heard that the American soldiers were closing in on the area. My father worried he would be taken captive.

"We used nearly all of our savings to have members of the local Taliban smuggle our entire extended family into Iran. Because there were so many of us, three trucks waited just over the border.

"After what seemed like miles of walking, we finally reached the vehicles. There was a sense of relief, and I caught sight of our mother smiling in the moonlight. I remember because that was the last time I saw her smile for a long time.

"At that moment, my father and one of my uncles just...sort of fell over, collapsed. I didn't even hear the shots. Suddenly, it was chaos, and everyone was scrambling to get in the trucks."

Omar spoke, the loathing evident in his voice, "I heard someone shout, 'It's the Americans!'"

"I thought Raziq was with Omar," Habib's voice broke and he swallowed several times, trying to keep his emotions in check.

"I thought he was with Habib," Omar added quietly. "I remember Habib calling 'Raziq! Raziq!' as he was pushed into one of the vehicles. One of the trucks took off, Habib in it. Our mother grabbed my hand—that's when I realized Raziq wasn't with either of us.

"I heard the roaring of the second truck. A cloud of dust formed as it took off. Then...there was this terrible thump, and I just knew." He paused and took a deep breath. "I knew Raziq was hit. We ran over, and it was clear he was...gone. My mother let out a wail, this...inhuman sound...I won't ever forget it. I had to drag her into the last car, afraid they would leave without us."

Silence.

Barakah turned his head away, surreptitiously wiping at his eyes.

Fakir spoke first, his voice low and earnest, "What would you say if I told you that Allah has provided a way to avenge your family?"

Chapter 17
Pineview Apartments, 6C, Malmö, Sweden
Day −2

Erik's footsteps echoed loudly on the pavement. He slowed himself down, trying to dampen the sound. Walking confidently, he stayed close to the shadows. His hat was pulled low on his brow with his head tilted toward the ground and angled away from potential CCTV cameras.

He felt grateful for the heavy mist hanging in the air and blurring the edges of his surroundings. He imagined anyone looking out their window would see a nondescript man in gray sweats and trainers, gym bag over his shoulder, walking purposefully to an early morning workout. He had passed only one other person since exiting the taxi a few blocks away.

As he neared her flat, Erik could feel his heart rate increasing in anticipation.

His thoughts turned to his plans for the evening. First, he would use a rubber ball to gag her, like the one used on him. This idea seemed appropriate somehow, like poetic justice. Then he would tie her hands tightly with nylon rope.

Imagining her humiliation and terror as he cut off her clothes, he could almost see the goosebumps on her porcelain skin. He would force her to look in the mirror as he sheared off her long, lustrous locks.

Ada's address was easy enough to find online. She was staying in a one-bedroom rental apartment in a large complex. As he approached the bland structure, he noticed peeling white trim and cobwebs drooping from light fixtures.

I thought you had better taste than this, Ada. How…disappointing.

Given that you are expecting to come into money, I can't imagine you staying here long.

It's remarkable what you can find online.

Within three minutes of searching, he had located a website with step-by-step instructions on how to make a bump key—a key that would open virtually any standard-size lock or deadbolt. There was even a helpful video link. It took time and patience to file the key into the correct shape, but it was worth it.

A few nights ago, when Sameer was asleep, he practiced the technique on his own front door. Following the online instructions, he pushed the key into the lock and slowly pulled, stopping when he heard two distinct clicks. He turned the key to the left, simultaneously striking the end of the key—hard—with a torchlight. It took some practice, but he was soon opening the door within seconds. Luckily, Sameer was a deep sleeper.

Erik seamlessly pulled his gloves on, grabbed his home-made key, and approached the building. He entered in one fluid motion, silently closed the door behind him, and stood in the gloom, letting his eyes adjust. He savored the feeling of anticipation as adrenaline hummed through his body.

To the left of the entrance was a sparsely furnished room with a tattered sofa and a small, boxy television.

He slipped booties over his shoes and pulled down the sheer nylon tucked under his hat. Ada would not be left alive to identify him, but the precautions would help minimize trace evidence left behind. He moved quietly toward the open door at the end of the hallway.

"Erik." The sound of his whispered name caused him to flinch in shock. Before he could fully turn toward the source of the sound, he felt an intense, fiery eruption in his neck.

Chapter 18
Pineview Apartments, Malmö, Sweden
Day −2

Ada felt the warm, arterial blood strike her face—once, and then again—before the scream ripped from her throat. She remotely registered the clatter of the knife as it hit the tile.

Erik's body crumpled slowly, almost gracefully, to the floor. He blinked furiously at the ceiling, as if in confusion. After a few seconds, his eyes squeezed shut and his face twisted in agony. In the din, she could faintly make out the rhythmic arc of blood pulsing from his neck. She watched, transfixed, as it became smaller and smaller with each beat of his heart.

She waited until the rise and fall of his chest completely stopped. Then, with shaking hands, she dialed 112.

⁓ᴠᴧᴧ

Two hours later, Ada was still trembling as she sat on the couch. Someone had draped a rough woolen blanket around her shoulders, but it seemed to do nothing to warm her still-freezing skin. Her hands were twisted in her lap and she could feel her icy fingers through her pajama bottoms.

"I know we've been over this, but could you tell us again about the events leading up to tonight's incident?" Detective Inspector Elias Lindell asked, not unkindly. DI Lindell's partner, DI Klara Nilsson, remained silent next to him, impassively taking notes.

Ada nodded and took a deep breath. "I have been living in fear since I left Erik several months ago. He was the sort of person…who wouldn't let things go. Looking back, I can see the warning signs I missed. He had trouble controlling his anger, and he seemed to lack…I don't know… human decency. I also came to realize he was incapable of real love."

She pulled the blanket tighter around herself. "I began to institute a few security measures. I couldn't afford an alarm, so I installed Wi-Fi motion sensors on all points of entry. If any of the doors or windows were opened, my cell phone would buzz a silent alert."

DI Lindell gave an encouraging nod.

"Using the money from the settlement, I was planning on leaving the country—go somewhere he could never find me."

Earlier in the conversation, Ada had told the detectives the details of the settlement, explaining that the pictures from the assault were on her phone, which was now on its way to the station for analysis.

"I guess I no longer need to leave," she said quietly. Her eyes darted to the stain painting the worn hall tiles.

"Please continue," DI Nilsson prompted.

"The more I thought about it, the more convinced I became that he was going to come after me. I began carrying a can of wasp spray everywhere I went. I read somewhere it works as well as pepper spray. I started sleeping with a kitchen knife under my pillow, but I still didn't feel safe. I couldn't sleep through the night. I couldn't paint.

"That's when I started sleeping on this cot behind the couch. I figured at least he couldn't surprise me in my sleep. I feared for my life every minute of every day."

DI Lindell and Nilsson exchanged a look that Ada was unable to read. Tears fell down her cheeks and she angrily swiped them away.

"When my motion alarm woke me up, I grabbed the knife and peered around the couch. I could see right away it was Erik."

"How could you tell it was him in the dark?" DI Lindell interrupted.

"I couldn't see his face, but I recognized his build and the way he moved. I keep a night light plugged in in the hallway." A brief pause, then she said softly, "I saw him put covers over his shoes." She suppressed a shudder and pure panic rose in her chest. A strange hiccupping sound escaped her lips, surprising her. She thought for a moment she might come undone, like a spool of thread. She stared at the floor as she took in a steadying breath, then another. She continued breathing in and out for a full minute before she could speak.

"There was no doubt he was here to hurt me, to kill me."

"Why didn't you call the police at that point?" DI Nilsson asked. "You said yourself that you had your cell phone."

"I didn't think the police would get here in time. I can't explain it, but I felt I needed to act. I knew he would get the better of me if given the chance. He is—was," she corrected, "so much stronger than me…and ruthless. I felt my only advantage—the only possibility I had of survival—was to take him by surprise."

At that moment, the door swung open and hit the wall with a sharp bang. All three heads turned to look at the woman filling the doorway. Ada sagged with relief as she recognized her lawyer. She had managed to tap out a frantic text to her before the police arrived and confiscated her phone.

"Not another word," Julie said forcefully to Ada, wild, scarlet curls fanning out from her head. She entered the room, pushing the yellow scene tape aside.

"This is a crime scene," DI Nilsson growled. "You can't come in here!"

Ignoring her, Julie said calmly, "I need some time alone with my client. After we have talked, she can give you her official statement. Let's meet at the station in, say, two hours?"

"Absolutely not," DI Nilsson said.

"I'm afraid Ms. Ekstrom will need to ride with us, but you can have all the time you need to talk—privately—at the police station," DI Lindell said reasonably, almost amicably.

Good cop, bad cop, Ada thought, suppressing a hysterical giggle.

Julie turned to Ada. "Do not say a word, *not a single word*, until we have had a chance to talk. Do you understand?"

Ada nodded weakly.

Julie made arrangements to follow the detectives in her Mercedes.

Ada, lost in her own thoughts, involuntarily searched out the hallway floor. The blood was starting to dry and darken into a tacky, reddish brown. Ada knew she would never set foot in here again.

Chapter 19
Holdings Condominium Complex, Malmö, Sweden
Day −2

Sameer awoke early and automatically began preparing for the dawn prayer. The water hit against the metal basin as he turned on the faucet and yawned, not quite fully awake. Then, he froze. There was a subtle change to the atmosphere.

He looked toward the front door. Erik's coat and shoes were gone, his keys absent from the silver Nambe bowl on the side table. In a few swift strides, he was over to Erik's door, flinging it open.

He stood there for a long moment, his mind running furiously through the possibilities. He couldn't comprehend that Erik would leave without his final payment, the *one million dollars* —it didn't make sense. He called Fatima and told her to come immediately, hanging up before she could reply.

Sameer began systematically wiping down the apartment. He thought carefully back to the surfaces he had touched. He had Fatima pull the linens from his bed and then gather the towels from the bathroom and kitchen. Wearing gloves, she replaced the sheets and towels with clean ones from the cabinet. They loaded and started the dishwasher; the swooshing of water filled the otherwise quiet space.

Sameer quickly gathered the waste from the bin and threw his belongings haphazardly into his overnight bag. It took two trips to get everything to Fatima's car. Within forty-five minutes of waking, they left, seeing no one.

Fatima waited nervously in the car as Sameer dashed inside the lab, disappearing in the thick fog. It was early morning, and the streets were mostly quiet and still. Fatima cracked the window, the fresh, cool air calming her nerves a fraction.

Sameer unlocked the door and went directly to the decontamination chamber. He pulled on his biohazard suit, coaching himself to slow down and remain vigilant. He duct-taped the sleeves over the gloves, just as Erik had taught him. The silver gleamed in the dim light, reminding him of handcuffs. Shaking off the image, he double-checked the integrity of his suit and entered the chamber.

There, in the medical fridge, stood three vials.

Three of Allah's soldiers, ready and waiting to do extraordinary work.

He removed the test tube container and positioned it on the table. Using a sterile pipette, he painstakingly transferred the contents of the vials into three empty travel-size Dove liquid soap containers. Then he disinfected the outside of the containers and gently, reverently, placed them in a battered red-and-white Igloo lunch box, into which he added ice cubes, one by one, until the containers were fully surrounded. He slid the top shut with a click.

The outside of the cooler was sprayed generously with disinfectant and encased in a plastic bag. He cinched the top and triple-knotted the ends, then covered the bag in disinfectant. He repeated the process two more times and then carefully placed the bundle outside the chamber.

Sameer turned his attention to the cages. The four cats were in various stages of decay. One of the cats was missing much of its skin and shiny, iridescent tendons were visible amongst the dark red muscle. Its yellow teeth were bared, as if hissing. What was left of its lungs were speckled with black spots—he couldn't tell if it was dried blood or something worse. He quickly doused everything in disinfectant and triple-bagged the carcasses. He vacuum-sealed them in containers and placed all three bags into a large box, keeping the flaps open.

He went through the familiar disinfection process and finally stepped out into the main lab. He stuffed the biohazard suit in the box and taped it shut. He hurried over to the supply table and, after a second's hesitation, grabbed a handful of syringes, gloves, alcohol wipes, and vials of normal saline.

Over the last several weeks, he had lain awake in Erik's guest room on numerous occasions. His mind remained active, searching for weaknesses in their plan. He kept returning to one concern—the unpredictability of human behavior and the innate human need for self-preservation.

He imagined the suicide hosts as they traveled long hours alone, experiencing the fear and uncertainty that would inevitably surface. He needed a way to make them feel safe and eliminate the perceived threat to self.

After careful consideration, he formulated a plan to ensure they didn't succumb to their potential misgivings. He would inject them with normal saline—saltwater. He would explain in scientific detail that he was injecting them with a "vaccine" which would impart complete immunity to the virus they were carrying.

The decision did not come lightly; he felt an acute discomfort in being dishonest to fellow Islamic brothers. He concluded, partly because everything had fallen into place so perfectly, it all had to be Allah's will. He assuaged his guilt by reassuring himself that this was bigger than him, bigger than all of them. They couldn't risk anything to jeopardize what had clearly been Allah's work. Above all, it was their duty to stop the spread of immorality propagated by the American infidels. He would have his place in Islamic history, and forever change the world.

He placed the cooler and other supplies inside a crisp Design House shopping bag and covered it with several random pieces of clothing. He was ready.

∿

Fatima looked relieved when Sameer finally emerged from the thinning fog and pulled open the car door. He placed the Design House bag on the footwell behind the passenger seat.

"*Do not* touch that bag," Sameer said. "Drive one block and park in the first available spot. I'll meet you there when I'm done." Sameer shut the door and turned away. Though he felt like sprinting, he forced himself to walk calmly and normally.

He spent the next hour wiping surfaces and gathering materials for disposal. He was determined to leave behind no evidence of their work. Once satisfied, he made several trips to different industrial dumpsters in the neighborhood.

The air was heavy with moisture and, as he walked, a light rain began to fall. Impatiently, he shook off the drops of water that beaded on his eyelashes and peppered his hair. He threw the sealed box containing the cats in the next dumpster he came upon, eager to be rid of them.

Once this was completed, he locked the door for the final time, walked briskly to Fatima's car, and jumped into the passenger seat, ignoring her white face and anxious expression. He leaned back and glanced behind the seat. The bag looked untouched.

"Where to?" she asked hesitantly. She was desperately hoping he would say home, because her bladder felt close to bursting.

Sameer turned to her, the pupils of his eyes so dilated they appeared black in the dawn light. The rain suddenly intensified, the silence morphing into a muted roar.

"The airport," he replied firmly, his jaw set in determination.

Chapter 20
The Centers for Disease Control and Prevention, Atlanta, GA
Day –2

The atmosphere of the CDC lobby was somber, grim even. Mallory's heels echoed loudly on the smooth marble as she walked, amplified by the area's near-empty state. Gone were the usual animated conversations and polite smiles.

She climbed the stairs and was surprised to see Rory already at his desk. She couldn't recall when he had ever made it to the office before her. He glanced up and immediately stood to give her a hug.

"Any word from Brooke?" he asked, his expression tense. He knew how much Brooke meant to Mallory and her sister.

Mallory shook her head. "She's still listed as one of the thousands missing."

She cleared her throat, swallowing back tears. "Kate wants to fly to California to look for her in person. I was able to convince her, at least for now, to leave it to the professionals. I can't imagine there's anything she could do."

She placed her bag onto her desk and began unpacking. "They aren't letting anyone into the flood zones except the military and emergency services. At least, that's what they're reporting on the news."

Rory frowned. "The media is more focused on pointing fingers. In my opinion, that can wait. Someday, it will be important to analyze what went wrong and prevent this from happening again. In the here and now, I wish they would concentrate on updating the public on the rescue efforts. They need to communicate to people how they can help. I'm sure there are many who would like to donate money or resources."

"I've noticed the same thing." Mallory sighed. "It seems like the never-ending supply of political 'experts' to spout their personal opinions. As is typical, the Democrats are blaming Republicans and vice versa."

She clicked on her computer and grabbed a bottled water out of the mini-fridge. There was a moment of silence, both of them deep in thought.

"These conditions produce a fertile breeding ground for disease," Mallory said. "To get to safety, people inevitably needed to wade through the flood water. Damage to sewer lines can lead to leakage and exposure to intestinal bacteria, like E. coli. Also, the lack of running water prevents hand washing, which can further spread contaminants."

Rory glanced at Mallory. "You're on call in a few weeks. Do you think the government will ask the CDC for prevention assistance, or will they wait until people are sick?"

"Hmm, it depends." Mallory considered this. "Obviously, prevention is always preferable. We should ask Dr. Lee if he's heard anything. Maybe he can contact someone out there to get a better read on the situation and make a recommendation."

The rest of the morning passed with agonizing slowness. Mallory found it difficult to concentrate and caught herself repeatedly glancing at her phone.

After spending several hours using statistical software to analyze her latest Marburg data, she needed a break. She answered a text from Marcus and then composed one to Kate, asking how she was doing. Afterward, she decided to eat an early lunch. She was glad she had planned ahead and packed a Caesar salad and chicken wrap last night. She pulled the wrap out of her lunch bag and offered half to Rory.

"Thanks, but I was just about to run down and grab something from the canteen. Could I get you a coffee?" Rory rose from his desk and stretched.

Mallory smiled gratefully. "Yes, light cream with no sugar, please."

"Gotcha. I actually need to do a few things in level four today. Do you want to head there after lunch?"

She nodded, swallowing a bite. "I'm scheduled to run PCR on my samples today. First, I'd like to talk to Dr. Lee. I'll meet you downstairs in a few?"

"Sounds good." He grinned and was gone.

The rest of the day passed uneventfully. Mallory tracked down Dr. Lee, who promised to talk to the director about recommendations on assistance in California.

She met Rory in the lobby, and they walked over to the lab together. Rory typically worked in the BSL-2 lab; however, his work occasionally required the extra precaution of level four. Other than Mallory, there were currently only two other researchers utilizing the BSL-4 lab for their projects.

She was grateful for his company that afternoon. She often spent long hours alone in the sterile, silent space, fighting the claustrophobia of decontamination on her own. Several years ago, the lab helmets had been equipped with wireless communication. His familiar voice in her ear was a welcome change.

Chapter 21
Sturup Guesthouse, Malmö, Sweden
Day −2

Fakir paced the room. He paused intermittently to part the semi-sheer curtains, his eyes searching the parking lot expectantly.

Omar and Habib sat on the edge of the expansive bed, discussing how well they had slept on a mattress as soft as a cloud.

Barakah was sitting across from them at the rich mahogany desk. He heard the glass in the window rattling, reminding him of chattering teeth, as another plane took off with a low rumble. He had one leg tucked under him, the other leg absentmindedly swiveling the chair back and forth. All three were feigning nonchalance, as if they hadn't noticed Fakir's behavior.

In truth, Fakir's constant pacing was making Barakah more and more apprehensive. He continued to banter with the others, instinctively not wanting to show any sign of weakness.

Suddenly, there came a staccato-like double-tap on the door. Barakah flinched and tried to cover it by stretching and getting to his feet. Fakir unlatched the solid door and swung it open, a broad smile on his face.

He embraced the tall, clean-cut man, and clapped him on the back several times. The three younger men stood in anticipation, facing the newcomer. Barakah noticed a battered, red and white lunch box in his hand.

Fakir turned toward the others and declared proudly, "This is my brother, Sameer."

Chapter 22
Mission Beach, San Diego, CA
Day −1

CNS NEWS

Tsunami destruction more severe than first predicted

Los Angeles, (CNS)—Officials report the number of confirmed dead at 21,909, with thousands still unaccounted for after Tuesday's San Diego tsunami, making it the deadliest natural disaster in recorded American history. The structural damage estimates are in the billions, with a projected 440,000 people lacking access to basic necessities such as water, food, and shelter.

The Federal Emergency Management Agency (FEMA) has established a displacement camp in the open area bordering lower Colina Lake, near Chula Vista, CA. There are reports the camp is currently over-capacity, with an estimated 17,000 occupants and enough supplies for approximately half that number. According to FEMA director Edward Martin, "Those with accessible friends or relatives are strongly encouraged to seek temporary shelter elsewhere."

Medical centers surrounding San Diego are overwhelmed with patients, and wait times are reported at thirty hours or more. Temporary medical centers have formed at various school gymnasiums in areas bordering the flood zones. Ridgeway High School in Chula Vista is thought to be housing more than 1,000 overflow patients.

FEMA has been widely criticized for being unprepared for a disaster of this magnitude. Martin cited longstanding budget cuts as a reason for the apparent lack of optimal response.

Chapter 23
Airspace, North Atlantic Ocean
Day −1

Barakah looked out the window and was greeted by impenetrable darkness. He closed his eyes, picturing the vast ocean hurtling by beneath him. His eyes shot open as a wave of vertigo washed over him.

He had never before been on an airplane and, under different circumstances, flying would have sparked a certain level of excitement. Instead, as he looked down, his hands were clammy and trembling.

In expectation? Fear? Excitement? No, definitely not excitement. Regret? This thought came to him unbidden. He sat up as if struck.

After a long moment, he was able to sadly acknowledge that regret was precisely what he was feeling. He closed his eyes, asking Allah for strength, and felt only marginally better. He wondered how Omar and Habib were faring on their flight to Omaha. At least they had each other.

"Are you okay?" a child's voice asked him in Swedish. A girl with light brown hair and large brown eyes looked at him curiously. When he didn't answer immediately, she resumed coloring enthusiastically. Barakah saw a picture with a smiling pig in a bright red dress alongside another pig clutching a dinosaur the color of green beans.

Barakah shot a glance at the child's mother sitting in the aisle seat. She was absorbed with work on her laptop, her fingers flying over the keys.

"Yes, I'm fine," he answered awkwardly.

"Honey, don't bother the nice young man," the girl's mother said without looking up.

"I, um, no… She isn't bothering me."

The woman looked up at him, fingers at a temporary standstill, and smiled warmly. One of her front teeth was slightly crooked. She had a smattering of freckles over her nose and a single dimple on her right cheek. Her brown eyes were the same milk chocolate shade as her daughter's.

"I used to get nervous flying too," she said. "Now I'm used to it." She resumed typing on her laptop and continued matter-of-factly, "Distraction always helped me. I have a Reader's Digest if you want to borrow it."

Without waiting for a reply, she deftly pulled the magazine from her bag and handed it to Barakah. "I can't promise it's thrilling reading but, hey, it's better than nothing."

Eyes still on the screen of her laptop, she reached into another bag and pulled out a squeezable applesauce. She twisted off the top and handed it to her daughter ,who said, "Yum! Thanks, Mommy."

"Thank you," Barakah said finally. He opened the magazine, the easy manner of the mother and daughter putting him at ease.

"You could also color with me," the girl said, plopping her coloring page in front of him. "This is Peppa Pig and her brother, George." She handed him a crayon.

He looked at the crayon for a long moment. Surprising himself, he picked it up and began coloring. The next few hours of the flight passed by quickly as he chatted in Swedish with the girl and her mother. He learned the girl's name was Maddy.

"Short for Madeline," she informed him with a solemn expression.

After a while, Maddy tired of coloring and fell asleep on a worn-looking stuffed animal that may have been a rabbit.

Barakah wadded up his sweatshirt and laid his head against the cool window. He closed his eyes and, instantaneously, his stomach clenched and cramped with unease. He feared he would need to make a quick break for the bathroom.

His thoughts turned to the night everything began for him, at the tobacco lounge nearly a year ago. Since then, countless evenings were spent crowded around the rickety, uneven table at the mosque. The four stayed up late into the night, reading from the Quran, drinking bottomless cups of coffee and tea, and ironing out the specifics of their mission.

The Imam would join them at times, praising their bravery and devotion to Allah. Barakah was barely able to contain his pride at the Imam's words. He saw a similar sentiment reflected on his friends' faces. Being a part of something significant made Barakah feel important, needed even, for the first time in his life.

They initially planned on launching a multi-location vehicle attack. Travel visas for Omar and Habib were secured several months ago after starting a laborious application process.

Omar and Habib's devout Muslim mother supported her two sons' travel to America to study, especially after receiving special attention and praise from the Imam. With his careful and practiced coaxing, she willingly gave up custodial rights, citing her financial inability to further care for them. On paper, they were scheduled to stay with a maternal aunt and uncle in Omaha, Nebraska, during which they would finish their school coursework and eventually return to Sweden.

Barakah's visa proved harder to obtain. His student permit request was repeatedly denied. He was eventually provided a genuine visa and passport belonging to a young man close in age and very similar in appearance. He never learned the details surrounding the purchase of the documents. He figured they were sold by someone who didn't plan to travel outside the country and desperately needed money. He was also unsure of the source of the funds, but it seemed there was no shortage of money for the mission.

His thoughts returned to the whirlwind events of the day.

Sameer announced that, according to Allah's will, a remarkable opportunity had arisen. Their plan, once a three-vehicle assault, had now changed to a coordinated, large-scale biological attack. The tsunami was another of Allah's blessings, a sign that it was time to strike. They felt compelled to take advantage of the circumstances and end the dark seeds of corruption propagated by the West.

They filled the hours before the flight refining the new plan in minute detail.

As they packed their meager belongings, Sameer explained he was sending them with a vaccine. He painstakingly went through the steps they would need to inject themselves. He made them practice before he was satisfied. The vaccine would protect them from the ill effects of the virus while still allowing transmission to others.

Barakah didn't understand the logistics of how everything worked. Science wasn't his strong suit. He did understand that the virus was very deadly but, with the grace of Allah, he would be protected.

∿∿∿

In his airplane seat, Barakah awakened to the sound of rubber striking pavement. The rumble of the thrust reversers startled him, causing his pulse to bound wildly in his neck, and his body to shift forward and rock on its own accord as the plane braked sharply. A sense of dread enveloped him so completely that, for a moment, he couldn't move. With his eyes still closed, his hands resumed shaking. Anxiety-laced adrenaline coursed through him.

He tried to avoid thinking of familiar surroundings—he was sure he would never see his home again. The more he tried to put it out of his mind, the sharper and more vivid the scenes became. The recreation room at the mosque with its perpetual scent of coffee, sweat, and dust. The cramped apartment where he would toss a ragged, orange Nerf ball with his brother, ignoring the protestations of his sisters. He almost smiled as he pictured the used ball they had found on the street. It looked as if it had been attacked by some type of foam-devouring insect.

Don't think. Just follow the plan.

"You're awake!" Maddy said happily when he finally opened his eyes. She pulled off her bubble-gum pink headphones, and, without waiting for a reply, began rattling off the sites they were going to see in Chicago.

Maddy's mother quickly stuffed her laptop, book, and water into her carry-on. They began walking down the aisle toward the cabin door. She looked at Barakah with concern. "Do you have someone meeting you? Do you speak enough English?"

"I'm meeting my cousin," he lied. "I know a little English—enough to get by." This last part wasn't a complete lie. He actually knew English quite well. It was the only class he had ever received a high mark in. He had always been secretly intrigued by America.

He hesitated. "Thank you for helping me…on the flight, I mean. I guess I was a little nervous." He turned to Maddy and grinned. "Have fun on your vacation," he said. They were swept along in the crowd exiting the plane and were soon separated.

"Barakah, Barakah!"

He heard his name and turned. Maddy, having let go of her mother's hand, was dashing toward him, a purposeful look on her face.

"You forgot this." She held out the coloring page they had completed together.

He crouched down next to her. "I think you should keep it. You did such an excellent job."

"No," she replied firmly. "I really want you to have it. Please—take it."

"How can I say no? Thanks, Maddy." He gave her a final smile and walked away.

Before he fully comprehended what he was doing, he felt his feet moving toward the wall, out of the stream of travelers. He set his bag on the ground and pulled out the sealed bag containing the soap container and disposable phone. Unceremoniously, he turned toward the trash can and threw both in. He re-slung his bag over his shoulder and resumed walking, holding the paper carefully in his hands so as not to crease it.

Chapter 24
Los Angeles International Airport, Los Angeles, CA
Day +16

Mallory shifted uncomfortably in the too-firm seats of the economy rental car as she pulled out of the LAX parking garage. She exhaled in relief—at least the flight was over. The anxiety she felt at takeoff intensified over the course of the flight, leaving her with a residual feeling of utter exhaustion. She reached over and took a cautious sip of the steaming coffee from the Starbucks airport kiosk.

LAX was the busiest she had ever seen it. Exiting the airport took twice as long as usual. She had to wade through huge throngs of people. As reported by CNS, there was a high volume of people coming into the area to look for those still missing, even though FEMA strongly recommended against it. Regional hotels were completely booked, and resources were still scarce.

Mallory's heart sank as she thought of Brooke. There was still no word from her. Kate was losing hope she would ever be found.

Deciding she needed some distraction, she used voice recognition software on her phone to call Marcus. Disappointed he didn't answer, she left a message letting him know she had arrived safely.

As Google Maps directed her to the highway, she began a mental checklist of what she wanted to accomplish today. After several weeks of bureaucratic roadblocks, the CDC had finally gotten the green light to send in a Medical Officer for a field evaluation.

It took over two hours to reach the outskirts of Las Colinas National Park, the site of the temporary refugee camp for tsunami survivors. As

Mallory wound around the northernmost tip of the lake's dark waters, she caught her first glimpse of the camp. She knew it housed tens of thousands of people; however, the sheer enormity of it took her breath away. Thick forest-green canvas tents, in neatly lined rows, stretched as far as she could see. The landscape surrounding the camp consisted of brown hills spotted with squat creosote bushes, and mountain peaks visible in the distant background.

She located the lot for temporary parking. After circling several times in search of a spot, she finally found an unmarked opening on the gravel. She pulled on two large medical bags, positioned the straps to crisscross the front of her light-blue scrub top, and, spotting a sign for "Reception," quickly followed the arrows. She passed several men and women in familiar camouflage fatigues, postures at ease, guns slung over their shoulders.

Two young men dressed in identical BDU's were positioned at the end of the lot. She noticed one of the soldiers nudge the other and say in a low whisper, "Check out that nurse."

Mallory continued walking, fighting the urge to roll her eyes. She was mistaken for a nurse so frequently she was surprised it still irritated her. She also knew that many harbored preconceived notions about young attractive women like her with blonde hair. All in all, she didn't always fit others' physical expectations of a physician.

Mallory firmly believed nursing was a noble profession, attracting many exceptionally bright and hard-working men and women. But after four years of competitive pre-med courses in college, four rigorous years of medical school, three years of eighty-hour weeks in residency, and a two-year infectious disease fellowship with the US Army, she felt she had earned the title of MD.

During residency, when she lost count of how many patients asked her "Are you the nurse?" she seriously considered cutting or dyeing her hair.

She ultimately decided she wasn't going to change who she was for others.

After several minutes of walking, she came upon an enormous canopy-style tent with four soldiers stationed near the entrance. At least one hundred people were in a line that snaked back and forth at sharp ninety-degree angles, reminding her of childhood trips to the amusement park. The people in line looked tired and disheveled, and distress was etched all over their faces.

Mallory felt a rush of sympathy and paused to compose herself. It was reminiscent of something she would see in a developing country, not something she had ever imagined seeing in America.

It's been several weeks since the tsunami. Have these poor people been without shelter all this time?

After a moment's hesitation, Mallory walked to the front of the line and pulled out her CDC identification. The smell of unwashed bodies and stale urine harshly greeted her. An immense, harried-looking man with a red "Volunteer" sticker on his shirt sat perched precariously on a metal folding chair. Tired eyes flicked toward Mallory as she approached.

"Medical?" he asked without preamble.

"Yes, I'm—," Mallory began.

"Check-in over there, second table on your left." He waved her through and immediately turned to the next person in line.

Mallory located the table and was greeted warmly by a middle-aged woman, also wearing a red sticker, dressed in brightly patterned Wonder Woman scrubs.

"I'm Mindy Walker, one of the volunteer nurses," she said sticking out her hand as she rose from the chair. "You must be Dr. Hayes from the CDC. Thank you so much for coming."

"It's nice to meet you," Mallory said, returning Mindy's smile, and immediately liking the no-nonsense older woman.

"Let's swing by the medical bunkhouse first. You can drop off your personal gear and get settled a bit. After that, I'll give you a quick tour of the camp itself. Dr. Walsh would like to personally walk you through the clinic. He'll be free in about an hour." Mindy spoke the last words over her shoulder, having already walked out of the tent.

"I'm not familiar with Dr. Walsh," Mallory replied. "Is he also a volunteer?" Mallory quickened her pace, slipping out between the flaps.

"No, Major Gregory Walsh is a physician with The Army Medical Corps. Apparently, he has been with the Army for 27 years. He's in charge of the camp's medical services."

"I see. I was in Army Medical for two years. We never crossed paths," Mallory said, concentrating on balancing her over-sized bags while keeping up with the energetic woman ahead of her.

Mindy stopped abruptly. "Here, let me help you with that." Without waiting for an answer, she removed one of the bags and hooked it over her shoulder.

"Thanks."

Mindy continued. "Dr. Walsh has been here since day one," Mindy continued. "He hasn't left the camp or stopped working, except to eat or sleep, of course. He has a Medical Corps team of two physician assistants and three RNs. There have been a few volunteer physicians and nurses to help over the last several weeks, but Dr. Walsh has taken on the bulk of the responsibilities."

Mallory noted a hint of admiration in Mindy's voice. "It sounds like the camp is lucky to have him."

"We are." Mindy nodded, her smile faltering. "The anguish here is still so raw. Nearly everyone has lost loved ones…." She took in a deep breath, visibly trying to rein in her emotions.

"I'm so sorry," said Mallory. She patted Mindy awkwardly on the back, attempting to comfort her.

Mindy slowed to a stop in front of one of the tents, which was indistinguishable at first glance from the thousands of others. Only then did Mallory notice a laminated paper pinned to the thick canvas. A quick glance to the neighboring tents confirmed they were similarly marked. Each tent was labeled with a single letter followed by a numerical designation. The tent they entered read *M 114*.

As if reading her thoughts, Mindy explained, "The *M* stands for medical and one hundred and fourteen is the tent number. The tents are labeled in a grid beginning with number one. The majority of tents have an *F*, for family, followed by a number. Each family has a unique number, like an address. Residents without any family are separated into tents by gender, designated by *W* or *M*, followed by the tent number. It's a crude way to track who lives where, but at least they can be easily located when needed. As of yesterday, there were finally more refugees leaving than entering."

"Where are they going?" Mallory asked.

"We have over fifty social workers helping people connect to any living family members or friends who may be able to take them in."

Mindy pointed to one of the empty bunks; white linens were folded neatly on top. A single open cubby was positioned at the foot of the bed. Mallory set the bag containing her clothes and toiletries on the bare mattress and promptly announced, "I'm ready."

Mindy proceeded with a quick tour, efficiently showing her the basic organization of the camp. As they walked, Mallory noticed a number of FEMA employees, their blue polo shirts with the agency name on the front and back, making them easily recognizable.

"Latrines and showers are spaced in a line running west to east, basically bisecting the camp directly down the middle. There is at least one facility for every ten tents. This maximizes access for all residents of the camp. The camp layout follows recommendations as outlined by the United Nations Refugee Agency. Dr. Walsh said you would be specifically interested in the hygiene and water facilities."

She handed over a short stack of papers and Mallory was surprised to see specific sections highlighted for her in bright, neon yellow.

"You can see that the bathrooms and showers are at least twenty feet away from the closest dwelling, with no single tent more than one hundred and fifty feet away. There are also pre-filtered water tanks spaced strategically along the entire length of the south border. Engineers are currently working on borehole development and plan to implement water taps over the next few weeks."

Mallory scanned a few of the highlighted passages as they walked, again adjusting her pace to keep up. She would have to look over the specifics in detail and take some measurements herself, but it seemed as if the camp had been constructed with sound public health and safety recommendations in mind. Mallory was relieved major changes in structure and layout were likely not necessary.

Impressive. Dr. Walsh seems to be on top of his game. No wonder Mindy holds him in high regard. She is quite knowledgeable about the camp set-up and regulations, especially since she is just a volunteer here. He must have prepped her when he found out I was coming.

They passed a string of trucks unloading crates near a building constructed of prefabricated materials. The unadorned corrugated metal glinted in the sun, causing Mallory to squint.

"That building is the food distribution center. Everyone is issued a ration card upon acceptance into the camp, which reminds me…" She rooted around several pockets of her scrubs before pulling out a small white card with a barcode in the center. She handed it to Mallory. "Here's your card. Keep close track of it—it's *not* easy to get another one issued." She rolled her eyes as if speaking from experience.

"How many calories per day are provided the men and women?" Mallory asked, sidestepping a group of children barreling toward her, giggling as they disappeared behind the building.

"2,000 for women and 2,500 for men. Caloric recommendations for children are based on age groups as recommended by the US Department of Health and Human Services."

Mallory nodded, satisfied.

"What's that?" She gestured to a crowd of people clustered around a small tower. Mindy followed her gaze. "Those are strategically placed charging stations. Electronic devices keep families in touch and help combat some of the boredom that inevitably arises."

After what seemed like an infinite number of tents, Mindy stopped in front of another prefabricated building, nearly identical to the food distribution center but significantly smaller. An unassuming red sign with "Medical Services" above the entrance was the only clue to the building's identity.

"This is it," Mindy said, opening the door and ushering Mallory inside.

The interior wasn't what she was anticipating. Excluding the exposed warehouse-style walls, she could have been standing in any urgent care center in the country. Back-to-back utilitarian chairs with curved black hand-rests and washed-out blue upholstery were grouped together, taking up much of the available space. Approximately one-third of the chairs were occupied, with a few patients flipping casually through magazines or using their smartphones. A large empty desk, complete with a sliding glass window, sported a tablet screen prominently labeled "CHECK-IN."

Without missing a beat, Mindy continued to the wooden door to the left of the desk, Mallory trailing behind her. The familiar scent of antiseptic and industrial cleaning solution was surprisingly comforting. The smells and sights reminded her of the medical bay at basic training.

She spotted Dr. Walsh immediately. He radiated a sense of authority, perceptible even across the room. He was tall, with a strong jaw, fashionable plastic frames, and neatly trimmed silver hair. He was talking to a group of women in scrubs.

At first, Mallory waited patiently while he continued to talk. After a few minutes passed without acknowledgement, she had the uncomfortable sensation he enjoyed making her wait.

She cleared her throat and smiled. "Pardon my interruption. I'm Dr. Mallory Hayes from the CDC. I believe you were expecting me?"

Walsh turned toward her, hesitated for a split second, then grasped her hand firmly. Mallory noticed his eyes were cool and his expression unreadable. His handshake lingered a moment longer than necessary. His hazel eyes flicked down her body almost imperceptibly.

"Ah, yes, the CDC is here to save the day." His tone was jovial and the others in the room obliged by laughing quietly or smiling.

Mallory acknowledged his comment with a brief, polite smile—always the consummate professional. In truth, she was beginning to think Walsh was going to make her short visit unpleasant. She was used to a certain level of bureaucratic resistance. After all, she did work for a civilian branch of the government.

Walsh gave her a perfunctory tour of the clinic. They walked past several patients, separated by standard hospital-issue curtains hooked on a latticework of metal rods. As she walked by, she could feel eyes on her, as if pleading for attention or assistance. One elderly man, his weathered skin and slack jaw in sharp contrast to his piercing blue eyes, held her stare as she passed.

The next cubicle contained two hospital beds. The curtain, normally pulled tight for privacy, was pushed against the wall. Two dark-haired teenagers lay facing each other, eyes closed in sleep. Their long, thin limbs were barely visible beneath the twisted sheets.

As Mallory watched, an RN strode into the room and plugged in a portable nebulizer, her movements brisk and efficient. The mechanical whir of the bed being raised caused the patient to stir. His eyes opened and, for a fleeting moment, Mallory caught a glimpse of panic in his eyes. The flash of emotion was replaced with a look of discomfort as he began coughing. Mallory made a mental note to check his chart. She needed to ensure that those caring for patients with respiratory symptoms wore masks.

Walsh halted abruptly at the end of the hallway.

"Any questions?" he asked, interrupting her thoughts.

"What type of patients have you seen over the last few weeks? Have there been many infectious disease cases?"

"Of course. There were the expected cases of infectious diarrhea, mostly in those who were directly exposed to or submerged in visibly contaminated flood water.

"There were also staphylococcal skin infections, presumed MRSA in a few cases that didn't initially respond to first-line treatment. All were ultimately treated successfully with oral antibiotics, I might add. Mostly, we've been dealing with illness and disease common to a population this size. We've had three myocardial infarctions, which were promptly transferred to the university hospital. We've also treated otitis media, diabetics in need of insulin, back pain, and so on."

"That makes sense. Did you perform any stool or wound cultures on patients with suspected infectious etiologies?" Mallory asked.

Walsh turned toward her and paused, as if measuring his words carefully. "I didn't think it necessary," he said, unable to keep the annoyance out of his voice.

"I agree, it's not clinically necessary given their response to antibiotics," Mallory replied quickly. "I was inquiring from an epidemiological, or public health, perspective."

During training, she had been exposed to older, male physicians who treated her with a certain paternalistic attitude. Most of them meant well. She didn't let it bother her. She was firmly secure in her medical knowledge and expertise. Walsh's reaction seemed to go beyond that.

He seems resentful of my presence here, as if he has something to prove...or hide.

Chapter 25
Las Colinas FEMA Temporary Relocation Camp
Day +18

Mallory unpacked several kits for sample collection and stacked them in neat rows, nearly filling the empty shelf of the supply cabinet she had commandeered. She added boxes of disposable paper gowns and masks, in case the need arose for barriers beyond the standard medical precautions.

Certain microbes, like influenza, spread easily via invisible respiratory droplets. Others, like Clostridium difficile, a cause of potentially severe healthcare-associated diarrhea, infect people by direct contact with contaminated surfaces. They live on inanimate objects like doorknobs for days, even weeks. Both pathogens have the potential to travel rapidly in healthcare settings, especially if patients are in close quarters.

The next several days passed quickly. Mindy assisted her, anticipating her next steps as if they had been working together for years. Walsh, on the other hand, barely acknowledged her. Mallory was actually relieved she could work without interference.

By Mallory's third afternoon at the camp, her comprehensive CDC report and final recommendations were complete. She anticipated a brief meeting with the medical staff first thing in the morning.

I can reserve a flight out of LAX around midday and be home in time for dinner with Marcus. The thought of flying again so soon made her stomach tighten and her breathing quicken. She took a few slow, deep breaths and felt slightly calmer.

She walked through to the waiting room, absently thinking about grabbing a cup of coffee, when she slowed to a stop.

The room was packed.

Chapter 26
Las Colinas FEMA Temporary Relocation Camp
Day +22

"Code 45, room eight, medical center; repeat code 45—all available medical personnel, please proceed to room eight of the medical center." The sudden, impersonal voice projected through the PA system startled Mallory. She sat frozen, a bite of eggs, red with tabasco sauce, suspended halfway to her mouth.

Code 45—Cardiopulmonary arrest. She dropped her fork, food already forgotten, and ran.

By the time she reached the open curtain of room eight, it was almost completely packed. It radiated a frenetic, barely contained energy.

She pulled on protective gear and deftly maneuvered her way into the room. Walsh had taken a position at the head of the bed, obviously in charge. A crash cart had been pushed haphazardly into the corner. The lips of an RN moved silently as she counted each chest compression.

"Mindy, you begin bag-mask respirations. Remember, slow and steady. Make sure you have a good seal. Deja, put on the AED and draw up 1 milligram of epinephrine, then wait for further instructions. Jake, start a large bore peripheral IV and begin normal saline, wide open. Continue compressions." Walsh spoke quickly and calmly, his face impassive.

Mallory joined him and they turned to look at the cardiac monitor. It was emitting a loud, insistent warning.

"Hemodynamically unstable ventricular tachycardia," Mallory said automatically. VT has a distinctive ECG appearance, and the importance of its quick identification and treatment were drilled into all medical students during training.

Walsh nodded. "I agree, he needs to be shocked." He turned back to the room and called, "Stop compressions."

"Do not touch patient. Analyzing heart rhythm. Please wait." The automated defibrillator repeated these instructions twice, artificial yet disconcertingly confident. "Shock advised. Move away from patient. Shock will be delivered in 3, 2, 1…."

The unconscious patient jerked once.

All eyes instinctively turned toward the monitor. The ECG reading had flattened to a single wavering line, as if drawn by a tremulous hand. Mallory could visualize the quivering heart in his chest, the normally graceful muscle contractions now twitchy and uncoordinated.

"Jake, give Allison a break and resume compressions." Walsh didn't miss a beat. "Deja, administer the epinephrine now. We will re-analyze and shock again in two minutes."

The code continued for another 45 minutes before Walsh called 9:20 am as the time of death. The room was suddenly quiet, the disappointment tangible. There were a few audible sighs of frustration as the room emptied.

Placing the oxygen mask aside, Mallory leaned in to take a closer look. The patient was young, with the long gangly limbs of a teenager. The beginning wisps of facial hair sprouted in patches from his face, like an untended garden. His jet-black hair was unwashed and in need of a trim. He could be asleep, except for his absolute, perfect stillness. She recognized him as one of the two brothers she had recommended for respiratory precautions on first arriving.

She turned toward the curtain separating the two beds. It was drawn, shielding the other brother from view. As if sensing her gaze through the fabric, she heard a weak but urgent voice in a Middle Eastern language she couldn't identify.

"Could someone please get an interpreter on the line?" Mallory asked.

Mindy didn't hesitate. "I've got it." She turned and left the room.

A long moment passed.

Mallory broke the silence. "What are your thoughts on cause of death? I'm not very familiar with this patient."

Walsh spoke quietly. "Omar is a 15-year-old male of Middle Eastern descent with a history of asthma who presented with a productive cough, fever, wheezing, and shortness of breath. He was diagnosed with pneumonia after a chest x-ray confirmed an infiltrate in the right lower lobe.

"He demonstrated signs of an asthma exacerbation and was treated with steroids and albuterol nebs. He didn't initially respond to oral antibiotics—he remained febrile—and was switched to intravenous broad-spectrum antibiotics. Sputum was sent for analysis yesterday; susceptibilities are currently pending."

He took a deep breath and shook his head. "I was going to transfer him to the university hospital today. His oxygen requirements increased significantly this morning, but his vitals were otherwise stable. It doesn't make sense; he should have been covered no matter what the bacterial susceptibilities showed."

"Do you know where he's from?" Mallory asked.

"Sweden. Apparently, he had recently traveled to the area with his twin brother, Habib, to visit family." He shrugged and continued, "Anyway, to answer your first question, I'm guessing he developed an acute pneumothorax or pulmonary hemorrhage from infectious damage to the tissues. Acute respiratory distress syndrome is another possibility, although, I have to say, I have never personally seen this clinical picture in a previously healthy young person. The autopsy should give us more information."

"It sounds like you did everything in accordance with medical practice guidelines. I can't think of anything I would've done differently." Mallory tilted her head toward the closed curtain. "I can break the news to Habib if you want."

Walsh nodded. "Thanks."

For the first time since meeting him, she could see signs of fatigue on his face. He looked as if he was going to say more but changed his mind. He gave her a final nod as he left.

Mallory logged in and checked the name on the chart: Omar Nazari. She scanned his medical record as she waited for Mindy.

After a few minutes, Mindy returned, passing a phone to Mallory. "Because of the translation, you will have to pass the phone back and forth. Sorry, I know it's not ideal, but it's all we have."

"No problem. Thanks, Mindy."

Taking a deep, fortifying breath, Mallory parted the curtain. Two things surprised her. The first was the abject hostility in Habib's expression. The second was how thin and frail he appeared. He was nearly unrecognizable from a few days ago. A large section of his lower face was covered with a bulky white bandage. Raised, violet papules dotted every visible patch of skin. She noted significant lymphadenopathy. Nodes trailed down his neck like a string of pearls.

She checked in with the interpreter, introducing herself and briefly explaining the situation. She handed the phone to Habib, who took the phone silently, his cool eyes never leaving Mallory's. It took time, but she was eventually able to communicate to Habib that Omar had died from complications of pneumonia.

At first, Habib's expression didn't change. It became clear he didn't believe her. After passing the phone back and forth several more times, he suddenly let it slip from his fingers, and it dropped to the floor with a sharp crack.

Mallory was instantly on her feet, knowing the phone was their only means of immediate communication. She picked it up and assessed the damage. The screen was now cracked and dark.

Habib leaned forward and retched, cupping his hands in front of him as if to catch the vomit. He let out a slow moan and then collapsed on his side, sobbing.

"I'm sorry for your loss." Mallory knew he couldn't understand but felt she had to say something.

He abruptly sat up, his eyes locked intently on Mallory's. He began whispering something over and over in his native language.

"Allahu akbar, Allahu akbar."

He pointed emphatically toward the door, his eyes shining with tears.

Mallory stood there frozen, debating her options. When she didn't move right away, the volume of his voice increased, and he was suddenly shouting. She flinched imperceptibly and backed out of the room, pulling the curtain closed.

"What's going on? Why is he yelling?" Mindy was by her side, a look of concern on her face.

"He is, understandably, having a difficult time with Omar's death," Mallory replied reassuringly, peeling off her mask and protective gear. She couldn't shake the feeling there was more to his anger than that.

Mindy's gaze trailed to her hand and she realized she was still clutching the broken phone. Using a disinfectant wipe, she gave it a thorough cleaning. "This wasn't yours, was it?"

"Luckily, no," she said,."It's the Army's." A pause. "Did he throw it at you?" Mindy sounded protective, the hint of anger in her tone unmistakable.

"No, nothing like that. It slipped out of his hand." She tried turning it on, but the screen remained black.

"Hmm. Maybe it can be fixed," she said doubtfully. "Anyway, thanks for your concern, Mindy. I think he just needs some time. I'm going to give it a few hours and then check back in with him."

As they turned to walk away, Mallory noticed Mindy's drawn face and the smudges of purple discoloration under her eyes. She looked exhausted, which wasn't surprising considering the lack of sleep they had all experienced recently. Mindy took a small container of Tums out of her pocket. She popped the top with her thumb and dropped several tablets directly into her mouth.

Crunching on the tabs, Mindy said, "I have been having the most awful heartburn the last few days. It must be the stress and long hours. I haven't worked this much since, well, let's just say since I was a lot younger." She smiled wryly at Mallory. "What's next?"

"I'm going to go check in with Dr. Walsh. You should rest for a bit. You've barely slept the last few days."

"Look who's talking. I'm just glad that your boss let you stay and help out for a little longer. It's crazy the cases we're now seeing. We went so long without having to transfer anyone and then, all of a sudden, we're inundated with patients." Mindy sighed.

"That's part of what I wanted to talk to Dr. Walsh about. There's been a higher than normal number of patients with unusual symptoms. Now we have an adolescent die from community-acquired pneumonia? That's rare in itself," Mallory said.

Mindy suppressed a yawn and Mallory gave her a pointed look.

"Okay, Okay. I see when I'm not wanted." Mindy smiled. "I'll head back to the tent for a quick nap."

Mallory found Walsh in the physicians' small office located at the back of the clinic. The door stood partially open. Mallory knocked on the jam and paused, respectfully waiting for permission to enter.

"Come in," a baritone voice boomed.

She pushed the door open and entered. He glanced up briefly and gestured toward a chair. "Have a seat. How can I help you, Dr. Hayes?"

"Please, call me Mallory," she replied as she sat down. She noted he didn't extend the same informality to her.

"All right, Mallory. I'm glad you're here, and I wanted to thank you again for talking to Habib. It's never easy to lose a patient so young. How did he take the news?"

"Not well, I'm afraid. He became quite agitated, almost combative. I'm planning on letting him process things for a bit. I'll check back in with him in a few hours."

Walsh nodded. "To be honest, that doesn't surprise me. Since arriving here, the two brothers have barely responded to questions. They either gave vague responses or totally ignored us. Social services tried contacting their aunt and uncle several times but, as far as I know, haven't received a response."

"Were you able to get any sort of environmental or exposure history?" Mallory asked.

"Not even close. We were able to glean that they came from Sweden, but where they flew in or how they came to be here is anybody's guess. Per the computer records, they arrived at the camp six days ago. They didn't register a vehicle, so I assume they either arrived on foot or took one of the shuttles. They were admitted into the medical center the next day. We have a phone number for the aunt and uncle. The area code corresponds to Omaha, Nebraska, but no address." Walsh frowned, as if fully realizing the unusual circumstances.

"Maybe it's mistrust of the medical community. I'll try to get some more information from Habib when I talk to him. I noticed he had a generalized rash and lymphadenopathy. Do you suspect an infectious cause or a drug-related side effect?"

"At first, I thought it might be an allergy, but the lymphadenopathy was just documented this morning, making infection much more likely, unless it's a rare allergic reaction, such as DRESS." Walsh looked thoughtful and then scanned his medication list. "He hasn't been on any of the typical inciting medications. Also, there's no elevation of eosinophils."

"Infection seems the most likely. I can obtain swabs and have them sent off for culture."

"Sounds good. I'll keep you updated on Omar's microbiology results." He turned back to his computer, obviously ready to get back to work.

"Just one more thing, Dr. Walsh. Have you noticed the increase in infectious cases over the last several days?"

He slowly turned back, unable to hide the annoyance on his face. "Yes, obviously I noticed. Many patients are exhibiting symptoms of the common cold, not unexpected in such a large group kept in close quarters."

"Agreed," Mallory said carefully. "But there have been clinical presentations that I suspect may be from rare pathogens."

Walsh studied her for a moment. "Have you heard the saying, 'When you hear hoofbeats, think horses, not zebras?'"

Standing abruptly, Mallory replied. "Yes, I have. I'll leave you to it then." She could only take so much of his condescending attitude.

I need to talk to Rory and Dr. Lee.

Chapter 27
Malmö, Sweden
Day +22

Fakir paced the room, the muted soundtrack of an American news channel murmuring in the background. His distress was obvious. His jaw muscles were clenched and his movements were fast, jerky, and uncoordinated.

"Brother, sit down," Sameer said in a calm voice. In truth, he felt just as worried as Fakir. He was, however, far more adept at compartmentalizing his emotions. He always had been.

Fakir hesitated for a moment, shrugged, and sat down.

Sameer spoke, using the same measured tone. "I know we expected news by now-"

"It's been 23 days—*23 days* since they left Sweden. Something happened. Something is wrong. I know it. How do we explain this to the Imam? Or to all those devout servants of Islam who donated money. What do we tell them?" He shook his head in frustration, tapping his fingers nervously on the edge of the chair.

Sameer spoke softly; the steely edge in his voice was barely detectable, "We need to leave it in the hands of Allah."

This had the desired calming effect. The two sat in silence for a moment. Sameer finally stood, gazing out the window. He saw the familiar sight of the Malmö City Theatre and the lush green of the football fields beyond.

The sun has finally decided to make an appearance. He closed his eyes and tilted his head towards the warmth.

The light and view triggered a long-buried memory which floated to the surface of his mind, like a dream slowly realized upon awakening. It was about his first symphony.

He imagined he could see his father and his childhood self walking hand-in-hand on that crisp fall day, so many years ago. That was the day he fell in love with classical music.

Sameer had just seen his first performance of the Malmö Symfoniorkester (the Malmö Symphony Orchestra). Afterward, he felt different, as if the music had changed him in some fundamental but unexplained way. They walked slowly, in no particular hurry, while his father, his mood uncharacteristically light, discussed the rich history of the theater.

It wasn't often he was treated to time alone with his father. His mother and younger siblings, Fatima and Fakir, were a constant presence. They filled their cramped apartment with noise, spilled milk, and the smell of dirty diapers.

Sameer recalled the unrestrained joy he felt when his father surprised him with a used, slightly battered violin a few days after the concert. He also arranged for private lessons, which they could hardly afford. Sameer had played nearly every day since then, except, of course, the weeks he spent with Erik.

His father was strong in both personality and physical strength. He built a life for his family based on principles rooted firmly in the Islamic faith. He often spoke of the day when unbelievers and their Western ideologies would be completely destroyed—wiped from the earth. It became his passion, his focus, his life.

He died three weeks before Sameer's twelfth birthday. It was a sudden cardiac arrest, the doctors told his mother. Sameer experienced near-crippling grief.

Just like that, he was the head of the house. Filling this role helped him cope with his grief and provided a sense of purpose. He vowed to serve Allah and lead the family in Islamic faith and traditions, just as his father had.

Fakir's voice pulled him from his reverie. "What are you thinking?"

Sameer turned from the window, gripped by a sudden sense of optimism. "There is a strong possibility that the mission is still alive. We have no idea how long it takes a human host to experience symptoms. Remember, it was only tested in cats. We need to give it time."

Chapter 28
Las Colinas FEMA Temporary Relocation Camp
Day +22

enry Rodriguez slowly picked his way through the maze of tents, concentrating on each step. Suddenly, his body swaying, he paused to consider his situation. His headache was bad—no, worse than bad. It had taken on an eager, pulsating quality, causing his thoughts to become blurry and indistinct.

Earlier in the day, when he had attempted to venture out of his tent, the light from the cloudless sky increased the pounding in his head to an unbearable level. Hot tears leaked involuntarily from his lids and he was forced to stagger back to his cot. He lay there for several hours, dozing fitfully in sweat-soaked sheets.

After the sun dipped low over the hills, painting the sky a muted orange, he was finally able to leave the tent again.

Henry squinted, struggling to focus. He could just make out the outline of a couple walking ahead of him, their hands clasped together. The man was pointing a flashlight at the ground as they walked.

"S'cuse me," Henry asked, raising a finger to them. His finger hovered in the air as he tried desperately to recall what he was going to say.

The flashlight jerked up, blinding him. A wave of electric pain gripped him mercilessly, traveling from his head to the tip of his spine. An image of a tropical fish, its soft flesh pierced lightning-fast with a spear, entered his mind. He scrunched his eyes shut, fighting down a surge of nausea.

What's happening to me?

"Keep walking," the woman urged the man in a loud whisper, tugging his hand. "He's obviously drunk." They both began to turn.

"Medical!" The word came out loudly, almost triumphantly, startling all three of them.

Henry's hand dropped to his side. He began lumbering closer to them, his movements uncoordinated. The couple instinctively stepped back.

"Straight down this aisle and to your right," the man said, gesturing vaguely before hurrying away.

Henry managed a final shaky step before his vision began to fade. He stopped and blinked furiously. A feeling of helplessness morphed into all-consuming panic as he sensed he was going completely blind.

Alone in the darkness, his eyes becoming two bright-white orbs staring at nothing, he crashed onto the dirt. Fragments of gravel bit into his cheek, drawing beads of bright red blood.

Tonic-clonic movements rocked his body in a grotesque rhythm. His bladder released. Warm liquid spread around him, saturating the dirt as he continued to convulse.

Chapter 29
Las Colinas FEMA Temporary Relocation Camp
Day +23

Mallory picked her way through the dense fog. The row upon row of identical green tents added to the surreal atmosphere the thick mist created.

She had spent over an hour the previous night updating Rory on the events of the last few days. He agreed that many of the details she presented were unusual, but he didn't seem to share her sense that she was missing something. He asked her to call as soon as she was notified of the culture and pathology results. Barring any major surprises, she estimated she would be on her way back to Atlanta sometime in the next 24 hours.

After ending the call with Rory, she decided to try Marcus again. Since arriving in California, they had been able to talk only briefly, and the few times they had connected, he seemed distracted. Mallory attributed it to some level of continued grief and shock from the tsunami.

Nearly everyone in America had been affected by the loss of a family member, friend, or acquaintance. The staggering loss of life had left many angry—angry that a more effective warning system hadn't been in place.

Mallory sighed when her latest call to Marcus went to voicemail. She hung up without leaving a message. As soon as she tucked the phone under the corner of her pillow, she felt the vibration signaling a new text message.

Sorry, babe, out with the guys for a few drinks. Talk later?

She sighed again, writing and re-writing various responses. In the end, she decided not to reply. She tossed her phone on the bed and rolled onto her side, trying in vain to find a comfortable position on the ultra-thin mattress.

∿∿∿

As the medical center slowly materialized through the fog, she saw a group of people standing in a semicircle, looking at something on the ground.

She recognized the distinctive salt and pepper hair of Dr. Walsh. When someone in the group shifted, she caught a fleeting glimpse of a figure lying in the patchy weeds. His skin had turned an unnatural shade of gray and his eyes had sunk back into his skull. She moved to stand by Walsh, her brain trying to process what she was seeing.

Walsh spoke in a low voice. "Henry Rodriguez, age 62. Driver's license lists an address in Chula Vista, California, which I assume is now under water or was at some point." He gestured vaguely. "He was found here about 20 minutes ago, in between these two tents. He's registered to a tent of single men."

"No family or friends?" Mallory asked.

"He appears to be here by himself. We're working on notifying his next of kin and obtaining his medical history."

"Umm, any foul play suspected?" Mallory cringed once the words left her mouth. It sounded like a line from a bad detective movie.

Walsh didn't seem to notice. "Upon first inspection, there is no obvious cause of death." He shrugged. "Just playing the odds, but in a gentleman of this age, the most likely cause of death is a cardiac event. The scene will be processed by the Army forensic team and an autopsy will, of course, be conducted." As he spoke, a white sheet was carefully draped over the body to shield it from view.

Mallory heard murmurs behind her and turned to see a group of around twenty people. They milled about, some with concerned expressions. Many were in pajamas and holding small containers of toiletries, their morning trip to the showers interrupted.

Knowing she had nothing to contribute, Mallory entered the medical center and walked through the mass of people now filling the waiting room. She had just started to duck through the clinic door when she heard several startled exclamations.

She turned and saw a young woman stretched out on the floor, unconscious, one leg folded at an unnatural angle.

Her training automatically took over. She yelled for assistance, sank to her knees by the prone figure, and was relieved to feel a carotid pulse. She worked with the team to quickly stabilize and transfer the woman to a monitored bed.

"What happened overnight? Why is the waiting room so full again?" Mallory asked, holding the door open as the metal gurney carrying the woman squeaked through.

"I'm not sure, Doctor," Deja, one of the Army nurses said. "I just got here myself and it was like this."

Mallory made her way to the storage bay and slipped on gloves and a disposable gown. She grabbed a box of masks and snapped one over her face, straightening it to make sure she was covered, and returned to the waiting room.

She handed a mask to each patient, instructing them to put it on immediately. In her quick circuit of the room, she noted several of the patients seemed disoriented—a few were barely conscious.

She stood a moment, feeling suddenly chilled to the core, as if she'd been injected with an ice-cold saline solution.

What's going on? There is absolutely no way an upper respiratory infection would present this way.

Taking a deep breath, she forced herself to focus. Grabbing a marker from the reception desk, she began to implement a triage system using different-colored sticky notes.

The next several hours passed by in a blur. They had run out of curtained rooms and were forced to line the hallway with cots. After the second wave of patients was stabilized, Mallory sank into a chair at the nurses' station.

Craving caffeine, she took a long sip of her now-cold coffee. It was only then that she realized she hadn't seen Mindy at all that morning. She thought back a moment. The last time she saw her had been yesterday afternoon.

The tent had been dark and silent when she slipped out that morning. She assumed Mindy was still sleeping, but she hadn't checked her cot.

She felt the blood drain from her face and her pulse quicken. She stayed in her seat, trying to think of a reason why Mindy, who had barely taken time to eat or sleep this past week, would still be in bed.

Mallory jumped up, almost knocking over her coffee.

Get a grip. She's probably just catching up on some much-needed sleep.

"Have you seen Mindy yet today?" Mallory called to Dr. Walsh, who was examining an elderly woman, one of the unlucky patients stuck in an overflow cot.

"Nope, not since yesterday," he answered, continuing his exam as he spoke. "Allison called the university hospital to give them a heads up. I'm transferring Jeffries, Lopez, Berger, and Garcia. Would you be able to find the admitting physician and hand-off these patients?"

"Of course," said Mallory. "I just need to run and check on Mindy. I'll be right back." Not waiting for a reply, she hurried through the still-crowded waiting room and into the cool air.

The mist had mostly evaporated, but the sky remained a dusky gray. She broke into a light jog, retracing her steps, the matching green tents the only point of color in the washed-out, earthen landscape.

She arrived at the medical tent and pushed the thick canvas flap open. The interior was gloomy. Shadows stretched and filled the corners of the room. She made her way to Mindy's bed, barely noticing when her knee collided with the sharp angle of a storage locker.

"Mindy?" Mallory whispered, not wanting to startle her.

Mindy lay on her side, facing the tent wall and unmoving under her blanket. Mallory studied her for a moment, holding her breath. Squinting, she could see the nearly imperceptible rise and fall of her chest. Not taking her eyes off the sleeping form, she slipped on a mask and crumbled nitrile gloves.

She shook her gently. Nothing.

"Mindy," Mallory said in a loud, firm voice.

"Hmm? Oh." Mindy's voice was soft, halting. "Hi, Doctor." She turned her face toward Mallory, who stifled a gasp.

The whites of Mindy's eyes were a deep red, bringing to mind her childhood pet rabbit, Marshmallow, with its snow-white fur and distinctive ruby eyes. Her lips were cracked and peeling, open sores visible at the corners.

"Mindy, what's going on?" Mallory asked, forcing her voice to sound calm. "How long have you been like this?"

"I don't know. I have this terrible headache and my vision is blurry," Mindy murmured. Her head fell back on the pillow, as if this short interaction had drained her of energy. "I can't swallow. It's too painful." Her pillow appeared to be soaked through. She couldn't swallow her own secretions.

"Well, we'll get you feeling better in no time." Mallory tried to smile reassuringly. "Let me contact the medical center and get a stretcher here."

Mindy didn't reply, but lay gazing at the wall, trying to moisten her peeling lips with her tongue.

Mallory pulled a clean mask out of her pocket and carefully placed it over her friend's mouth and nose. "All right, I'll be right back."

Within ten minutes of her call, four volunteers were holding a bright orange plastic stretcher, the straps unclipped and dragging on the ground. She stopped them at the door, instructing them to put masks and gloves on prior to entry. They obliged without comment and were soon backing slowly out of the tent, Mindy securely strapped in.

Mallory let out a long breath. She couldn't believe her friend had gotten so sick so quickly. She was obviously dehydrated, but had what caused her symptoms in the first place? She remembered Mindy complaining of heartburn yesterday, but she otherwise seemed well. Now, Mindy was a patient at the Medical Center, where she had volunteered so many hours.

I need to take a step back, look at this from a public health perspective. I know there is some kind of infectious process causing these illnesses. But what? There are no unifying symptoms that point to one particular microbe. It seems as if the bug is affecting people in vastly different ways, which doesn't make sense.

Most infectious organisms tend to infect and produce symptoms in specific areas of the body, causing a clinical presentation in a fairly predictable pattern.

For example, Legionella bacteria, a rare contaminant in air conditioners and other water sources, causes an infection in the lungs. This manifests itself in a clear-cut way, with symptoms of cough, fever, and shortness of breath. Two other bacteria, Staphylococcus and Streptococcus, are responsible for the majority of skin infections. These classically cause signs and symptoms of redness, warmth, and pain in a well-demarcated section of skin.

After we get Mindy onto intravenous fluids and her basic work-up underway, I need to call the lab and get some answers.

∿∿∿

Mallory tapped her pen on the cheap, Formica-coated desk. She had retreated to the relative quiet of the back office to call the Army's central lab. Bland instrumental music flooded her ear as she glanced at the time on the screen—eleven minutes on hold. She blew out a breath and leaned back, her chair squeaking noisily in protest.

She should have expected this. Military inefficiency was something she experienced regularly during her years in the Army. If the samples had been sent to the CDC lab, she would have had the results yesterday.

"Sergeant Greenberg, Central Lab," said a terse female voice.

"Hi, Sergeant. Dr. Mallory Hayes here, I'm calling to obtain culture results for several patients from the Las Colinas FEMA camp."

"Please hold."

Of course. Cue the elevator music.

Mallory grabbed an old copy of *The New England Journal of Medicine* from the corner of the desk and settled back in the chair.

She had just flipped it open when she heard a man's voice. "Dr. Hayes, I'm Dr. Lombardi. I was just picking up the phone to call you guys. We have some interesting results from your cultures."

Chapter 30
Las Colinas FEMA Temporary Relocation Camp
Day +23

"I'm telling you, Rory, this is way beyond anything we've ever seen before. I've cross-checked the culture results with the histories, exams, and labs." A pause. "These patients are immunosuppressed."

"I think Dr. Lee needs to hear that. Give me a second to get to his office, and I'll put you on speaker."

She heard shuffling papers and the creak of a door, then faint voices.

She glanced absently at her nails and was surprised to see a drop of blood beading at her cuticle. She watched as the drop swelled and slid down the side of her thumb. She had bitten all of her nails down to the quick.

She silently chastised herself. To minimize the spread of germs to mucosal membranes, touching the face should be avoided altogether.

"Go ahead, Mallory. You're on speaker with myself and Dr. Lee."

"Hi, Dr. Lee. Thanks for speaking with me." Mallory held the phone between her shoulder and ear as she scrubbed her hands in the sink.

"Hi, Mallory. Of course, anytime." Mallory thought she detected a hint of concern in his voice. Using a sterile applicator, she placed a small amount of antibacterial ointment on her thumb and covered it tightly with a band-aid.

As her direct supervisor, Dr. Lee had been regularly updated via email. It was their usual and preferred form of communication. Her prior reports contained information regarding the public health aspects of the camp, such as the physical set-up, water sources, and waste removal.

Then, as she was about to depart the camp two days prior, he had electronically approved a temporary extension to evaluate the sudden surge of patients.

"I know you're busy, so I'll get right to it. When I first arrived at the camp, the medical center had few patients and, according to the Army physician, Dr. Walsh, just a small number of infectious cases, all easily treated with antibiotics. Then there was this sudden rush of patients. Their symptoms were, at first, consistent with a viral upper respiratory infection, largely unconcerning, really."

She swallowed, gathering her thoughts. "Something, however, seemed to change. Several patients quickly became very ill, and we even lost a young man to presumed pneumonia. I called the Army lab to follow-up, and they informed me the cultures and tissue samples revealed some very unusual pathogens. For example, the young patient who died was found to have Pneumocystis pneumonia."

Mallory paused, letting that sink in. Pneumocystis is a type of yeast-like fungus that causes infection exclusively in patients with a poorly functioning immune system, mostly patients with HIV or those on immunosuppressive drugs. It's classified as an opportunistic pathogen. It doesn't infect people with healthy immune systems.

"Was he on corticosteroids for some reason or HIV positive?" Dr. Lee asked as if reading her thoughts.

"The lab actually ran a reflex HIV test. It's protocol for any patient with an opportunistic infection, and it was negative. The unusual thing is that his white blood cells were at the low end of normal, with the differential showing a drastic reduction in the number of lymphocytes. I asked the lab to run a quantitative T and B cell panel. Results are pending."

There was silence as Dr. Lee and Rory seemed to take all this in.

Rory spoke first. "Sometimes severe infection can lead to a paradoxical decrease in lymphocytes instead of the typical increase the body naturally produces to fight infection."

"Agreed," said Mallory. "However, looking back at several of the seriously ill patients with an infectious picture, it appears that the one thing they had in common were very, very low lymphocytes—nearly undetectable in some cases."

Mallory plowed on, eager to fully update them. "Several of these patients have grown opportunistic organisms on culture, like toxoplasmosis, mycobacterium and, this is interesting, the twin brother of the deceased patient I just mentioned, developed a large skin ulcer, generalized rash, and severe weight loss. A tissue culture obtained from the ulcer grew Bartonella."

Bartonella causes a rare type of local bacterial infection associated with lymph node swelling. It is known in the medical community as "Cat Scratch Disease" and is usually treated easily with antibiotics. In comparison to patients with a normal, functioning immune system, immunodeficient patients exposed to certain strains of the bacteria experience a more widespread, potentially serious infection.

"All patients were reflexively tested for HIV and were found to be negative."

Silence. She could imagine Rory and Dr. Lee looking at each other in surprise.

"I asked the lab to scan in all the results and email them to me as soon as possible," Mallory said.

"I guess the question is, Mallory, what on earth do you think is going on?" A pause. "To me, it sounds like these patients are immunosuppressed. Other than HIV, I'm not aware of any infectious process that exclusively depletes lymphocytes. As you know, HIV causes a drop in a subset of lymphocytes—CD4 T lymphocytes to be precise. B lymphocytes aren't affected."

Dr. Lee spoke the last part softly, as if deep in thought. "It will be interesting to see the T and B cell subset results."

"The other thing is," Mallory said, "it takes years for HIV patients' CD4 cells to drop to such a level that opportunistic pathogens thrive. In these patients, it seems to have happened extraordinarily quickly."

Rory spoke then. "It's obvious that some kind of infectious process is in play, likely viral given the pattern of presentation, but how's it spread? It can't be body fluids like HIV. I can't imagine all of these patients have had sexual contact."

Mallory felt an icy dread as the virus' potential, and possibly devastating, effects dawned on her. "It seems to be similar to HIV in that it destroys the immune system. The difference is this virus depletes lymphocytes in a matter of days, not years, and spreads quickly through casual contact and contaminated surfaces, like door handles."

Rory whistled softly. Mallory remained quiet.

"Let's not get ahead of ourselves," Dr. Lee said. "We need more information to make any firm conclusions and, Mallory, you need some help out there. I will brief Director Quinn. I need her approval to mobilize a team. Let's touch base again in about two hours."

Mallory rushed back to the medical center. She found Walsh talking to one of the nurses in the corridor. She interrupted the pair without preamble. "I need to talk to you. It's urgent. We can't transfer those patients."

Walsh gave her an incredulous look. "What are you talking about? They are critically ill and have been accepted by UC Irvine. They are being readied for transport as we speak."

"We need to stop them." Mallory pulled Walsh aside. She gave him a synopsis of her conversation with Rory and Dr. Lee.

Walsh studied her skeptically. "It must be some sort of lab error; it just doesn't make any sense. Could you have the lab re-run the samples?"

He turned away. Before she realized what she was doing, Mallory instinctively reached out and grabbed his arm, her sense of urgency increasing with each passing moment.

Walsh looked down at his arm, then said coolly, "Please remove your hand, Dr. Hayes. Do I need to remind you who's in charge here? The Army, in conjunction with FEMA, are running this camp, not the CDC. Please verify the results with the lab and have them re-run the samples. Once this is complete, we can discuss the results. I'm not going to put these patients' lives in danger by holding them here. They need treatment at a fully equipped hospital facility."

Mallory could tell she wasn't going to change his mind, at least not right away.

"We need to at least make sure they are treated there as highly contagious," Mallory said. "They need strict isolation with airborne precautions. We also need to institute similar precautions on all of our patients here and anyone who has come in contact with someone sick, including the medical staff."

"I'll leave that to the CDC then," Walsh said. "Would you forward the information from the lab when you receive it?"

Mallory nodded, not trusting herself to speak.

"Excuse me," Walsh said. "I have orders to write."

"One last thing," Mallory said quickly. "We need to close the camp to new residents and delay anyone leaving—just for a day or so until we get everything sorted." She held her breath as she waited for him to curtly dismiss her suggestion. Instead, he turned and looked at her. To her relief, he nodded.

Chapter 31
I-5 North, near Irvine
Day +23

Alexa Garcia appeared to be sleeping peacefully and, at first, didn't stir with the inevitable bumps and jolts of the ambulance. Her dark lashes, fluttering periodically, stood in sharp contrast to her smooth skin. Alfie couldn't help but notice the perfect shape of her face and full lips. He instinctively glanced toward her left hand—no ring.

He finished taking her blood pressure and recorded the numbers in her chart. Whistling softly to himself, he continued the well-practiced ritual of recording other vitals. Temperature, heart rate, pulse, oxygenation—all stable.

He absently wondered what was wrong with Alexa. He hadn't gotten much history at the time of her transfer—just something about encephalitis of unknown etiology. A blonde doctor, in full hazmat gear herself, focused more on making sure he and the ambulance driver were equipped with gowns and respirators. She also discussed, in excruciating detail, how to disinfect the bay once they handed over the patient to the ER.

They did have the appropriate equipment—somewhere. He had never had occasion to use the respirator, and it took him several long minutes to locate it among the various drawers and lockers of the ambulance.

She helped them both suit up and personally checked to make sure everything was airtight. "I'm not a bloody idiot," he had wanted to say to her, but something about her serious tone and laser focus unsettled him.

Alfie had just leaned back against the plastic bench seat when a faint but insistent *beep, beep, beep* from the IV pump interrupted his thoughts. He checked the line and noticed it had pulled loose. The tiny plastic catheter hung limply by a lone piece of tape.

"Great," he muttered. He stood, steadied himself, and set about gathering supplies for a new IV.

"Alexa," he said in a clear, reassuring voice with a pronounced English accent, "if you can hear me, I'm going to place another IV in you. You may feel a little pinch."

Alfie crouched next to her and scrubbed at a fresh patch of skin. The familiar scent of alcohol filled his nostrils.

"One, two, three, pinch," he recited automatically.

At the exact moment he pushed the needle, the ambulance dipped sharply into a pothole. Alfie watched in disbelief as the needle jerked up and skimmed the edge of his glove, causing a tiny tear.

He didn't move for a second and then looked down at his hand. His bright blue nitrile glove definitely had a tear. He tore it off and pushed himself up to from the rumpled blankets. He examined his hand for any break in the skin. Nothing.

The needle didn't break her skin or mine. I'm fine. I'm completely freaking out over nothing.

He shook his head ruefully. He grabbed a clean glove and, distracted by the close call, forgot to wash his hands before snapping it on over his bare hand.

Chapter 32
Las Colinas FEMA Temporary Relocation Camp
Day +24

Rory, along with two other medical officers, arrived early the next morning. To Mallory's relief, things moved quickly after that. The lab results were confirmed, and all tissue and serum samples were sent to the CDC via a medical courier. Scientists in Atlanta would soon begin identifying and isolating the unknown organism.

Director Quinn approved a quarantine, effective immediately, for all individuals currently in the camp. No one would be allowed to leave or enter the camp until the quarantine was lifted.

After a rushed conference call with Mallory and Dr. Lee, the director also agreed to a voluntary home quarantine for residents and government employees who had been discharged or who had left the camp within the last fourteen days.

Those who had entered and left the camp prior to the fourteen-day cutoff would also be closely monitored for symptoms. Both groups would be instructed to take their temperatures twice daily and self-report any symptoms or rise in temperature. It wasn't perfect; Mallory was under no illusion that everyone would comply. However, it was the best they could do at the moment.

Director Quinn sounded tired. "Good work, both of you, but I need to go. Someone from the President's office is scheduled to call me in a few minutes for an update. I'll send more help as soon as I can. Talk soon." *Click.*

"Are you still there, Dr. Lee?" Mallory asked.

"Yes, I am." His voice was quiet, thoughtful. "Listen," he said, "I'm heading out there. My flight leaves in a few hours."

Mallory's shoulders relaxed a fraction. "I can't tell you how relieved I am to hear that."

"This is the largest quarantine in CDC history." He hesitated. "It's also the first time a quarantine had been instituted without a confirmed microbe. We'd better be right about this."

∿∿

"We need lists—lots of them," Mallory said. She stood at a white board in the cramped back office of the medical center, an open marker poised in her hand.

Rory and two other medical officers, Tanvi Krishnan and Nat Marjani, remained outside the quarantine perimeter in the CDC mobile trailer. They were linked into the room via a secure video feed provided by the Army. They sat attentively; their iPads balanced on their knees.

Three harried administrators from FEMA and two Army representatives were also present. One of the FEMA employees looked close to tears. She stared vacantly at the notepad sitting in front of her. Her shoulders slumped.

She was young, possibly just out of college. Her curly brown hair was shoulder length and pulled back in a practical ponytail. Her face was open and innocent, and she had a tiny gap between her front teeth. Mallory felt a surge of sympathy for her. Understandably, she had to be scared and feeling far out of her depth.

"First of all, we need a master list of everyone who has stayed, worked, or visited the camp." She turned to the white board and punctuated each task with a bullet point. "Next, we need to break that list down into those who have left in the last fourteen days, those who have visited the medical center at *any* point since its inception, and, finally, contacts of those who have visited the medical center, such as tent-mates and family members.

"It's not going to be easy," she continued. "We are talking about hundreds, maybe thousands, of people here. This is where we need FEMA's help. This information is crucial, and the sooner we get it, the better."

She briefly started at the screen. "Before we go any further, Nat and Tanvi, could you take the mobile unit to UC Irvine as soon as possible and set up the quarantine there?"

They nodded.

Mallory glanced down at her tablet, checking her list. "There were four patients who were transferred there: Garcia, Jeffries, Lopez, and Berger. They're currently under strict isolation. We need to quarantine anyone who came into contact with them without the proper infection precautions. You guys know the drill.

"The Army will help you set up the quarantine. A battalion of National Guard soldiers arrived this morning to assist the Army company already present. Director Quinn spoke to General Banks prior to this meeting."

"Who is General Banks?" Tanvi asked.

"General Banks is the general in charge of tsunami relief efforts, including this camp. He has a platoon, led by First Lieutenant O'Connor, ready to escort you and enforce the quarantine. They will establish a perimeter and act as gatekeepers, so to speak." Tanvi entered First Lieutenant O'Connor's direct cell number into her iPad as Mallory recited it.

"The Army medical team, headed by Dr. Walsh, will continue to evaluate and treat patients at the camp. They are bringing in two more physicians and ten more nurses. The CDC needs to focus on our primary goal—identification and containment."

"Will patients be transferred out of the camp if necessary?" Rory asked.

"Critically ill patients will be transferred to isolation rooms at UC Irvine. Any other questions?"

Mallory waited a beat. "Okay. Good luck. Keep us updated."

Nat stood and clapped his hands together.

"Tanvi and I will touch base this afternoon," he said.

"Perfect. I'll text you when Dr. Lee arrives. Rory, would you be able to suit up and assist me in the camp today?"

"Of course. Where should I meet you?"

"How about the main checkpoint in fifteen minutes? The media has heard about the quarantine and are out in full force. Director Quinn instructed us to stay quiet, so we'll leave communication to the media relations team."

"Thanks for the heads up." Rory gave her a small smile of encouragement and then, after a final nod, the screen went dark.

Mallory turned her attention back to the FEMA employees.

"One last thing." She cleared her throat. "I wanted to say, thank you. Thank you for your dedication to helping others and continuing to do your job in this difficult situation. It's not easy to be under quarantine in the best of circumstances.

"The CDC needs you and your colleagues to stay strong. I firmly believe we will be able to identify and, most importantly, stop this pathogen from spreading. Please pass this encouragement on to your respective teams."

Out of the corner of her eye, she saw the young woman with the curly hair sit up a little straighter.

"Let's reconvene in this room at..." She glanced at the time. "Ten o'clock. We need to come up with a plan to contact every single person on those lists."

Chapter 33
Outside Perimeter: Las Colinas FEMA Temporary Relocation Camp
Day +24

CNS: BREAKING NEWS

Thousands Quarantined in Southern California FEMA Camp

Los Angeles (CNS)—Upon recommendation by the CDC, the federal government has begun a record-breaking quarantine at the Las Colinas FEMA camp for a presumed viral outbreak. The camp is estimated to house approximately 16,000 residents displaced by the catastrophic Southern California tsunami earlier this month.

The news was announced this morning by CDC Director Quinn, who released this prepared statement exclusively to CNS:

"A mandatory quarantine, effective immediately, has been announced for the Las Colinas FEMA temporary relocation camp to prevent further spread of a possible virus.

"First and foremost, we want to reassure the American public there is no immediate threat. This quarantine was declared out of an abundance of caution and in the best interest of public health.

"We sincerely apologize for the inconvenience this will undoubtedly cause current Las Colinas residents and those working in the camp. Rest assured we are working around the clock to lift the quarantine as soon as possible."

"We are asking the public to exercise common-sense precautions, such as frequent hand washing and staying home if you aren't feeling well."

Visit CNS.com for updates throughout the day.

Chapter 34
Las Colinas FEMA Temporary Relocation Camp
Day +24

Mallory blew out a frustrated breath. "I can't talk now, Marcus, I'm sorry. I'll be back at my tent in about an hour. Will you be up?" She shook her coffee cup. Empty.

"No, I have an early meeting tomorrow. We've barely talked in days. Don't you have a few minutes now?" Marcus asked.

"I've had one of the longest days of my life, and it's not even over." Mallory walked a little farther down the hall, out of earshot. She pulled her phone from her ear to check the time. It was nearing midnight.

There was a heavy silence. "I just wonder...about your priorities," Marcus said. "I know you have an important job and everything—you're brilliant at what you do, and I get it. I guess...I just wish I was also that important to you."

"That's not fair, Marcus. How could you say that?"

There was another silence, even longer than the first. He had hung up.

I can't think about this right now. It's too much. I need to focus everything I have on this crisis. Hopefully, I can convey how dangerous this situation is to him, but not tonight.

Mallory pushed her phone into her back pocket and walked back to the cramped office. Dr. Lee and Rory were on the screen, already deep in conversation.

"Sorry about that. I'm back." Mallory collapsed into the desk chair. "What did I miss?"

"We were just talking about our plan of attack for tomorrow," Dr. Lee replied. "Right now, we have called in all non-essential CDC personnel in

Atlanta. They'll continue to contact those who have left the camp through-out the night. It's estimated they will be done by early morning. We're strongly recommending a two-week, voluntary home quarantine for those who have been inside the camp within the last fourteen days. For indi-viduals who've been in the camp at any point prior to the last fourteen days, we're recommending self-monitoring.

"It seems the script Rory came up with, detailing temperature monitor-ing and a checklist of symptoms, is working well. So far, no one has re-ported anything. Our team will check in with all possible exposures every twenty-four hours until the quarantine is lifted." He leaned back in his chair and rubbed his chin. "People have a lot of questions, which is under-standable. We just have to be honest with them. We don't have all the an-swers yet."

"Hopefully, we will soon," Rory said, clearing his throat. "The lab is processing the first wave of samples as we speak. Their plan is to work around the clock, with alternating twelve-hour shifts, to identify the mi-crobe. Walsh has agreed to send additional serum samples of any new or suspected cases."

"It sounds as if Tanvi and Henry have the isolation and quarantine at UC Irvine under control," Mallory said. "If anyone connected to the camp develops symptoms on the outside, they will be transported directly there via ambulance.

"The hospital CEO wasn't happy about the quarantine at his facility. He was even less happy that he may have more cases coming in that re-quire that level of isolation. Apparently, the cost is extremely high. In the end, Director Quinn had to personally call him and twist his arm a bit."

"Waste of our time." Dr. Lee shook his head.

Mallory stifled a yawn. "I'm going to finish going through the medi-cal center records. Our next priority is to form a line list and identify the index case. If we have any hope of stopping it, we need to figure out how and where this originated."

Dr. Lee thought for a moment and finally stood. "I think we all need to get some sleep; it will be another long day tomorrow."

Mallory agreed and signed off. She had one more stop to make.

Mindy was asleep when Mallory entered the dimly lit isolation room. A slice of ambient light illuminated her friend's face.

Mallory experienced a sudden ache deep in her chest. The visor on her mask clouded as she tried to consciously slow her breathing.

Mindy was unrecognizable. One side of her face was twisted into something resembling a grimace. Both of her eyes were taped, covered in thick gauze, and nearly soaked through with a yellow serosanguinous fluid. As Mallory watched, Mindy began to writhe in her bed, halfheartedly pulling at her medical restraints.

"Shhh," Mallory said softly. "It's okay. You're safe."

Mindy murmured incoherently.

Walsh had sent her a brief text earlier in the day. Mindy's serum viral PCR panel was positive for cytomegalovirus (CMV), so she had been started on a potent antiviral drug. Her T and B cell lymphocytes were nearly zero, leaving her body with no defense against CMV dissemination. The virus had taken over her body, infecting her retinas, esophagus, and brain.

In patients with healthy lymphocytes, CMV infection may not produce noticeable symptoms. If symptoms are present, they are typically as severe as the common cold.

Mallory said a silent prayer for her friend, along with one for herself. If Mindy was exposed, it's highly probable she was too.

Chapter 35
Las Colinas FEMA Temporary Relocation Camp
Day +25

Mallory awoke before dawn the next morning, her sheets drenched in sweat and her mouth dry. For a confusing moment, she didn't know where she was. She lay staring into the darkness, willing the disorientation to lift.

The past few days came back to her in a rush: the horrific infections, the patient deaths, Mindy, unresponsive and restrained in her hospital cot and, finally, the grim nightmares that plagued her overnight.

She groped for her water bottle, knocking it onto the floor, where it landed with a dull thud. Sighing inwardly, she got out of bed and finally located the water under a nearby empty cot. Now that Mindy was gone, Mallory was the sole tent occupant. Shaking off a pang of loneliness, she glanced at her phone—twenty minutes before she was scheduled to meet Rory.

The closest set of showers was empty at this hour. She turned the water as hot as possible to combat the chill in the air. She returned to the tent and dressed in the half-light, munching on a Clif protein bar. She craved coffee more than she thought possible. At least she hadn't experienced any claustrophobia-related anxiety since arriving at the camp. She looked toward the venting at the top of the tent. The circulating fresh air helped.

Before leaving, she took a moment to check her temperature with a forehead thermometer. Normal. She let out a puff of air. It didn't mean she was in the clear. Not all opportunistic infections cause a fever.

She spotted Rory. He was holding a large, steaming cup of coffee in his gloved hand.

"Please tell me you're willing to share," Mallory said, only partly joking.

"This one's for you. I had mine in the mobile unit. You know I can't remove my respirator to drink in here." She could hear the grin in his voice as he passed the cup to her.

"You're amazing, Rory. Thanks." She leaned forward. She could detect a hint of the delicious aroma through her mask. "This lack of sleep reminds me of residency. Give me a minute to take a few sips?"

"Take your time. I'm still waking up," Rory said.

Mallory moved to an open area of the camp and tugged her mask down. It was the best coffee she had ever tasted.

Equipped in yellow and white biohazard suits, the two headed to the medical center side-by-side. The day was clear and crisp, with the sun still low in the sky.

They passed several masked residents, who invariably stared at them or passed quickly, giving them a wide berth. She imagined the frustration, confusion, and anger the camp residents must be feeling. In a way, she didn't blame them.

Two long beeps filled the air. A mechanical voice echoed from speakers hung throughout the camp: "Could I have your attention please? This camp is under mandatory quarantine. Please wear a mask at all times and stay inside your assigned tent as much as possible. Proceed to the medical center immediately if you experience fever, headaches, fatigue, weakness, rash, runny nose, sneezing, muscle aches, diarrhea, vomiting, or other concerning symptoms. We appreciate your cooperation in this important matter." The announcement was scheduled to play every hour on the hour.

Six extra-large khaki tents, erected overnight, had been positioned in a tight semi-circle near the east end of the original prefabricated medical facility. Each tent was partitioned into twenty compact isolation chambers, complete with positive-pressure ventilation. Figures in matching personal protective equipment (PPE) suits were busy on the ground. Two helicopters dotted the sky, delivering supplies in a near-constant loop.

Mallory and Rory entered the medical center. They found Walsh leaning on the counter at the nurses' station, writing orders. Mallory introduced her colleague and asked if they could borrow the back office for a few hours.

"Knock yourselves out," he replied absently.

They squeezed two chairs into the small space and settled themselves at the computer. Their next step was to create what disease investigators called a "line list"—a collection of all confirmed and suspected cases. Cases would be listed confirmed if they had documented low, or absent, T and B lymphocyte levels.

They systematically searched each patient chart. When they came across a case to add to the list, Mallory dictated the details to Rory, who entered the information into a spreadsheet on his iPad. They recorded demographic information, symptom onset, lymphocyte levels, opportunistic microbe, if identified, and patient status.

Four exhausting hours later, they had a total of 31 suspected or confirmed cases. Twenty-seven of the 31 patients had died in the last three days.

Mallory was up and out of the room before Rory realized what was happening. He rounded the corner in time to see her making a beeline for Walsh.

"Why didn't you tell me?" Mallory demanded.

Walsh made no attempt to disguise his annoyance. As his eyes locked on Mallory's, he took an involuntary step back, surprised by the thunderous expression behind her visor.

"Tell you what?" Walsh asked, confused.

Mallory glared at him. "Twenty-seven patients have died."

"Yes, I'm well aware—"

"Well, I'm not aware. The CDC isn't *aware*," Mallory said sarcastically.

He shook his head in disbelief. "I had my hands full, trying to keep these patients alive. I'm sorry I didn't step out and update you," he said, mimicking her sarcasm.

Rory stepped in, his voice firm. "We're all under a lot of strain here. How about this? We have someone from our team check in with the medical staff twice daily for updates—from either end. That way, we can keep the lines of communication open."

Walsh raised his hands in a placating gesture. "Fine. Just so you know, most of those patients died late yesterday and overnight. It all happened extremely fast."

"Did they die from infectious causes?" Rory asked.

"It looks that way. Clinical pictures were mostly consistent with infection, in various forms. We won't know for sure until we have the culture and PCR results. The only common denominator for all the cases is low to undetectable lymphocytes. Even with prophylactic antibiotics and antivirals, these patients didn't stand a chance."

There was a moment of silence.

"Have you been able to send the blood samples to the CDC lab?" Mallory asked.

"We have sent out a total of 21 patient samples," Walsh said. "We just finished collecting the remaining 10 and are preparing them for direct courier transport. For what it's worth, Dr. Hayes, you did the right thing by closing down exit and entry to the camp." He sighed and rubbed his temples. "We need to figure out what is going on, and fast, before more people die."

Chapter 36
Las Colinas FEMA Temporary Relocation Camp
Day +25

allory, alone in the back office, munched on a dry turkey sandwich as she worked.

After compilation of the line list, it didn't take long to identify the index case among the 31 patients. The two brothers from Sweden were the first to develop symptoms, prior to any other patient by at least two days.

We need to interview Habib immediately. There must be a clue in his travel and exposure history, although, given our last interaction, I'm not sure he will cooperate. Maybe he would respond better to Rory.

Her heart sank as the reality dawned on her. Of the identified patients, only four were still alive. A staggering 87 percent of the patients on their list had died. A quick check confirmed her worst fears: Habib Nazari was deceased.

Mallory's phone vibrated. She checked the ID: Rory. "I was just about to call you."

"I have news." Without waiting for a reply, he barreled on: "The CDC lab has isolated a viral strain in 21 of the 21 patients tested. The remaining patient samples are still in transit."

"What kind of virus?" Mallory asked.

"You aren't going to believe this. It's a novel strain of adenovirus."

Mallory hesitated before answering. "That doesn't make any sense."

"I know."

"Adenovirus is one of many viruses that cause the common cold. It doesn't lower lymphocyte levels."

"I know." Rory sounded puzzled. "The molecular profile of this adenovirus doesn't match anything previously reported. Could it be some kind of mutation?" He didn't sound convinced.

"Hmm, I don't think so." Mallory was frantically trying to process this new information. Thinking out loud, she said, "When we went through the charts earlier today, most, if not all of, the patients had something in common. They all initially reported a runny nose, sore throat, sneezing— symptoms consistent with an adenovirus infection."

"That still doesn't explain why the lymphocytes are so drastically affected. The absence of lymphocytes is what allows the opportunistic infections to flourish, and those infections are the ultimate cause of death in these patients," Rory replied.

"I agree." Mallory's brow furrowed in concentration. "So...it seems when this specific strain of adenovirus infects a host, it must either suppress the production of lymphocytes or target and destroy them exclusively. Maybe even both. Those infected are then left without protection from the near-constant exposure to all of the viruses, bacteria, and fungi ubiquitous in the environment."

"The million-dollar question is, how in the world is adenovirus destroying or suppressing lymphocytes?" Rory said.

"I wonder if it's some kind of secondary immune response, possibly an autoimmune response. Could antibodies to the virus be attacking healthy lymphocytes, mistaking them for infected cells?"

"The lab is running more tests this afternoon and through the evening. Hopefully, we'll have more definitive answers soon."

"So, what's our next step?" Mallory asked. "Contact tracing?"

"Yep. We have to track down anyone and everyone who may have had contact with the infected. Dr. Lee, Nat, and Tanvi have already started. I'm going to join them shortly," Rory said.

"Great. I'll get to work contacting the Nazari family in Sweden. I think Walsh mentioned they also had family in... where was it? Omaha, I think."

"Sounds like a plan. I'll check in with you later."

Something was bothering her, a foggy memory at the edge of her consciousness. She sat for a minute, trying to clear her mind. It was something she had learned during her month-long CDC orientation.

That's it.

She spun to the computer, her fingers flying over the keys. She pulled up her Gmail folders, where she stored all her documents. It took her several minutes, but she was eventually able to find the chart she was looking for:

When to Suspect Bioterrorism: 1) A higher than normal number of people seeking care in a specific location; 2) A disease appearing rapidly, often within hours to days, in a previously healthy population; 3) A high fatality rate; and 4) An uncommon infectious agent.

Check, check, check, and no check. Adenovirus is about as common as you could get. But still, three out of four. It's definitely worth looking into. The potential implications are too terrifying to ignore. How could I not have suspected this before?

Chapter 37
Malmö, Sweden
Day +25

Sameer's forehead furrowed in concentration as he coaxed the soft, melodic notes of Tchaikovsky's violin concerto from his second-hand Stradivarius. Dust motes danced lazily in a stream of sunlight, appearing to move in time with the melancholic music. Three large windows, framed with peeling, putty-colored trim, filled most of the south wall.

The muted sounds of CNS drifted through the closed kitchen door. The ting of breaking glass caused Sameer's fingers to slip on the fingerboard, producing an unpleasant squeak.

Fakir rushed into the room, swinging the door open with such force that it hit the wall with a staccato crack. Sameer stayed silent, his gaze locked on Fakir, not daring to breathe.

"It's happening!" Fakir's voice had risen an octave, the words tumbling out in a high-pitched screech. For an uncomfortable moment, Sameer thought Fakir was going to begin jumping up and down.

"Shhh," Sameer said, struggling to keep his composure. He held a finger to his lips and pointed to the surrounding apartments. "Keep your voice down. What's happening, Fakir?"

"But when the forbidden months are past, then fight and slay the Pagans wherever ye find them, and seize them, beleaguer them, and lie in wait for them in every stratagem." Fakir's voice came out in a whisper. His face was flushed a deep crimson and his eyes shone with emotion.

"Surah 9:5," Sameer said. "Praise Allah." He slid down to his knees on the floor, overcome with emotion, as tears loosened in his eyes. He felt as if his heart was going to burst.

We did it, Father. Our dream is a reality. We've struck the heart of our Western enemy. I can only hope we've earned our place in Paradise, where we can be reunited once again.

Chapter 38
Cabernet Club, Los Angeles, California
Day +25

Alfie closed his eyes, allowing his body to move with the music. A kaleidoscope of color flashed behind his eyes. Each thump of the bass caused a pleasant vibration deep in his chest.

He opened his eyes and took a long swallow of his gin and tonic, tipping it high to catch the last drops. Bodies bumped against him as they jostled for space on the dance floor.

He noticed his friend, Matt, dancing with a woman he hadn't seen before. She was slightly overweight with dark eyes, bright red lips, and long, perfectly straight, brown ombre hair. They danced enthusiastically, occasionally leaning over to be heard above the noise.

His other friends, Everett and Tommy, approached a group of women. They were slightly removed from the rest, positioned near the corner of the dance floor. Their satin sashes, adorned with magenta feathers and sequins, advertised them as members of a bachelorette party.

Alfie watched as the women closed ranks, turning their backs and effectively shutting the two out of their circle. He suppressed a smile. *At least Matt is having some luck.*

He was glad they had talked him into coming tonight. At first, he had begged off, citing his stressful week, particularly Wednesday. That was a bad day. Right after the incident with the needle, Alexa had gone into tonic-clonic seizures. It had taken multiple IV pushes of Ativan to stop the convulsing.

A generalized seizure is a horrible thing to witness: facial contortion, frothy blood when the patient bites her own tongue, the undignified re-

lease of bladder contents.

Alfie wrinkled his nose, as if he could still smell the acrid scent of urine filling the ambulance.

If that wasn't bad enough, after the seizure was under control, Alexa had gone into ventricular fibrillation. He had spent the rest of the 30-minute drive administering CPR. Despite his efforts, she hadn't made it.

For prior nights out, his friends had done their best to wear him down, insisting he make at least a token appearance as their wingman. "With your accent, the ladies practically throw themselves at you."

Alfie had burst out laughing but remained firm. He was exhausted. Plus, his throat was a little scratchy. He popped the top off a Blue Moon and sank onto his threadbare but comfortable couch. He knew he should replace it, but it had sentimental value.

"I heard Cameron might be there," Matt said. Those six words had changed his mind in an instant.

His eyes scanned the room. No sign of her yet.

He pointed to his empty glass to signal he was getting a drink. Tommy caught his eye, shaking his empty glass toward Alfie, a grin on his face. For a moment, Alfie thought about pretending he didn't see—Tommy was a bit of a freeloader. Instead, he nodded and made his way to the bar.

He saw her first from behind, standing at the bar. He noted the sleek black dress and shock of short hair, so blonde it was nearly white. It was his ex-girlfriend.

He squeezed in toward the bar, snagging a spot near an attractive, middle-aged woman in a coral-colored silk blouse and gray pencil skirt. She swung around carelessly, narrowly missing him with her drink as he jumped back.

"I love this song!" She started moving to the music, inching closer to the dance floor. She raised her eyebrows at Cameron. "See you out there?"

Cameron laughed. "Be there in a minute."

Oblivious to the near calamity, the woman turned and pushed her way through the crowd, cocktail glass held high. Her body swayed to the rhythm as she walked, the amber liquid tilting precariously.

Cameron watched as the woman tottered on her heels, a small smile playing on her lips. The smile fell instantly when she caught sight of Alfie.

"Hi, Cameron. Been a while." He leaned in and gave her a hug. "Who was that?"

"That's my older sister, Kathy, visiting from New York." She returned the hug half-heartedly.

"Wow," was all he could think to say.

"Let's just say she doesn't get out much." They both laughed, relieving some of the tension.

"How have you been?" Alfie asked, working to keep his voice casual. He studied her, looking for signs she was happy to see him. He saw none. Her fine, elfin features and slim figure were as appealing as ever.

"Good. Really good, actually. How about you?" Her tone was neutral, giving nothing away.

"Fine," he replied. He hesitated, then looked directly into her eyes. "I miss you. I'm so sorry for...for what happened with Ellie. I made a mistake."

Without waiting for an answer, he leaned in to kiss her. When she realized what was happening, she turned her head and he awkwardly pecked a spot near her ear. She pushed him away.

"I need to catch up with my sister, make sure she isn't getting into any trouble." She stepped around him and turned back. "I'm sorry Alfie. Take care."

He stood there for a long moment, watching her walk away.

Chapter 39
Las Colinas FEMA Temporary Relocation Camp
Day +26

Mallory had spent the previous afternoon and evening with the phone pressed to her ear. Her first call was to Dr. Lee. She voiced her suspicions, explaining how she thought this outbreak could be the result of a deliberate terrorist attack.

His voice was contemplative as he replied. "Biological weapons are typically uncommon virulent pathogens such as anthrax, tularemia, botulism or, theoretically, something like genetically engineered smallpox.

"I can't see how adenovirus would fit into any kind of biologic weapon scenario. I think the most likely explanation is that this strain of adenovirus has stimulated an autoimmune response against the patient's own lymphocytes. My guess is that the antibodies target the virus' infected cells *and* healthy lymphocytes, destroying both indiscriminately. The antibodies see the two cells as one and the same, because the receptors are the same.

"Viruses are constantly mutating. It's possible that this particular strain has receptors that have mutated to closely resemble, or become identical to, human lymphocyte receptors."

Mallory didn't give in. "I completely agree. That does seem like the most likely explanation. But what if we're wrong? We don't have concrete evidence of anything yet. Even if the probability of a deliberate, biological attack is small, the consequences of not exploring it further are too great."

"Good point, Mallory," he said. "I'll call Director Quinn right away."

She spent the next two hours trying to find and trace any family, either in the US or Sweden, of Omar and Habib Nazari. She had FEMA forward her the registration and demographic information collected on them. It was a futile effort. She couldn't find anything for either boy, not even an Instagram page or Twitter account.

Maybe Nazari isn't even their real name. If that's the case, I have no hope of learning their travel and exposure history. And if the last name is phony, all the more reason to consider a biological attack of some kind.

She felt her phone buzz in her pocket as she stepped out from the canteen into the warm morning air.

"This is Dr. Hayes," she said, setting out toward the FEMA administrative offices.

"Hi, Dr. Hayes. It's Deja, from Dr. Walsh's team?" she said, sounding unsure. "He asked me to call you with an update."

"Of course. Thanks so much for calling, Deja. How are things going there?" Mallory pressed the phone to her ear, anticipating more bad news.

Deja cleared her throat. "Well, there have been no new cases overnight, which is a huge improvement."

Mallory paused briefly, processing this information.

No new cases.

She felt a surge of hope. Maybe they had this contained. As of yesterday evening, the team had moved into the isolation tents the last of the known contacts of the 31 infected.

"How are the remaining infected patients doing?" Mallory asked, resuming her brisk pace.

"Unfortunately, all four patients passed away last night and early this morning." Deja's voice sounded suddenly tired, dejected.

Mallory stopped walking. "Mindy?"

"I'm sorry, Dr. Hayes. She's gone, too," Deja said.

Before she knew what she was doing, Mallory abruptly changed course. She stumbled, caught herself, and made her way back to the privacy of her tent.

"Did anyone notify her family yet? She doesn't have children, but she talked about a brother who lives in Alabama," Mallory said quietly.

"Dr. Walsh is talking to him right now."

"Thanks for letting me know, Deja."

A single, silent tear escaped, tracing a line down her cheek. She sat motionless in the dim light of the tent, not bothering to turn on the impersonal, industrial-size lamp hanging from the ceiling. She waited, watching a brown spider crawl leisurely up the canvas, until she regained her composure.

She glanced at her phone, exiting the tent and quickening her pace when she realized she had only a few minutes to make it to the main administrative building before the next meeting was scheduled to begin.

The room was nearly full when she entered, the air heavy with anticipation. Everyone present was in biohazard gear, making it difficult for Mallory to recognize faces. There were multiple representatives from FEMA and the Army, including General Banks. Dr. Lee, Henry, Rory, and Tanvi were connected via a remote video feed on a large flat screen in the corner of the room. They sat in four chairs facing the camera, their faces neutral.

"Director Quinn?" General Banks spoke, leaning over a telephone in the center of a gleaming conference table.

"Yes, I'm here. Please begin when you're ready." Shannon Quinn's voice was clear, confident.

After brief introductions, each group took a turn updating the others.

General Banks discussed the response to criminal behavior in the camp. The army was dealing with a few isolated incidents, mostly involving theft of personal items. Camp tensions were high. Within the last two days, the Army had to break up several fights as tempers flared.

Mallory felt the sweat collecting in the small of her back. The plastic suit trapped her body heat, and the room temperature was high due to the number of warm bodies present.

Rory cleared his throat, his chair making a cringe-worthy scraping sound as he rose to speak. "As some of you may know, adenovirus is one of the many viruses responsible for the common cold, which we have all experienced at one point or another. In the vast majority of cases, infection causes the host to experience a sore throat, runny nose, sneezing, and fatigue for 2-7 days. The immune system recognizes the virus infected cells and utilizes antibodies to rid the body of it. Complete recovery is the norm. That is, of course, an over-simplified version," Rory explained, glancing at Mallory.

Rory looked and sounded confident, but Mallory knew he was nervous speaking in front of large groups. She could see it in the stiffness of his posture and his uncharacteristically formal speech. She gave him an encouraging nod.

"The difference is that this virus, in a way we have not yet identified, severely damages the immune system. The host is left defenseless against invading microbes." He took a deep breath. His glasses slid partway down his nose, and he used the back of his gloved hand to push them back into place.

"The immune system is extremely complex, and many don't realize the constant 'behind the scenes' work immune cells do every day.

"Organisms that we regularly encounter, some that even reside in and on our own bodies, are suddenly a serious threat to those infected." There was absolute silence as Rory paused to let that sink in.

"Scientists at the CDC have sequenced the strain and have partly identified the DNA as adenovirus, subgenus B, serotype 7. Part of the molecular sequence doesn't match anything previously reported in the literature, which they are calling 'x,' making this strain adenovirus B7x. Needless to say, they are focused on finding the significance of the unknown x sequence. There is a lot we still don't understand. It's unclear if this is a viral mutation or some type of adenovirus humans haven't come into contact with before."

Rory took a deep breath. "Thanks for your attention. I would be happy to answer any questions at the conclusion of the meeting."

Mallory stood when it was her turn. "Thanks, Dr. Wilson. We have identified a total of 31 cases, all positive for the same strain, which we are now calling adenovirus B7x. Tragically, all infected patients have died."

Someone gasped. Murmurs filled the room.

Mallory spoke over the noise. "There is some good news. There have been no new cases for more than 24 hours. All contacts of the infected are in isolation and show no sign of symptoms. We are cautiously optimistic the virus is contained."

The room was silent for a split second and then burst into noise. Several people hugged, and a few cheered.

It's truly a miracle that more health care workers didn't become infected. Mindy, a volunteer civilian, was the only one.

At the thought of Mindy, Mallory's eyes immediately filled with tears. She swallowed several times, trying to control her emotions.

This isn't the time or place. I need to remain professional.

Director Quinn cleared her throat, impatient to continue. "Great job— all of you. We'll have more definitive answers over the next several days. If things continue in this direction, we may be able to lift the quarantine as soon as thirteen days from today."

"There is one more subject I need to address." Director Quinn's voice was serious. "The Department of Homeland Security has opened an investigation into the origin of the virus."

A shocked silence hung over the room. Director Quinn continued, "There is absolutely no concrete evidence of bioterrorism, but that possibility needs to be ruled out. Special Agent Coleman and his team will be conducting video interviews from this room beginning at eleven. General Banks will be handing out an interview schedule at the conclusion of this meeting. Drs. Lee, Wilson, Krishnan, and Marjani, Special Agent Coleman will be speaking with you sometime this afternoon in the mobile unit."

The director took in a deep breath, her voice softening. To Mallory, she sounded suddenly older. "Our thoughts and prayers are with the families who have lost loved ones to this devastating infection."

~~/\~/\~~

That evening, Mallory and Marcus talked for nearly an hour.

"I'm sorry, Mallory. I know I overreacted. I just miss you. It's hard to be away from you for this long. I can't stand it when I'm not even able to hear your voice."

Mallory resisted the urge to point out there were times he was the one too busy to talk. "I know, Marcus. It's hard for me too. This has been an especially difficult week. It's not always going to be this crazy."

He listened attentively as she described what had been happening at the camp, right up to her interview with Homeland Security that afternoon.

"Are you feeling okay?" Marcus asked. "You don't think you were exposed, do you?" She could hear the worry in his voice.

"No, I've been careful from the beginning. Hopefully, I'm in the clear. In fact, if there aren't any new cases, I should be able to leave here in about thirteen days."

"Thirteen days? Why so long?" He sounded surprised.

"I'm officially in quarantine until then, just like everyone else in the camp."

"I understand, I'm just glad you're okay."

Mallory felt better after clearing things up with Marcus. She laid back on her bunk, blinking at the ceiling, feeling some of the tension leave her body.

The tent itself seemed eerily quiet. She strained to hear the comforting sound of human activity outside. She looked around at the empty bunks. A creeping sense of isolation slid over her, like an unwelcome snake. She needed a distraction.

She grabbed her phone, deciding to call her parents and Kate. Her parents were obsessively following news about the quarantine. She spent the majority of the conversation reassuring them that she was fine.

Kate had just gotten back from Southern California after attending Brooke's memorial service. Like many who perished in the tsunami, Brooke's body was never recovered. It was disheartening to have Kate so close but be unable to see her.

They both cried as Kate described the service to her. During the slide-show, there was a picture of the three of them playing dress-up, their smiles impossibly wide and carefree. They were each wearing faux pearl necklaces that hung to their waist. In the picture, Mallory's chin was tilted up, her tiny hand holding the brim of an enormous floppy hat. Brooke was in the middle, one arm around each sister, squeezing them tightly toward her. She was part of so many childhood memories.

"I'm so sorry I couldn't be there, Kate," Mallory said softly, absently picking at a loose thread on her blanket.

"It wasn't possible. I understand," Kate reassured her. "I know you wanted to be."

"Thanks for understanding, but I still feel terrible about missing it. How is Brooke's mom holding up?"

"As well as can be expected, I guess. She looks as if she has lost weight and probably isn't sleeping well. I explained to her where you were and why you couldn't come."

"Thanks for doing that," Mallory said. "I better get some sleep. Talk soon?"

Kate yawned. "Sounds good. I'm beyond exhausted. Love you."

"Love you."

Chapter 40
Los Angeles International Airport, Los Angeles, CA
Day +27

Cameron hugged her sister tightly. "Thanks for coming, Kath."

"Are you kidding me? Thanks for having me. That was the most fun I've had in forever. Yesterday was a little rough, though, I'm getting too old to drink that much. In fact, I'm still feeling a little under the weather." As if to illustrate the point, Kathy pulled a tissue from her purse and discreetly blew her nose.

"You deserve to let loose a little. You work way too much and way too hard," Cameron said as she embraced her sister again. "Love to little Mercedes from me. You should bring her next time." Mercedes was Kathy's six-year-old Persian cat. She doted on her, treating her as if she were her own child.

"Oh, she doesn't travel well, but thanks for offering," Kathy replied.

Cameron loved her sister, but she was the first to admit Kathy could be high maintenance. A part of her was relieved to have her time, and apartment, back to herself.

She watched as her sister walked to the security line. A shiver passed through her and she pulled her cardigan tighter. *I'm completely drained. Maybe I'm the one who can't handle a night out.*

Chapter 41
Los Angeles International Airport, Los Angeles, CA
Day +27

Kathy gave Cameron a final wave before handing her ID and boarding pass to the blank-faced TSA agent. She dreaded this part of the process. She simply wasn't good at waiting.

I can't believe they make us walk barefoot on this dirty floor. Shouldn't they provide paper booties or something like those disposable flip-flops used for pedicures? Ugh, and those filthy gray trays? I read somewhere they have more germs than a toilet seat.

She glanced at her Cartier watch, jiggling her wrist so the face was visible. As the line crawled forward, she waited impatiently, absently tapping her foot. She would much rather be in the Sky Lounge, relaxing with a drink.

I should order a Bloody Mary. They're supposed to help with hangovers. Why am I still feeling poorly? I feel worse today than I did yesterday.

She sneezed, then groped in her handbag for a tissue, dropping her boarding pass in the process. A faint current of air caused it to float to the adjacent security lane. A thirty-something hipster, his hair pulled back in a man-bun, picked up the pass and handed it to her. She noted his symmetrical face and his well-defined arms, which were sleeved in intricate tattoos.

He caught her looking and winked, his face breaking into a wide grin. She reached out and grasped the boarding pass, still holding a crumpled tissue to her nose. She turned quickly away, embarrassed, and mumbling her thanks.

By the time she reached the gate, First Class was boarding. She found her seat and collapsed into it, regretting her choice of footwear, although she would never admit that to Cameron. She smiled as she recalled her sister's face when pulling on her sky-high Louboutins that morning.

"Seriously, you're wearing stilettos? Have you ever *been* to an airport?" Cameron teased, genuinely perplexed.

Kathy exhaled and leaned back, glad to be off her feet. Out of the corner of her eye, she saw the man with the sleeve tattoos enter the first-class cabin.

Of course he's on my flight. Just don't make eye contact.

She busied herself getting settled while the rest of the plane filled. The next thing she knew, Mr. Man-Bun was sliding into the wide leather seat next to her, double-checking his ticket. He nodded, satisfied.

"Hi there. I'm Forest," he said confidently, holding out his hand.

Hmm, the only Forest I've heard of had a box of chocolates and liked to run. Ahh, I loved that movie. I shouldn't mention that, though. He's probably too young to have even heard of it.

"Kathy," she said in a brisk tone, giving his hand a quick, firm shake.

I mustn't encourage him. There's nothing worse than sitting next to someone who talks the entire flight. I don't have the energy for polite, meaningless conversation.

She pulled out her Kindle, immediately losing herself in the latest Liane Moriarty novel. He seemed to get the hint. It wasn't until they were nearing O'Hare Airport that he spoke again.

"So, Kathy, are you a Chicago native or just visiting?" he asked, grinning and giving her a sideways glance.

"Actually, I live in New York," she said. "Just here for a layover." *Like it's any of your business. Why do people think they can ask you personal questions, as if it's their right, just because you were randomly assigned to sit next to them on an airplane?*

"Ahh, that makes sense," he said, almost to himself, going back to tapping away serenely on his iPad.

Kathy began to nod, then stopped herself. "'Makes sense?' What do you mean by that?" She wasn't sure if she should be offended.

"You just seem like a New Yorker," he said, shrugging. "I'm from LA. I can usually spot someone from the East Coast a mile away. Not that it's a bad thing."

"Oh, I see," Kathy said. She hadn't realized she was that easy to read. "I guess you're right. I do kind of have 'New York' written all over me. So, what about you? Are you here to visit the Windy City?"

"I'm here on business. We're opening our third location." He continued to tap at his screen. "I'm the founder of Namaste House. It's an architectural firm, known for creating spaces that promote mindfulness in a spiritually nourishing environment. You may have heard of it." He looked at her expectantly.

Kathy blinked at him. "No, I'm afraid I haven't. I'm not very familiar with that sort of thing. I work in PR."

"Of course," Forest said.

Kathy fought the urge to roll her eyes. They didn't speak the rest of the flight.

Chapter 42
Las Colinas FEMA Temporary Relocation Camp
Day +27

Mallory and her colleagues stayed more than busy over the next several days. The direct contacts of those confirmed positive for adenovirus strain B7x, still sequestered within isolation tents, remained healthy. The majority of staff time was spent making daily contact with the long list of prior camp occupants.

Mallory was beginning to feel trapped in Walsh's tiny, impersonal office. Like everyone else in the camp, she was counting down the days until the quarantine was over. Rory, Tanvi, Nat, and Dr. Lee were planning to head back to Atlanta that afternoon. They would continue to assist her from CDC headquarters.

Mallory had just gotten up to grab a bite to eat when her phone buzzed with a text from Rory. One of the prior residents, Crystal Green, called the CDC hotline to tearfully report symptoms of sneezing, runny nose, and malaise.

According to Rory, Crystal, a twenty-nine-year-old cocktail waitress and single mother, sounded terrified. She had seen the news about the camp's deadly virus and been self-monitoring for symptoms since being contacted by the CDC days ago. Rory stayed on the phone with her, meticulously going through her recent movements to identify others who might have been exposed.

Mallory sank back into her chair, her stomach clenching.

She pulled up Crystal's social work notes. Crystal and her eleven-year old son were rendered homeless when the tsunami flooded the lower level of their apartment building, making the whole building uninhabitable.

They stayed at the camp for five days before a social worker was able to locate her estranged family in Madera. After some persuasion, they agreed to temporarily house the small family.

Within thirty minutes of her call, Mallory had arranged ambulance transport to the Medical Center at UC Irvine for each of the household occupants. She spoke directly to the paramedics en route to ensure they had the proper isolation equipment.

The family arrived at the University Hospital without incident and was immediately admitted into separate isolation rooms.

PCR viral testing quickly revealed Crystal to be infected with rhinovirus, one of the many viruses responsible for the common cold. She could have contracted the virus at the supermarket, work, gym—anywhere she had contact with infected people or fomites. Fomites—inanimate objects such as doorknobs or railings—are capable of housing and transmitting infectious organisms. Some viruses are adept at living on fomites for days.

Mallory exhaled a sigh of relief when notified of the results. Crystal was in no way linked to the deadly adenoviral strain. It was a false alarm.

After texting Rory and the rest of the team, she called Agent Coleman.

"Special Agent Coleman," he said, his voice clipped.

"Hi Special Agent, it's Mallory Hayes."

"Hi, Dr. Hayes. How can I help you?" His voice relaxed a notch.

Mallory could hear activity in the background. She imagined him sitting at a conference table littered with empty coffee cups, tie loosened, a large whiteboard on the wall filled with scribbled notes and mug shots of potential suspects. Then again, maybe she had been watching too much *Homeland.*

"As requested, I'm calling to update you regarding the possible case from Madera. I just received the results. It's not adenovirus B7x. It's just a typical cold from a completely different type of virus."

"That's great news. Thanks for letting me know," he said.

There was a momentary pause. Mallory heard the shuffling of papers and then Coleman asked, "Since I have you on the line, do you have time for a few questions?"

"Sure, no problem." She was curious as to how the investigation was going and secretly hoped she might be able to glean some information from the conversation.

"You said during your initial interview that Omar seemed openly hostile to you. What did you make of it at the time?"

Mallory thought for a moment before answering. She needed to be careful about patient confidentiality, but if a possible threat to others existed, she had a legal and moral responsibility to help. "Well, I initially thought his anger was his response to grief. After all, I had just informed him that his twin brother passed away."

"Initially?" Coleman prompted.

"In hindsight, it does seem like it may have been more...personal in some way. I'm sorry, I'm not sure I'm being very helpful."

"Any information you provide is appreciated," Coleman assured her. "Can you remember anything else Omar said? Anything that might give us a clue as to his mindset?"

Mallory thought back. The depth of Omar's hostility was unsettling, and, because of that, their interaction was burned into her memory. "We had to talk through a phone interpreter. At one point in the conversation, he dropped the phone, damaging it. We then had no way of communicating. He became very agitated and gestured emphatically for me to leave the room. But...there was something he did say as I was leaving. Something like 'Allahu akbar' over and over. I'm not sure what it means."

"God is most great," Agent Coleman replied quietly.

They were both lost in thought for a moment, processing the implications of this.

She waited a beat. "May I ask you a question?"

"Yes, but to give you fair warning, I'm not able to comment on an ongoing investigation," he said, as if reading her thoughts.

"Yes, of course. I understand." Mallory was disappointed, but, in truth, she hadn't expected otherwise.

"I can tell you we're taking this very seriously."

Mallory ended the call, promising to let him know if anything else came up.

Chapter 43
Zimala Community Center, Chicago
Day +30

Dust swirled around Barakah's feet. He swept faster, putting everything he had into making the floor of the Zimala Community Center shine.

After all, it's the least I can do.

Barakah emptied the dustpan, brushed off his hands, and opened the scuffed utility door. The scent of mold immediately overwhelmed him. Breathing through his mouth, he found the ancient janitor's bucket and filled it to the brim with hot, soapy water. The corresponding mop, presumably once white, was now a tangled, gray mass of string.

He wheeled out the bucket and got to work. He was nearly done with the first floor when he heard the Imam Khatib's deep, melodious voice.

"Hello there, Ahmed. Well done! I don't think The Center has ever been this clean or smelled so...lemon fresh." The Imam sniffed the air appreciatively and spread his arms. "You know you don't *need* to do all this." He smiled. "We certainly appreciate it, though."

He gave Barakah a fatherly pat on the back. "Any word from your cousin?"

"Um, no, not yet, Imam," he stammered. Two bright, pink spots appeared high on his cheeks. "I'm sure I'll hear from him soon."

"Yes, of course. I just worry about you here, with no family supervision. Would you mind very much if I called him?"

"Umm, I don't have his new cell phone number. He, um, told me he was buying an iPhone on eBay. He was supposed to email me the number. I guess he hasn't gotten around to it yet." He flushed a deeper shade of red.

He wasn't very good at lying.

"I know I've asked you this before, but … you don't have any other family in America? A distant great auntie? A family friend I could talk to?"

Barakah shook his head, swallowing a lump in his throat.

"Hmmm." The Imam had lost his smile. He looked deep in thought, a concerned expression on his face, and tapped a finger against his lips. "You have been here for almost a month. Your cousin was supposed to come and get you weeks ago. I feel uncomfortable with you missing this much school."

"Could I enroll in school here?" Barakah asked hopefully. "I'm learning more and more English every day."

The Zimala Center had Rosetta Stone available on two battered iPads, secured to the table with electric-blue bike chains. In the after-school hours, it wasn't uncommon to see a line of five or six people waiting to use them. The twenty-minute time limit was taken seriously by all. Barakah made a habit of getting up early to have an hour or two for undisturbed practice.

"Well, we need to go through the proper channels. My good friend, Sidra, is a social worker here in Chicago. She has dedicated her life to helping Muslim immigrants, particularly children and families. She can point us in the right direction."

Barakah nodded gratefully, unable to speak. He felt terrible lying, especially about his name. His name was the final link to his identity—his sense of self. When first introducing himself as "Ahmed," he felt a deep sense of loss, as if he had severed the last remaining tether to solid ground. The current isolation felt like a physical weight pressing down on him.

The Imam was smart and street-savvy. He had run The Zimala Center successfully for the last twenty-five years. Barakah held no illusions that he was fooling him. And yet, the Imam still wanted to help him and, even more incredibly, asked for nothing in return.

Thank you, Allah, for bringing me here. Barakah looked skyward. *I don't know what would have happened to me.*

The day he arrived in America, the only thing he could think to do was find a taxi driver who spoke Arabic. He spent nearly an hour wandering up and down the O'Hare arrivals section until he found one.

He asked to be taken to the public library in downtown Chicago. In a densely populated area, he felt more inconspicuous. At the library, he planned to research Arabic neighborhoods and locate a hostel or somewhere inexpensive to stay.

Fortunately, the taxi driver was a talkative, older gentleman who was happy to converse in his native tongue. He mentioned the Zimala Center and suggested Ahmed check it out. He had been there ever since.

At times, the guilt nearly destroyed him. He had resolved to confess countless times. The America he had seen since his arrival was far from the country of immoral behavior, debauchery, and frivolous excess he had been taught all his life. Everyone he had met was nice, often going out of their way to help him. Fear inevitably gripped him, paralyzing him into inaction. He knew Fakhir and Sameer were capable of having their American contacts track him down. He had to remain anonymous if he wanted to stay alive.

Barakah made his way across the black and white linoleum of the kitchen and down the narrow stairs to his tiny basement room.

He stopped at the threshold and examined his surroundings. The room was sparsely furnished with a scratched, imitation-wood desk, folding chair, and rickety bed. Each night, as he crawled onto the bed, it wobbled, creaked, and protested so much he considered it a small miracle when he made it through the night without it collapsing.

The room's concrete walls were painted an eye-watering lime green.

A faded gold Islamic Star and Crescent, slightly off-center, had been stenciled onto the far wall. For reasons unknown to him, there was also a lone freestanding sink of indeterminate color and three crates filled with old toys and clothes.

Barakah loved it. Never before in his life had he had space to himself.

"Alfie, it's Matt. Open the door!" After a full minute of knocking, Matt stopped, his knuckles stinging. He blew out a breath and raked his hands through his already-greasy hair.

I need to calm down. Think.

Even as he formed that thought, he was back to pounding on the door with a closed fist. *Boom. Boom. Boom.* The door shook in its frame. He paused to listen—nothing.

Where could he be? He hasn't shown up at work for days, and he isn't answering calls or texts. It's as if he disappeared off the face of the earth.

Alfie and Matt had become close friends since Alfie's arrival from the UK six years earlier. They were assigned to the same first responder unit and quickly bonded over their mutual obsession, *Game of Thrones*.

Cameron used to get annoyed with the two of them because they had to dissect each episode after it aired. Matt had also introduced him to *Call of Duty.*

They had spent many nights sipping craft beer and playing *COD* until the early hours of the morning. Matt's parents died in a car crash when he was in high school. With no siblings or family in the area, Matt thought of Alfie as family.

He heard the click of a lock disengaging behind him. He turned, wiping his nose on his sleeve. The door opened a crack. A striking blue eye, surrounded by deep wrinkles, peered at him suspiciously.

"If you don't stop that banging, I'm going to call the police." The voice was surprisingly clear and firm. It reminded him of his elderly, extremely strict fifth-grade teacher, Mrs. Richardson. He stood a little straighter.

"I'm sorry to disturb you, ma'am. I'm just trying to get a hold of my friend, Alfie. Have you, by chance, seen him?"

"Oh, that English chap? No, I can't say that I have. Not recently at least."

"Do you remember when you last saw or heard him?" Matt asked anxiously. "It's important. I'm worried about him."

"Hmmm...it must have been a few weeks ago. It's been pretty quiet over there. I figured he was on vacation."

Matt felt a sinking feeling in his stomach. "Well, he didn't say anything to me about a vacation. He has been a no-show at his shifts for over a week. It's really unlike him."

The woman was silent for a moment, contemplating. "The super, Remi, lives in number 115. I guess you could try him. He'll probably let you in if you're listed as an emergency contact."

Why didn't I think of that? I have to be one of his emergency contacts. Who else could he have put down?

Before Matt could thank her, she shut and locked the door with a curt, "Good luck."

Without wasting any time, Matt trotted down the stairs to level one.

Remi, who answered the door in an old gray T-shirt with yellow pit stains, appeared put-out by Matt's request. He left Matt standing at the open door and walked to his computer, grumbling to himself in Russian. After several long minutes, he managed to locate Alfie's file. He confirmed that Matt was, indeed, listed as an emergency contact.

Remi closed and locked his door. He walked toward the stairs without another word. When they reached the top of the landing, Matt swayed slightly on his feet. He felt Remi's eyes on him.

"You sick or something?" Remi said with no trace of sympathy. "You're as pale as shit. You look like you're going to keel over. What's wrong with you?" He eyed Matt, backing away a step.

Matt pushed past him onto Alfie's floor. "Just getting over a cold. I'm fine. Maybe a little dehydrated."

Matt's insides coiled with anxiety as Remi unlocked the door. The door squeaked open and the smell hit him—hard. It was unmistakable—the smell of death. A small moan escaped his lips.

No, no, no!

The interior of the apartment was in complete darkness. Matt fumbled along the wall until his fingers connected with the light switch. He snapped it on and rushed toward Alfie's bedroom door. Remi, right behind him, looked excited to have the monotony of his day interrupted.

Matt hesitated for a fraction of a second, took in a deep breath, and pushed the door open. He didn't think the smell could get any worse, but he was wrong. Remi gagged loudly and turned for the door, his face pinched in disgust.

Alfie was lying on the bed, his mouth stretched open, as if in a silent scream. His skin looked loose, surreal, as if it could slip off his body at any moment. It was the color of ash—both waxy and shiny in appearance. Matt took a small step closer, staring at circular, reddish-brown scabs covering the majority of his body.

Something about his fingers looked strange. He leaned a little closer, holding his breath. It appeared as if his fingertips and knuckles were covered in small, warty growths.

Matt stood frozen, his eyes tearing. He would never be able to erase this horrific image from his mind. He lifted his phone and, his eyes fixed on the scene before him, called 911.

He felt instantaneous grief.

He also felt fear.

Chapter 45
Los Angeles
Day +38

Cameron coughed and reluctantly pushed herself up off the mattress. A silver slice of light peeked through a crack in the blackout curtains, slightly lessening the total darkness she preferred while sleeping. She had never felt such exhaustion in her life, but she had to get up. She couldn't sleep in bedding drenched in sweat. She kicked away the tangled sheets and flung her Tommy Bahama duvet onto the floor.

Even the duvet is soaked. What's going on with me? I must have gotten the flu or something from Sheryl. She was sick last week and missed work for a few days.

Slowly, Cameron stripped the bed, tossed the wet sheets toward the corner of the room, and grabbed two clean ones from the closet.

Ugh! I feel terrible. If only I could stop coughing. This pain in my muscles reminds me of the time I ran the Los Angeles marathon. Even my skin hurts.

Without thinking, she rubbed the exquisitely tender, dusky-pink nodules covering her shins.

Maybe I should take my temperature. No wait—I can't. I don't even have a thermometer. I really need to get to the doc-in-a-box tomorrow.

She spread the clean sheets over the mattress. A coughing spasm overtook her, squeezing her chest. She leaned forward, her palms flat on the mattress, arm muscles quivering. After a minute, she caught her breath. She crawled into bed and curled into the fetal position, too tired to grab a pillow. She drifted asleep, her cheek pressed against the soft sheet smelling faintly of fabric softener.

Ten minutes later, a distant buzzing pulled her from her slumber.

What the hell? Who is calling me in the middle of the night?

She kept her eyes closed, deciding to ignore the call.

What if it's an emergency? What if something happened to Kathy?

Releasing a groan of frustration, she rolled over and plucked the phone from her nightstand. She checked the screen: Matt.

Matt? I don't know a Matt. Oh, this must be Alfie's friend. Weird. Why would he be calling me at this hour?

She tossed the phone down in frustration and collapsed back onto the bed.

Whatever he has to say, it can wait until morning.

Her eyes flew open as another coughing spasm took hold of her. She sat up and swung her legs to the floor, her chest muscles tightening. She groped blindly for a tissue, pressing it to her mouth. She gagged as thick, warm liquid filled her mouth and spilled onto the tissue. She squinted in the semi-darkness. The tissue, and her hands, were completely covered in bright red blood.

This isn't happening. This is a bad dream.

Her heart hammered in her chest and she nearly succumbed to overwhelming panic. She couldn't take a deep breath. It was as if she was underwater.

She coughed again, leaning forward to release another stream of blood from between her lips. The rich coppery taste was too much. She heaved helplessly as the contents of her stomach spattered onto the hardwood floor. She gasped for breath.

"Help me!" she tried to yell but only managed to mouth the words. She felt frantically for her phone. Her wet fingers slid over the screen.

Please, please, please.

After a few attempts, her home screen appeared. Dark spots clouded her vision and she held the phone until it nearly touched her nose. With shaking hands, she dialed 911.

Chapter 46
Las Colinas FEMA Temporary Relocation Camp
Day +39

There was muted applause in the camp when, at eight a.m. sharp, the loudspeakers announced the official end of the quarantine.

For a moment, Mallory felt like cheering. Then, just as suddenly, the smile fell from her face.

How could I be happy when Mindy and thirty other innocent people have died? She felt overcome by emotion as she imagined the suffering their loved ones must now be experiencing.

Could I have done more to save them? Truthfully, she didn't think so, but this belief did nothing to stop the guilt from creeping into her consciousness.

Sighing, she stood up, more than ready to go home, sleep in her own bed, and spend some quality time with Marcus. Lately, things had been good between them. They were back to the comfortable, easy way their relationship had been before she left.

She tried to suppress the familiar, burning anxiety she always experienced when flying. Each time she awoke the night before, thoughts of her upcoming flight immediately filled her head and she had trouble falling back asleep.

She glanced at her watch. She had five hours until take-off. Perfect. There was plenty of time to drive her rental car to the airport, grab some lunch, and get lost in her book. She grabbed her bags and made her way to the main entrance, deciding to skip the camp's hot breakfast.

There was a growing line of residents waiting to exit. It looked as if many of them had been there for hours.

A middle-aged Caucasian man in jeans and work boots lay curled on a dirty blanket, his head resting on a mustard-yellow JanSport backpack that had seen better days. She passed hundreds of men, women, and children. Many of those waiting sat on the dirt, their backs pressed against the fence.

These poor people seem as eager to leave as I am. They must have gotten up early and staked a place in line. It's encouraging that this many people have found somewhere more permanent to stay.

Yesterday afternoon, FEMA announced over the loudspeaker that they were working to make the checkout process as smooth as possible, but given the number of people expected to leave, long wait times were predicted. Each adult resident was required to provide identification and updated contact information before departure.

Dr. Walsh and his team were stationed at the final exit point. They were to perform abbreviated assessments before the residents were released.

Mallory stood on tiptoe, surveyed the clusters of people, and finally located Dr. Walsh's distinctive salt and pepper hair. She waited while he finished talking with a family of three.

"Goodbye, Dr. Walsh." She stepped forward, extending her hand. "I know we had our differences at times but, well, I wanted to say, I admire your dedication. I hope we get to work together again in the future, although not under these circumstances," she hastened to add.

Walsh took her hand and shook it firmly. "I would be honored to work with you again. Take care of yourself." His lips formed a small smile and he dipped his chin in farewell.

Mallory found herself smiling as she walked away.

So much for a relaxing hour of reading before departure.

Mallory ran for her gate, her suitcase wheels squeaking and bouncing behind her. She had a matter of minutes before take-off. There had been a major accident on I-5, where she found herself stuck in standstill traffic for hours.

"...paging Mallory Hayes. This is the final boarding call for passenger Mallory Hayes." She heard the disinterested voice as she approached the gate.

"I'm here, I'm here," she said breathlessly, thrusting her boarding pass toward the agent.

"You just made it, lucky lady," the agent said, smiling wryly.

Mallory tried to work on her *Journal of Virology* paper while in the air, but soon gave up. She couldn't concentrate. There was too much turbulence. She gripped the armrests, her heart hammering harder with each dip, sway, and bounce of the aircraft.

Only when the plane was back on solid ground and taxiing to the gate did she breathe a sigh of relief. She was drained and slightly sick to her stomach. Though it was still early, she couldn't wait to put on her pajamas, grab a glass of Meiomi pinot noir, and curl up in bed with her new book, *The Last Mrs. Parrish.*

On the way home, she received a text from Kate: "How was the flight? U home yet?"

Instead of pulling over to text her back, she used voice recognition to call her. Kate answered on the first ring.

"Hi, Mal. You back in Atlanta?" There was something in her tone that made Mallory instantly on edge.

"Yep. I'm on my way home from the airport right now. Why? What's going on?"

"Could I come over? I need to talk to you."

"About what? Can't you tell me over the phone?" An unexpected note of hysteria crept into Mallory's voice. "Oh no, are Mom and Dad okay?"

"They're fine. Everyone is fine. Nobody is hurt. I promise. I just have to talk to you," she said cryptically.

"Kate, I'm exhausted. Can't you just tell me over the phone?"

"I would rather not. I'll be over in twenty." Without giving her a chance to reply, she hung up.

Strange. What does Kate need to tell me in person? I just want to collapse in bed.

Frustrated, Mallory tried to call Kate back. It went straight to voicemail.

After a tense drive, Mallory finally pulled into her underground parking. When she opened the door to her apartment, Kate was already there, staring out the window and holding two glasses of red wine.

Before Mallory could speak, Kate said, "It's about Marcus." She handed Mallory one of the wine glasses. "Let's sit."

Mallory's stomach tightened.

"You know my friend Miriam Freeman, right? She's the one who's living with her parents in Johns Creek while she's job hunting."

"Of course. What does she have to do with anything?" Mallory's words came out colder than she intended. Kate didn't seem to notice.

"She was at Trattoria Blu for a family birthday party yesterday and, well, she saw Marcus...with Phoebe."

"Phoebe? I don't understand. Marcus can't stand her. It was probably someone who looked like Marcus."

She held out her phone. "They were holding hands."

Mallory leaned over, studying the photo. "Miriam took a picture? What a nosy…" Mallory stood up quickly, some of the wine sloshing onto the floor. "Sorry, it's not her fault. I'm projecting. I just can't believe he would do this to me."

Mallory shook her head in disbelief and felt hot tears forming in her eyes.

"I'm going to be sick." She pushed her glass toward Kate and rushed toward the kitchen. Kate followed closely behind, rubbing her back and murmuring sympathetic noises.

Mallory gripped the edge of her farmhouse sink and closed her eyes. She took several deep breaths, silently counting to herself.

After a long minute, she straightened up. "I will never forgive him—it's over."

Chapter 47
Whole Foods, Midtown Manhattan, New York
Day +42

Kathy pushed the shopping cart down the snack aisle of Whole Foods, weaving around a woman in yoga pants scrutinizing a packet of chocolate-covered almonds.

She stopped to rub her eyes. Strangely, her right eyelid was drooping, and both her eyes were sore, as if they had been struck by some object. An elderly man behind her clipped the back of her leg with his cart.

"Watch it!" she shrieked.

The man jumped in surprise. His face reddened, in either anger or embarrassment. Kathy didn't know which.

"Excuse me," he mumbled, walking quickly around her.

She gripped the handle of the cart. She could feel every detail of the smooth plastic with her right hand. Her left hand was a different story.

It began yesterday—a tingling, pins-and-needles sensation. It was more of an annoyance, and easy to ignore. But then, when she woke up this morning, her entire left hand was completely numb. She also had the worst headache of her life.

She held out her hand, flexing her fingers. All moved normally. She placed her left index knuckle in her mouth and squeezed down hard. After a moment, she pulled it out and studied it in horrified fascination. Two white indentations were visible—crescent moons surrounded by a halo of red. She should be howling in agony, she thought. Instead, she felt nothing.

The throbbing in her head increased suddenly, demanding her attention.

I need a pain reliever, extra strength, like, right now.

After wandering around the store for several infuriating minutes, she located the vitamin and supplement aisle. Her eyes scanned the shelves. She tried to concentrate despite the pounding in her head. She winced; the pain was becoming nearly unbearable. Her breath came in ragged gasps.

I must be having a migraine. Where is the Tylenol? Ibuprofen?

She grabbed a bottle of turmeric tablets. *What is this homeopathic crap? Where is the real medicine? If I could just stop this pounding in my head, everything would be okay.*

Suddenly, she was angry. The feeling was unlike anything she had ever experienced before. The rage rose in an intense wave, a grotesque crescendo. Her skin felt uncomfortably hot, as if it was prickling with electricity.

"Where. Is. The. Tylenol?" she bellowed, punctuating each word.

There was a moment of total silence. Then a tall, wiry clerk with a smattering of acne and a pristine green apron rushed in her direction. He reached the end of the aisle, stopped, and peeked warily around a display of dried fruit.

Kathy threw the turmeric at him, missing by several feet. It clattered to the floor, the sound echoing in the now quiet store. The clerk yelped as if he had been hit.

She watched him skitter away, her vision blurring. His retreating form separated into two figures and, just as quickly, merged back into one. For a moment, she felt cut off from reality, as if she was floating underwater and all her senses had left her.

Her hand darted out, swiping a handful of plastic bottles to the floor. The crashing sound partly satiated the burning inside her. She slid down among the debris and her foot caught the edge of an economy-size bottle of B6. She watched as it rolled lazily away. She drew up her knees, dropping her head to her hands.

Several minutes passed. Then she could hear, as if from far away, the frenzy of activity around her.

"Ma'am." A gentle shake of her shoulder. "Ma'am, can you hear me?"

Keeping her head down, Kathy moaned. She whispered, her tone childlike, "My head." Tears rapidly fell down her face. "It hurts."

A voice, brimming with authority, rose above the din. "Tell me exactly what happened."

"I don't know," a high-pitched voice replied, sounding strained and nervous. "I heard yelling—something about Tylenol, I think—and came to check it out. As soon as she saw me, she let loose a bottle…right at me! I ran. I mean, I was worried. What if she had a gun or something? That's all I know." A dramatic pause. "Oh, one other thing I did notice. One of her eyes was, like, half-closed."

"Which eye?"

A moment's deliberation. "Umm, her right."

"Thanks for your help," the authoritative voice said.

"Does anyone here know this woman?" a male paramedic asked as he crouched next to Kathy, unzipping a large canvas medical bag.

Silence.

I should speak. Tell them who I am.

She remained slumped over, mute. Her head hurt too much to do or say anything. The all-consuming pain was her only focus. She was vaguely aware of efficient hands fastening a cuff to her arm, then cool, dry fingers checking her pulse.

Chapter 48
Namaste House, South Loop, Chicago
Day +43

Using voice activation, Forest called his personal assistant.

"Yes?" Sierra's voice was low and modulated, the way she answered all calls from him. They had dispatched with pleasantries long ago.

"I need you to find me a primary care doctor in the South Loop. Get me in over the lunch hour. Tell them I'll pay cash, double their normal rate." He pulled a monogrammed handkerchief from his pocket to mop his brow.

Forest rubbed his eyes gingerly. It felt like his eyelids were lined with sandpaper. "I'm not getting any better. Actually, I'm feeling worse today, which I didn't think was even possible." He swallowed, stifling a cough, his voice hoarse. "My fever was up to 102 this morning. I need antibiotics, and I don't have time to sit in an ER or urgent care center."

Forest and Sierra had dated briefly in the past but quickly realized they weren't compatible outside of the office. Against all odds, they had maintained a close and effective working relationship. Sierra knew what Forest needed before he realized he needed it.

Forest ran a hand over the clean lines of his reclaimed wood desk. The surface was bare except for an iPad Pro and his iPhone—the newest model not yet released to the public.

Paper is strictly taboo at all Namaste House locations. Each of the Chicago building's five floors are outfitted with plastic and glass recycling bins. On the main floor sits a single, lone garbage bin. An enormous chalkboard sign hangs above it, sporting a message written in near-perfect calligraphy:

*Namaste House **challenges you** to reduce your personal waste.*

*This garbage can will be emptied once monthly and the contents weighed. The location that produces the least amount of waste will enjoy a group dinner at **Oriole**, compliments of Namaste House.*

The investors loved it.

"You don't sound good." She fought to keep her voice even. "Are you at the office?"

Forest opened a drawer and pulled out a spray bottle. He began a circuit of his office, spraying peace lilies, succulents, and spider plants as he spoke.

"Of course, I am. How could I miss—" he was cut off by a fit of coughing.

"Okay. Okay. As you no doubt know, that isn't typically how medical offices work...but I'll see what I can do." Forest could detect a hint of bemusement in her voice. "Not even the man-flu can bring the big guy down."

Forest couldn't muster the energy to reply. He hung up, knowing she wouldn't take it personally. She never did.

Abandoning his spray bottle on the floor, Forest slipped off his shoes and sank into his brand-new custom sofa to wait.

He closed his eyes and tried to concentrate on his breathing. He willed his body to relax and his mind to clear, but he couldn't suppress the ongoing urge to cough and rub his sore eyes.

Five minutes later, a text message came through. He knew, without looking, that Sierra had worked her magic.

Dr. Reddy, 1430 S. Michigan Ave, Suite 202.

12:30. Bring cash. —S

ᴧᴧᴧ

As he sat in the empty waiting room several hours later, Forest couldn't recall how he made it through the remainder of the morning. He had never felt so terrible in his life, even as a child. His chest and ribs were exceptionally sore from three days of near-constant coughing.

I've worked too hard on this opening to be sick now. I just need antibiotics and a good night's sleep. I'll be fine by tomorrow.

He glanced at the clock, eager to get back to the office. He would have to skip lunch. That was fine. He didn't have much of an appetite anyway. His tongue and mouth felt as if they were on fire, as if he had gulped a full cup of hot tea.

"Forest?" a young woman in scrubs called from the doorway.

Forest nodded. He stood and silently followed her to an exam room, coughing into his elbow.

He noted her slight, almost imperceptible frown as she took his vitals. He remained quiet, swallowing small sips of water from his smart hydration bottle, afraid speaking would trigger more uncontrollable coughing.

Dr. Reddy entered the room moments later, awkwardly pushing a cart with a computer. His forehead wrinkled and the corners of his mouth turned down as he stared at the screen. He looked to be well past retirement age, small and stooped, with a bald pate as shiny as a polished bowling ball. White tufts of hair sprouted from the sides of his head, reminding Forest of a baby bird.

He closed the door behind him and looked straight at Forest, not saying anything for a moment.

"What brings you in today?" he finally asked, not breaking eye contact.

"I've had this annoying cough and fever for a few days. It seems to be getting worse. This morning, my mouth and lips began to hurt, and my eyes feel gritty."

He shifted uncomfortably on the exam table.

"Anything else?" the doctor asked.

"Well, this is kind of embarrassing, but my skin is irritated and painful, umm, down below. It hurts to pee." Forest shrugged.

"There is nothing I haven't seen before," he said simply. "No need to be embarrassed. How high was your fever?" he asked.

"It was around 102 this morning." Forest turned to cough into his elbow.

"Any sick contacts?" Dr. Reddy's gaze had returned to the screen. His voice was dry, professional.

"Not that I know of. But there is something going around the office. There were a number of people who called in sick today."

"It says here that you don't take any medications. What about herbal supplements, vitamins, anything over the counter?"

"When I remember, I take a multivitamin. No herbal supplements."

"Any recent travels outside the country?" Dr. Reddy eyed the computer with mistrust as he pulled it closer. He pecked at the keys with one finger, looking up to the screen and back to the keypad with each letter.

"No, I live in LA. I'm here on business, but I haven't been out of the country in at least a year."

"Hmm." The doctor stood slowly, his knees cracking. "Let's take a look at you," he said as he washed his hands.

Dr. Reddy was silent as he examined Forest. After listening to his heart and lungs, he took his time examining his eyes, throat, and genitalia with a penlight.

Finally, he sat back on his stool. He looked at Forest with a serious expression, his eyebrows pushed down into two fuzzy punctuation marks.

"We need to admit you to the hospital right away," he said without preamble.

"But—"

The doctor held up a hand. "Let me explain. First, you have signs and symptoms of community-acquired pneumonia. There are extensive crackles throughout your lungs and your oxygenation saturation is below normal. Your temperature is currently 101.5. This alone would be enough to send you to the hospital for IV antibiotics." He looked at Forest sternly.

Forest remained silent as panic and desperation seized him. He had put everything he had into this project; he had a million things to do before the grand opening tomorrow. He couldn't miss it.

"Second, on examination, you demonstrate classic signs of a rare type of secondary response, probably due to the infection, evidenced by distinctive erosions and ulcers on your mucosal membranes—eyes, mouth, and genital area. This is called Stevens Johnson Syndrome and it's something we take very seriously. SJS is classically triggered by medications but, in your case, I suspect it's from infection with a specific type of bacteria called mycoplasma pneumoniae."

Forest opened his mouth to protest but closed it again as the gravity of the situation washed over him. He felt the first stirrings of fear as he studied the doctor's solemn expression. Suddenly, he wanted to sleep. He wanted it more than he had ever wanted anything before.

"All right," he said.

Dr. Reddy rolled his stool toward the door. He opened it without rising and called into the hallway, "Katie, please place Forest on four liters of oxygen and recheck his pulse oximetry."

He turned back to his computer as he continued to speak. "We need to directly admit him to the hospital. Please have reception call an ambulance, and then contact Northwestern to give them a heads up. I'll put in an admission note." *Peck. Peck. Peck.*

Forest cautiously lowered himself back on the table, the white paper cover bunching and tearing. His lower legs hung uncomfortably over the side. He stared at a small brown stain on the tile ceiling. Katie entered and wordlessly placed him on oxygen, looping the tubing behind each ear.

How did I get here? I was absolutely fine a few days ago. Running four miles and doing strength training every single day. In the best shape of my life. Now, I feel like...like I'm dying.

Chapter 49
The Centers for Disease Control and Prevention, Atlanta, GA
Day +43

"Hi, this is Dr. Marjani. How may I help?" Nat asked distractedly.

Where is it? I just had it.

His hands fumbled around the papers and books strewn haphazardly on his desk.

"Hello, Dr. M. I have a Dr. Ware on the line for you. Apparently, she has some concerns regarding an autopsy she performed. She'd like some input from the CDC."

Maybe it slid off the desk?

"You're the fellow on call, right? It's your name on the list but..."

"Sorry about that. I'm here and yes, I'm on-call. Thanks, Alisha. You can put Dr. Ware through."

Nat leaned down, straining to see the dark corners beneath his desk: a stress ball covered in cobwebs, an empty Flamin' Hot Cheeto's wrapper, one chewed-up pen cap, and no paper.

"Dr. Marjani," he said. He swiveled his chair around, holding the phone to his ear with his shoulder.

Ahh, I bet I set it back here.

"Yes, hi. This is Dr. Melinda Ware from the University of California Los Angeles Pathology Department. Do you have time for me to run a few cases by you?"

"Of course, happy to help," he mumbled, eyeing a precarious stack of books and loose papers on a wooden chair by the door. He scooted his chair over and craned his neck to take a closer look.

"Well, we have had a few bizarre deaths in otherwise healthy, young adults."

Nat sat up straight, bumping his head on the edge of a floating cabinet, the paper search momentarily forgotten. A burst of apprehension squeezed his chest.

"Oww." He rubbed his head absently. "Sorry, did you say you're from UCLA?"

Stop jumping to conclusions. The probability that it is related to ade-novirus B7x *and the FEMA camp is extremely low. It's probably something like bacterial meningitis which, as every infectious disease expert knows, can happen within the close quarters of a university.*

"Yes, I'm a pathologist at UCLA," she said slowly.

"Tell me about the cases concerning you." Nat, picking up on her hesitation, replied in a professional tone.

"All right, thank you." Nat could hear typing and the clicking of a mouse.

Still sounding slightly hesitant, she continued, "Ahh, here it is. Case number one is Alfie Hughes, a 29-year-old man with no significant past medical history who was found deceased in his apartment by a concerned friend seven days ago. Given his age, and the condition of his body, the county coroner was called to investigate. He determined the cause of death to be natural, secondary to an unspecified illness. Following procedure, an autopsy was requested.

"Unfortunately, we have been short-staffed for the last several months and Mr. Hughes didn't make it to my table until six days ago, seventy-two hours after the estimated time of death.

"External exam revealed lesions consistent with disseminated herpes zoster and significant mucocutaneous candidiasis affecting his eyes, nose, mouth, and genitalia. There were also peculiar, warty growths covering eighty percent of the dorsal surface of his hands." She took a deep breath, warming to her subject. "To be honest, I've never seen anything like it in person— only in medical textbooks. There were some similar, small verrucous lesions just beginning to show around the nares—"

Adrenaline surged Nat's bloodstream. He hunched over the notepad balanced on his lap, scribbling furiously as she talked.

"Three different opportunistic pathogens in a single patient: disseminated shingles, covering large areas of skin instead of the usual single dermatome; a fungal infection, commonly called thrush, involving all visible mucosal parts of the body; and, HPV-related warts disfiguring both hands and beginning to work on the patient's face, only to be stopped by the host's death.

"All three microbes are ubiquitous in the environment. They are extremely common infectious agents, typically causing mild infection. Shingles may cause immunocompetent patients' significant neuropathic pain; however, it is usually isolated to a small area of the body and is typically not life-threatening. The majority of people are infected with one or more of these pathogens at some time in their life. However, in this case, it's the extent of the infection that is unusual. It's unequivocal evidence of immunosuppression in some form. If the immune system is working properly, it wouldn't allow these particular organisms to replicate and infect the body unchecked and—"

Typically, Nat liked to have the consulting physician present the entire case before asking questions. That way, all information the presenter deems important is included. This approach decreases the likelihood of missing something. In infectious disease investigation, small details often prove crucial.

In this instance, he found it impossible to keep quiet. Interrupting her mid-sentence, he blurted, "Did you test for HIV?"

There was a brief pause. "Yes, obviously, that was my initial assumption. It was negative. Otherwise, I wouldn't be calling you," she replied coolly.

Chastened, Nat replied, "Of course. Please go on."

"As I was saying...ah, yes. There were warty lesions noted around the nares. Internal exam demonstrated signs of inflammation in the setting of otherwise healthy organs. PCR testing revealed an extremely high herpes zoster viral load, which I ultimately determined to be the cause of death."

"I know you said the patient was previously healthy. Do you know if there was any family history of immunosuppressive disease?" Nat asked.

It's possible the patient had an undiagnosed immunodeficiency. Primary immunodeficiencies typically present in childhood, but not always.

"Given the unusual circumstances, I did attempt follow-up with the deceased parents. They're in England. I left a message earlier today, but I haven't heard back from them. I'm guessing they may be en route to the States."

"What about medications?" Nat asked. "Was he taking anything?"

"The paramedics didn't find anything in his apartment,' she replied and waited a moment. "Do you have any other questions, or shall I present the other cases?"

"How many cases have you flagged?"

"Two others."

"I promise this is my last question for the moment. You aren't able to obtain a CBC postmortem, are you?"

"Well, no. We don't typically perform CBCs postmortem. The results can be quite variable."

Nat took a deep breath, resisting the urge to bombard her with questions. "Please continue."

"Case number two is a 30-year-old woman, Cameron Davis, with a past medical history of migraines. Five days ago, she was admitted to UCLA, intubated, and unresponsive. She was found unconscious in her apartment after dialing 911. Per the hospital notes, a chest CT revealed extensive thin-walled cavities and infiltrates in both lungs. This is, presumably, what led to respiratory failure and unconsciousness. Also noted in the physical exam, and my post-mortem, were dusky, raised nodules on her lower extremities bilaterally, consistent with erythema nodosum.

"She died three days after admittance. I performed the autopsy yesterday. I found considerable pulmonary disease consistent with the CT description. Curiously, there was a lack of lymphocytes. There was utterly no visible pus at the sites of presumed infection—just areas of necrosis and hemorrhage.

"Scrapings of lung tissue were consistent with coccidioidomycosis fungal infection, which, ultimately, I named as the cause of death. The weird thing was, microscopically, there was a near-complete absence of white blood cells. Naturally," placing emphasis on the word, "I was concerned about immunosuppression, but HIV was negative."

"Hmm, that is strange," Nat replied.

Nat knew these cases had to be related to adenovirus B7x. It was just too big of a coincidence. There were no cases of contagious, viral-induced immunosuppression that he was aware of outside of HIV. This was unlike anything described in the medical literature. He placed his CDC-issued cell phone on speaker and began texting frantically.

"Before you ask, the patient was a life-long resident of southern California, but mostly stuck to the city and populated areas, at least according to her family. No recent instances of camping in the desert, as far as I can tell. She took Sumatriptan as needed for migraines. No other known medications. There is no family history of immunosuppression."

Coccidioides is a fungal organism endemic to the desert areas of southern California, Arizona, New Mexico, and western Texas.

I wonder if she had prior exposure, even years ago. Maybe the fungus, even a single fungi, lay dormant in her lung and reactivated when her immune system stopped producing lymphocytes to keep it in check. It's unbelievable to think about the billions of microbes that reside in and on the human body, some of which can be deadly in the absence of particular immune cells.

"The third case is Matthew Cooper, a 28-year-old gentleman with no significant past medical history who presented to the ER three days ago with cough, fever, and diarrhea. He was treated for a presumed bacterial gastroenteritis with antibiotics and IV hydration. It appears the ER doctor was going to treat and release, but then his lab results came back. His WBCs were near zero. He was admitted and underwent a full work-up.

"His chest x-ray showed bilateral infiltrates. An infectious disease consult was obtained, but they couldn't find a reason for his low WBCs. He was screened for a long list of opportunistic pathogens, and mycobacterium avium complex came back positive. HIV was negative.

"Despite treatment, he experienced multi-organ failure and was transferred to the ICU. He passed away late last night. I performed his autopsy this morning. Findings were consistent with death secondary to disseminated MAC caused by immunosuppression of unknown etiology."

Nat glanced at his phone. No reply yet. He stood quickly, heading down the hallway toward Dr. Lee's office.

"You may not know the answer to this, but is it possible these three individuals came into contact at some point with one another during the last two weeks?" Nat asked as he walked.

"Well, I only know the answer to this because I spoke to Dr. Perez from Infectious Disease. He was able to obtain an exposure history from Matthew before he was transferred to the ICU. In fact, he was the one who suggested I call you. Apparently, Matthew Cooper and Alfie Hughes were close friends. Matthew was the one who discovered Alfie's body, and Cameron Beckett was Alfie's ex-girlfriend. Apparently, Alfie ran into Cameron at a club a few weeks ago."

At this, Nat broke into a run.

Chapter 50
The Centers for Disease Control and Prevention, Atlanta, GA
Day +43

Mallory and Rory hurried to the conference room, sipping from identical venti iced coffees. Mallory couldn't recall ever being summoned to an emergency meeting at the CDC. She was exhausted, both physically and emotionally, and had planned to leave work early, wanting nothing more than a hot bath, a glass of cool, crisp pinot, and eight hours of uninterrupted sleep.

She had spoken to Marcus briefly a few nights ago. When he answered her call, she immediately informed him she knew about Phoebe. He denied it so adamantly at first that Mallory momentarily faltered in her conviction. When she mentioned the picture Kate had shown her, he changed tactics, begging for forgiveness and swearing it would never happen again. She told him it was over between them, hung up, and blocked his number. She would never be able to trust him again.

Kate offered to stay the night and Mallory accepted gratefully. Despite her resolve, she had lain awake most of the night, alternating between sadness, fury, and regret.

It never even crossed my mind that he might be cheating on me. Those phone calls from Phoebe that morning—why did I take his word for it? She suspected she knew the answer. She was a fiercely loyal person. She had projected her traits onto him and trusted him implicitly. She would not make the same mistake again.

Mallory slid into a seat and turned expectantly toward Dr. Lee. He sat at the head of the gleaming black conference table, absorbed with something on his laptop. His mouth was set into a hard line, an abrupt deviation from his normally open, relaxed face.

Mallory felt unsettled.

Please, please don't let it be adenovirus B7x.

The team had received semi-regular updates from the lab director. Since the identification of adenovirus B7x, they had worked nonstop to complete the molecular sequencing.

This phase complete, they were now comparing the molecular sequence to known, previously sequenced adenoviral strains. In this way, the unknown components of aB7x could theoretically be identified and isolated. The researchers hypothesized that the novel sequences might be responsible for the depletion of lymphocytes.

What about vaccine development? Mallory knew the virology lab had made adenovirus B7x a priority given its previously unheard-of mortality rate. They had only a small sample size, but in the small FEMA camp group, it was one hundred percent lethal. In the last update she had heard, they were beginning phase 1 of animal studies. She made a note to ask Dr. Lee about it.

Dr. Lee finally looked up. "Thanks for coming on short notice. We're here because Nat just received a concerning phone call from a pathologist at UCLA. Nat, if you could please summarize what you've learned."

Nat nodded soberly and stood.

Mallory listened in rapt attention, taking notes as Nat spoke. She swallowed, though her throat suddenly felt dry. They needed to get back to L.A. as soon as possible.

"...and, here's a key part of the history." Nat paused to ensure he had everyone's attention. "All three fatal cases knew each other *and* had confirmed recent contact. As I'm sure you guys are thinking, adenovirus B7x is a possible, if not probable, cause of the immunosuppression." He took a deep breath and, his voice vaguely ominous, said, "It looks like aB7x has traveled outside the camp."

The back of Mallory's neck tingled, as if traced by icy fingers. She suppressed a shudder, repositioning herself in her seat.

"Thanks, Nat. Great work." Dr. Lee stood. "I spoke to the head of Infectious Disease at UCLA. They are currently quarantining all personnel who came into contact, or may have come into contact, with either Cameron Beckett or Matthew Cooper at the hospital. Dr. Ware, the pathologist who performed the autopsies, along with the entire staff at the morgue, are also under voluntary quarantine." He moved to the white board, saying over his shoulder, "I just briefed Director Quinn, so she's aware of the situation and is awaiting an update."

He uncapped a red marker with a snap and wrote "NEXT STEPS" in quick strokes. "We need to track down anyone who may have come into contact with the infected, prior to death in Alfie's case, or prior to hospitalization in the others. We also need to pinpoint exactly when, where, and how the virus left the camp." Dr. Lee's words were clipped, efficient. "Nat and Tanvi, since you are on-call and familiar with the situation, the three of us will take the first available flight to LA."

Why does the name Alfie sound familiar? I feel like I've heard it recently.

"Pardon my interruption, Dr. Lee," Mallory said. "Was Alfie a resident of the camp at some point? Maybe he came through the medical center? For some reason, the name sounds familiar."

Dr. Lee leaned over his computer. "Hmm, it doesn't look like we have that information yet. Could you track down—"

The conference room door burst open. Adam Rossi, a medical officer from Dr. Powell's team, leaned into the room. His expression was a complex mix of disbelief and apprehension.

"You guys need to see this."

In confused silence, Mallory and the rest of the room scrambled out of their chairs to follow Adam.

He led them to the main media room, nicknamed the M&M Room, partly because of the initials and partly because Fintan, the head of IT, could often be found there, tinkering with equipment while crunching on chocolate candies.

The M&M was outfitted with enormous wall-mounted screens and three rows of identical, wide-screen computers. The overhead lights glowed muted spots of orange, dimmed to the lowest setting. The majority of the room's illumination came from the blue glow of the monitors, giving the room an eerie atmosphere.

CDC employees streamed quietly into the room, their eyes riveted to the screens.

A CNS broadcaster, her nasal voice slightly breathless, assaulted Mallory's ears as she entered the M&M.

"I repeat, breaking news, folks. A mysterious, deadly illness has been reported in multiple US cities. Emergency rooms in New York, Chicago, and Los Angeles are experiencing an unexpected surge of patients.

"Some are speculating this could be the same virus that prompted the record-breaking quarantine at the Las Colinas FEMA camp, which ultimately resulted in dozens of deaths." She paused, tilting her head slightly while pressing a delicate, manicured finger to her ear. She looked directly at the camera, lowered her voice, and rearranged her features into a mask of faux gravity. "This just in. We have confirmed that Orange County Medical Center in Anaheim, California has officially closed its emergency room doors. They are at capacity and will not be accepting new patients. You heard it here first…"

Mallory locked eyes with Rory. She imagined them to be a mirror image of hers, reflecting both shock and disbelief.

It's not just Southern California. Chicago and New York also have the virus. Maybe other big cities. Probably others.

A powerful sense of foreboding overcame her, and for several long seconds, she was frozen in panic. An image flashed in her mind: her beautiful and vibrant sister, Kate, lying on a gurney, soiled sheets twisted like snakes around her legs. She was unconscious and deathly ill, her body ravaged by invisible and seemingly invincible organisms.

Mallory clasped her hands to her stomach and took a few shuddering breaths. She felt sick.

Dr. Lee muttered, his words angry. "How the hell are we just learning about this? From the *media* no less?"

He retreated to a corner of the room, speaking animatedly into a cell phone. Having seen and heard enough, Mallory maneuvered her way out of the room, her stomach a knot of anxiety; Rory, Tanvi, and Nat were close behind her.

He must be talking to Director Quinn. We need to close the airports, quarantine whole cities, deploy the National Guard...

Mallory's mind swam with the work ahead as her thumbs flew over the keys on her iPhone. She needed to text her family: "DON'T LEAVE THE HOUSE. Make sure all doors and windows are locked. Don't let anyone in ... I'll explain later."

She crossed the threshold and entered the same conference room they had vacated minutes before. As she sat, she briefly closed her eyes, saying a silent prayer for her parents and Kate. She hoped they saw the text right away. Her mom was known to leave her phone at random spots within the house for hours at a time. Mallory used to tease her about it.

If the virus was in Chicago, LA, and New York, it might already be in Atlanta.

It could be anywhere.

The first thing Mallory did was send a mass email marked "urgent" to the three other teams, headed by Drs. Powell, Perez, and Greene.

The subject line: **EMERGENCY MEETING**ALL MEDICAL OFFICERS, CONFERENCE ROOM C. The message was blank.

Adam was the first to make it to the conference room, still appearing slightly dazed. Over the next several minutes, the other medical officers and team leaders trickled in, many looking pale and shaken.

Dr. Lee arrived last, looking as if he had aged years during the past several minutes. His shoulders were slumped, as if in defeat. His jaw alternately tightened with stress and then slackened to incredulity. He repeatedly swept his hands through his hair, leaving it looking greasy and unkempt.

Mallory was surprised by his reaction; he usually radiated a reassuring and calm confidence. Admittedly, though, they had never come close to a crisis of this magnitude. She hoped the others in the room didn't pick up on his distress. It was essential that they stay focused.

They then brainstormed tasks to be undertaken by groups to be assembled. Rory volunteered as scribe and filled the white board quickly and efficiently. He divided the board into four groups, one section for each team.

They would send one team each to LA, Chicago, and New York. The fourth team, Dr. Greene's, would stay in Atlanta to coordinate specific recommendations for a national press release. They would connect with the various state-level CDC offices and public health departments. They needed all the help they could get.

Mallory knew the dissemination of accurate information, while keeping panic at a minimum, would be key to slowing down the rate of infection. If the public could be persuaded to stay indoors and follow precautions, their chances of beating the virus would improve dramatically.

They would eventually need to split the teams into smaller groups, sending team members one by one to new hot zones as they emerged, and there was no doubt other pockets of infection *would* emerge.

An average adult comes into contact with around five to twenty people daily. This can vary widely depending on the circumstances, with heavily populated areas generating hundreds of potential exposures from a single person. Each of those contacts would expose countless others. The number of infected would exponentially increase.

It wasn't just person-to-person contact they needed to worry about. Viruses could be transmitted by fomites. Any surface that infected individuals came into contact with could be a potential contaminant. Adenovirus had been proven to live on surfaces for weeks.

Forty-five minutes after the breaking news story, Mallory was in her car, her mind spinning. She planned on throwing some clothes and toiletries into a bag and get on her way to Chicago within the hour.

She used voice recognition to call Special Agent Coleman. After four rings, it went to voicemail.

"It's Mallory Hayes, from the CDC. I'm afraid I have some bad news. It seems adenovirus B7x may have spread to parts of Southern California, New York, and Chicago. This is not confirmed, though we have a high level of suspicion and I wanted to give you a heads up. I presume Director Quinn has notified your bioterrorism division but, well, I wanted to make sure you were also aware." She recited her cell phone number, thanked him, and ended the call.

Next, she called Kate. Mallory blew out a breath of relief when she answered. She updated her as quickly as she could. She made her find a pen and write down specific instructions to keep herself and their parents from exposure over the coming days.

She spent the remainder of the twenty-minute drive reviewing isolation procedures with a public health representative at Stroger Hospital of Cook County, in Chicago. She would call the other Chicago hospitals on the way to the airport. Deploying the Illinois, California, and New York state-level CDC officers was the first priority of Dr. Greene's team. According to protocol, the state teams should be on their way to the major medical centers.

Her mind was a million miles away, mentally composing her to-do list, when she pulled into her designated parking spot. She didn't immediately see the figure, shrouded in shadow, leaning against the pedestrian gate.

"Hi, Mallory." Marcus stepped forward, a slice of light illuminating his face.

Mallory yelped in surprise, dropping her keys. They hit the concrete with a musical clang.

"Marcus, you startled me."

"We need to talk." His voice was curiously flat, his face blank.

For the second time that day, Mallory experienced a frisson of fear. *What is he doing here unannounced? Why does he look so cold, so devoid of emotion?* She kept her eyes on him as she leaned down to snag her keys.

"There isn't anything to talk about. I'm never going to be able to trust you again. It's just...non-negotiable. I'm sorry." *Why am I the one saying sorry?*

"You can't just ghost me like this. I deserve better."

Mallory's eyes flashed in anger. "I'm handling a major national emergency at work. I don't have time—"

There was a short, loud bark of laughter. She flinched involuntarily. "Of course," he said. "Busy, busy, busy little bee."

She had never seen Marcus like this before. *Where was the sparkle in his eye? The cheeky grin?*

Mallory's eyes flicked to the elevator, only ten feet away. She tried to step around him, but he shifted to block her way.

In a flash, his hand shot out and clamped down on her wrist. She bit back the urge to scream, sensing this would only serve to incense him further. As she locked her gaze on his, it was as if she was looking into the eyes of a wild animal.

She spoke, surprised at how calm her voice was. "Marcus, let me go."

They stood staring at each other for a long moment, his grip unyielding. Then he reddened and began blinking rapidly, as if trying to hold back tears. His face twisted, and he slid down to the dusty concrete. Wrapping his arms around Mallory's legs, he let out a few shaking sobs.

"Mallory, I'm so, so sorry. It was beyond stupid. I made the biggest mistake of my life. *Please*, give me another chance."

Mallory's legs felt rubbery from adrenaline. She leaned down and pried his hands off her. Without missing a beat, she fled toward the stairwell. The door slammed behind her with a reverberating thud, raising her heart rate higher than she thought possible. A tiny winged insect seemed to be fluttering in her chest and she briefly wondered if she was having palpitations. As she sprinted up the stairs two at a time, she strained to hear, over the echo of her footsteps, for sounds of pursuit.

Chapter 51
Malmö, Sweden
Day +43

"Fakir, come here!" Sameer called breathlessly. "I've just received word from Abu himself."

Fakir had been resting on his bed, staring at the ceiling. He jumped up and rushed out of the room.

Sameer spun from the window and tossed his phone onto the couch. With two quick strides, he was in front of Fakir, squeezing his shoulders in excitement. He looked squarely into Fakir's eyes, tilting his forehead until it was nearly touching his. "It's time for the world to see what we, as devout Muslims, have always known—that Allah's power is omnipotent!"

Fakir clenched his fist in a show of triumph, unable to speak. Embarrassed, he pressed his fist against his lips, trying to suppress the tears that threatened to pour forth. *How was Sameer so adept at controlling his emotions?*

He took a few steadying breaths and managed to whisper, "Allahu akbar."

"Yes, my brother, God is great indeed," Sameer said, his voice infused with excitement. They embraced, clapping each other on the back.

"Father would be proud," Fakir said as he surreptitiously wiped his face with the back of his hand.

"Yes, I'm sure Alab *is* proud." Sameer pressed his hands together and gazed at the ceiling. "He is looking down on us approvingly from Paradise."

"Yes. What happens now? Where are we going to do it?" Fakir replied.

"I have somewhere in mind. Grab your thawb and dupatta. We leave in ten minutes."

Chapter 52
O'Hare International Airport, Chicago
Day +43

O'Hare Airport was strangely quiet. Discarded McDonald's bags, plastic sandwich wrappers, and abandoned newspapers littered the rows of chairs. *Maybe the cleaners called in sick, or just left when they heard the news.*

Mallory, Tanvi, Nat, and Rory followed the throng of passengers toward Baggage Claim, their masks, gloves, and protective gowns firmly in place. The non-breathable plastic had made the already uncomfortable and anxiety-riddled flight that much more uncomfortable.

An odd sense of detachment descended over Mallory. The events of the previous hours felt surreal, as if they had happened to someone else. She wasn't sure why, but she hadn't mentioned what happened with Marcus to the others, not even Rory. *Maybe I don't want to waste another moment thinking about him. I have more pressing matters to occupy my mind.*

And yet, she had to admit that his actions had scared her—really scared her. When leaving for the airport, she asked the building's concierge to walk her to the waiting Uber. There was no further sign of Marcus.

Inside the O'Hare concourse, they passed the distinctive Bubbles Wine Bar. The piano was silent and the black leather barstools empty. A small cluster of people were gathered around a TV to the side of the bar, their faces tilted toward the screen. Mallory felt Tanvi nudge her.

She gestured toward the TV, her eyes wide. "Look."

A man, clad in a robe that skimmed the top of his bare feet, filled the screen. His hair was covered with a checkered white and black wrap, and dark sunglasses obscured his eyes. A square of black cloth was tied over the lower half of his face.

He gestured animatedly toward the camera. In the background, a green flag with a white Islamic star and crescent was carefully tacked to a weathered, wood-paneled wall.

"This disturbing video was posted on Facebook mere minutes ago. It has since been taken down, but not before copies were re-posted on various online sites. Our experts continue to work on translating the video in its entirety. The bottom line is…"

Mallory sucked in a breath. She knew what was coming.

"…that the Islamic terrorist group, ISIS, has taken responsibility for the manufacture and distribution of a particularly virulent virus that has already killed dozens in California."

The anchor's voice remained professional, but his pinched expression didn't fully cover his distress. "It is feared the virus has now spread to major US cities, including New York and Chicago."

The camera panned to an anchor with a dark blonde bob, sprayed and gelled into immobility, and her thin lips pulled down into a frown. "In related news, at four p.m. this afternoon, the TSA, acting on orders from the President, made a shocking announcement: All out-bound flights from O'Hare, Midway, JFK, LaGuardia, and Newark have been grounded. This comes in the wake of the controversial shut-down of all central and southern California airports earlier this afternoon. Tens of thousands are stranded, many of them far from home."

The screen cut to an exterior view of an American Airlines departure terminal. Mallory noticed the red banner at the bottom of the screen: O'Hare International Airport, 4:17 pm.

Above the banner, the video showed a continuous stream of people flowing from the exits. The camera panned outward. The United and Spirit airline terminals showed a similar mass exodus. Crowds of people filled the sidewalks and spilled out onto the drop-off lanes, blocking the few cars attempting to get through. Most were either typing on their phones or had them pressed to their ear, seemingly oblivious to their surroundings.

The camera suddenly jerked and zoomed in on two men. One man wore a tailored suit. The other was an older man, possibly a retiree, with bright white hair and tanned, leathery skin wearing a sky-blue golf shirt and khakis. The two pushed each other, roughly jostling for one of the few remaining cabs. The white-haired man's sun visor was knocked askew.

Without warning, the man in the suit dropped his shoulder and lunged forward, like a defensive football player, connecting directly with the older man's center mass. As Mallory watched in disbelief, the man's feet flew high into the air as he fell, the curb hitting him squarely in the back of his neck. His spine appeared to compress like an accordion as the weight of his lower body pressed down above him.

The man appeared to groan; his eyes squeezed tightly in agony. Out of the corner of her eye, she saw Tanvi cringe as, a split-second later, the momentum of the fall caused the man's head to whip back and bounce twice on the concrete. His feet were the last to land, his white athletic shoes finally thudding to the pavement.

"This video shows one of several physical altercations that have occurred outside the airport, thought to be due to the overcrowded conditions and lack of ground transportation for passengers of cancelled flights." The anchor shook her head, her face serious. "Per the Chicago Transit Authority, the majority of stranded passengers have since been moved to hotels or to one of five temporary shelters near the airport.

"The Chicago, New York, and Central/Southern California airports are to remain closed to outbound flights for the foreseeable future." She turned to another camera, her frown set firmly in place. "Coming up, the experts weigh in."

A woman in a navy-blue business suit and beige heels pushed through the crowd, a panicked expression on her face. "My children are in New York with our nanny. I have to get to them." She nearly collided with Mallory and then visibly recoiled when she noticed her protective gear.

The woman skirted around Mallory, slipped off her heels, and set off at a jog, her stockinged feet slapping the tiled floor.

It was as if a spell was broken. The majority of the small crowd dispersed, scattering like a startled flock of birds.

Turning away themselves, the CDC group resumed walking, Nat in the lead and setting a brisk pace.

After a few minutes of walking, Rory spoke. "The crazy thing is, I'm not surprised. I'm just...really, really angry on behalf of the innocent people targeted. Whoever did this...well, they have to be pure evil." His fists clenched and unclenched.

"Anyone who can kill children has to have a black heart," Nat said softly.

Tanvi and Mallory nodded in agreement, temporarily at a loss for words. It was difficult to comprehend why some work so hard to end the lives of others simply because they are different from them.

"The question we need to be asking is: How does this change our approach? Now that we know it's bioterrorism—a virus made synthetically—does this help us in some way?" Tanvi asked, her forehead wrinkled in concentration.

"That's a good point," said Mallory, "but can we even say definitively that ISIS created the virus? What if they're taking advantage of this situation to cause panic and terror? But honestly, I do think the way this virus is acting...it fulfills the criteria for a biological weapon."

"It seems anything could be possible. At this point, we can't know for sure if it's man-made or natural," Rory said, shaking his head. "Hopefully, we'll have more concrete answers from the lab soon."

They continued walking, each lost in thought.

"Let me try Special Agent Coleman. Maybe there's *something* he can tell us." Mallory called him, leaving another voicemail when he didn't answer. *I'm sure he has his hands full.*

"All right, until we have more information, I vote we continue doing what we were trained to do—contain and eradicate this bastard," Nat said forcefully, grunting as he pulled his luggage off the carousel.

"Sounds good to me," Mallory said quickly. Nat and Tanvi nodded, a look of determination on their faces.

"What do you have in there, rocks?" Mallory said, trying half-heartedly to lighten the mood.

"Nope—books. Textbooks to be exact. It's always good to have a hard copy." He paused and then shrugged. "Just in case."

Just in case...what? We lost power? Society collapsed and the internet was no longer available? Mallory shuddered. *Could things really get that bad?*

Their National Guard escort greeted them the moment they passed through security. It was strange to see the normally packed lines completely devoid of people. Even though Dr. Lee had given them a heads up, the three men and two women decked out in pristine combat gear, complete with vests, helmets, and service rifles, still managed to rattle her. Mallory herself felt comfortable around firearms; she had plenty of training in the Army.

Is this really necessary? It seems like overkill.

After brief introductions, they walked toward the exit. The rhythmic swishing of their plastic protective gear seemed to fill the cavernous space of the terminal, which felt even larger in its near-abandoned state.

The automatic doors slid open. Humidity immediately engulfed Mallory, descending over her like an unwelcome blanket. She experienced a fleeting moment of panic when her plastic shield fogged with condensation. She waited a few seconds for it to clear, taking deep, controlled breaths.

There was a hint of ozone underlying the pungent scents of diesel and asphalt. Mallory caught a flash of lightning to the north as she climbed into the Humvee behind Rory.

Conversation was difficult over the rumble of the engine. Mallory found herself staring out the window as they drove, fully occupied with her thoughts. There were twenty-three emergency rooms within the city limits of Chicago. They had decided to split up to cover more ground, starting at the four largest. Cook County Department of Public Health employees would be assigned the others.

Dr. Lee and the other team leaders were to remain in Atlanta for the time being. They were hard at work gathering information remotely. Dr. Lee offered to collect passenger lists for all outbound flights from the quarantine zones over the last seventy-two hours. They would meet with Director Quinn every four hours to make recommendations based on their findings and the findings of their respective teams.

Mallory leaned forward, her seat belt straining across her chest. "Excuse me, Corporal Parker. How much longer until we reach the quarantine line?"

She saw the Corporal shoot a glance toward the driver, who remained expressionless, staring at the road.

"Ma'am, I thought you knew. We're already in the quarantine zone. It encompasses Chicago and all surrounding suburbs. An estimated 9.5 million people."

Mallory sat back, surprised.

Director Quinn isn't messing around. Good.

As they approached downtown, Mallory noticed faint lines of distant smoke. They curled lazily into the air, disappearing into the night sky. It looked like the remnants of oversized birthday candles had just been blown out.

Rory craned his neck and repositioned his glasses on his nose. "What's that?" he asked, his voice incredulous. "Is that smoke?"

Without turning, Corporal Parker answered, his voice projecting over the roar of the engine. "Yes, sir. Riots and looting are occurring in parts of the city, mostly the south side. We've also had several attempted breaches of the quarantine line."

In the reflection of the passenger window, Mallory noticed the corporal's eyes. They flicked right and left as he spoke, constantly scanning their surroundings for danger.

I was wrong to question their presence. If things are already this bad, what's going to happen over the next several days or weeks? I'm a trained officer. However, I can't be both soldier and doctor right now.

"It's just happening so fast. I mean, the news broke, what, like seven hours ago?" Tanvi said.

"If you think about it, it makes a sad sort of sense," Mallory said, gazing out the window at the tendrils of smoke. "Nobody likes to be legally restricted to a specific area. It's an affront to their human rights. They feel trapped, in a city with a deadly virus no less. They must be utterly terrified, which is, frustratingly, exactly what the terrorists want. Not that I condone rioting or looting. They're putting even more people in harm's way and probably contributing to the spread of this virus. I just...I wish there was another way."

Rory said, "It comes down to being informed. The public *needs* information. It's the only thing that may help calm people down and possibly prevent further panic. I hope Dr. Greene's team has been in regular contact with the press. People need to be advised to stay inside, remain isolated, practice good hygiene—washing hands, using hand sanitizer liberally and often, and, of course, wearing protective gear if available.

"People also need to know how adenovirus spreads, the incubation period, how long to expect before symptoms appear, how long they should stay isolated...I could go on and on. These recommendations could save lives."

"Dr. Greene is a professional," Mallory said. "I'm sure he's on top of things." A flash of lightning caused the strands of smoke to stand out in sharp, ghostly white relief.

"We'll find out soon enough," Nat added. "As always, there will be a certain percentage of people not able, or willing, to listen."

At that moment, the skies opened up, the water droplets condensing, and finally growing too heavy to win the war against gravity. The water surrounded the Humvee, covering it and making Mallory feel as if they were underwater.

As they drove, Corporal Parker passed out packs of protective gear. The soldiers dressed wordlessly in the moving vehicle, occasionally bumping into each other as they slid arms and legs into coveralls.

Rory was assigned to cover Northwestern Memorial Hospital, their first stop on the way from the airport. They dropped Rory and one of the National Guardsmen off at the emergency room entrance. Rory squeezed Mallory's hand as he climbed out, slamming the door behind him. She watched as the two figures melted into the rain, suitcases trailing behind them.

An alarming thought surfaced. *This is the last time I'll ever see Rory.* Her stomach clenched. *No, stop. I can't think like that. If I have any hope of remaining focused, I need to stay positive—stay in the moment.*

Next up was Rush University Medical Center, Tanvi's assignment.

"Let's check in at midnight," Tanvi said, somewhat wearily, opening her door. "We'll obviously still be up." The humidity and rain had untamed her soft chestnut waves of hair.

"Sounds like a plan," Mallory replied and Nat nodded. "I'll let Rory know."

"Be careful, Tanvi," Nat said, his voice serious.

Tanvi flashed a brief smile and was gone.

The rain slowed to a steady drizzle and the night landscape came into sharper focus. Mallory caught sight of a stone building, imposing in both its size and architecture. It appeared abandoned, graffiti and streaks of black mold marring a previously regal facade. Mallory didn't believe in ghosts, but she couldn't help thinking: *If they do exist, that's definitely where you'd find them.*

"What is that?" she asked, leaning forward to avoid yelling.

"That's the old Cook County Hospital. It's been abandoned for years. The County built a shiny new one just up here," he said, gesturing straight ahead. "I'll be your escort. Please gather your things. We're just about there." He turned, giving her a subtle wry grin before pulling up his mask. "Call me Park. Everyone else does."

Mallory opened her mouth to answer but an explosive crack at her right ear caused her to instinctively pull away from the window. Her hand shot toward her belt, groping for a weapon that wasn't there.

The Humvee slowed for a fraction of a second, but the two men in the front appeared unaffected.

Park called over his shoulder, "That sound was some type of projectile hitting the window—probably a rock or piece of concrete. Not everyone is happy that we're here. Either way, nothing to worry about, ma'am.

This glass is bullet-proof."

Mallory squinted out the window. She didn't see anyone lurking in the shadows. There were a few people walking purposefully in the light rain, hoodies pulled up and shoulders hunched against the wind. One woman, in pink scrubs, hurried along the sidewalk, her rainbow-striped umbrella bright against the shades of gray surrounding her.

"Mallory," she said, attempting to quell her racing heart. "Call me Mallory."

Chapter 53
Zimala Community Center, Chicago
Day +43

Barakah had seen the news reports. It was impossible not to, even though he had tried his best to avoid them. He sat on his rickety bed, alone in his room, as far away from the communal TV that he could get.

His knee bounced.

He thought about venturing out to the pantry for a snack, but his stomach immediately protested. He hadn't been able to force down a single morsel of food since yesterday. A cramp rippled through his abdomen and he eyed the door, thinking he might need to make a quick break for the bathroom.

He pulled over one of the crates he used to store his sparse belongings, rummaging for the nearly empty bottle of Tums. He noticed a piece of paper, wedged between two mismatched pairs of socks. He reached for the paper, his movements hesitant, unsure.

He thought of his mother, who was, at this moment, most likely cleaning their cramped apartment, scrounging together an inexpensive meal, or working a double shift at the fish cannery at the harbor.

Barakah's father had left when he was four years old. He often wondered how different his life would have been if he hadn't. Barakah clung to a single, vague memory of a man with a full beard in traditional Muslim dress, carrying him on his shoulders to the market. He bought Barakah a small square of halva—sesame candy which they ate together outside on the dusty street. He couldn't remember many of the details, but he could still recall the happiness he felt.

His mother had remarried and gone on to have five additional children. Eventually, his stepfather had also left, causing their already struggling family to slip further into poverty. After that, his mother, remote and ill-tempered at the best of times, seldom engaged meaningfully with her children. In fact, she rarely spoke, except to assign chores or errands.

Throughout Barakah's childhood, she remained a devout Muslim, praying five times daily and reading the Quran nightly before bed. On Fridays, she would become slightly more animated, pleased to attend services at the mosque and, of course, see the revered Imam.

The polite knock on the door startled him from his reverie. He shot straight up off the bed. His body seemed to be saturated with a near-constant anxiety, making him flinch at the slightest noise.

The Imam Khatib's distinctive low voice floated clearly through the flimsy wood-veneer door. "Ahmed, are you here?"

Barakah realized he was on his feet, staring at the door.

"Yes, Imam, I'm coming." He rushed to open the door, holding it open wide in deference to the Imam's rather large frame.

Imam Khatib smiled, the skin around his eyes crinkling. "I have good news. I spoke to Sidra this morning. She has put in a request for a temporary replacement visa with the Swedish consulate. Even better, she thinks she may have found the perfect foster family for you." Ahmed felt the blood slowly drain from his face. "Of course, we need to have proper identification and an approved visa before Sidra can put you officially into—" His voice halted abruptly. "Ahmed? Are you ill? What's wrong?"

Instead of answering, Barakah walked purposefully back toward the crate. He felt a small measure of peace now that he had finally made his decision. He grabbed the crumpled piece of paper and placed it reverently on the bed, carefully smoothing down the edges.

Still looking at the picture, Barakah spoke. "Imam, I have something important to tell you."

Mallory fell into the worn blue chair, the cloth so thin that the yellow foam was visible between the silver threads. *This must have been brought over from the old building. How many residents have spent their nights entering orders and returning pages while sitting in this chair?*

Mallory looked around the unoccupied call room she had commandeered. It looked much like the call rooms she had spent every fourth night *not* sleeping in during training.

Park had been her shadow during her emergency room work that evening and, after ensuring that her door lock was functioning, retreated to a mirror-image room directly across the hall. Park had insisted that no one else be allowed down their corridor and that the other four call rooms in that section remain empty, with the double doors to their hallway locked.

Mallory initially objected, worried the residents might not have enough call rooms for themselves.

"You—your work—is too important to take any chances. That's why I'm here," he said, leaving no room for further discussion.

Mallory sighed. She signed into her email, located the invitation that Tanvi had sent, and clicked into the conference call.

"Sorry I'm late," she said immediately, trying to hide the weariness in her voice.

"No problem," Tanvi said. "We're still waiting on Rory."

"I'm here," Rory broke in, sounding slightly out of breath. "My apologies."

"Who wants to go first?" Nat asked, yawning.

"Well, I have something to report," Rory said.

"Go for it," Nat said simply.

"Okay. Well, I think I've found the index case for Chicago. The patient's name is Forest Chang, who was the founder and CEO of Namaste House, an architectural firm with a branch in the loop. He was the first person to arrive at the Northwestern ER with the suspected virus. Unfortunately, he passed away a few hours ago, but he was coherent enough when I first arrived to give me a pretty complete exposure history."

Rory's voice was measured as he continued. "Mr. Chang was a thirty-three-year-old man with no significant past medical history who was admitted with suspected SJS and bacterial pneumonia. His lymphocytes were found to be near-zero, though his viral PCR is still pending. When I interviewed him in the ICU, he was in pretty bad shape but wanted to help." He paused, his voice breaking slightly. "It's heart-breaking, really. He had lost skin over ninety percent of his body, was completely blind and, even with an enormous amount of morphine on board, remained in pain, but he still wanted to help."

Rory cleared his throat, his voice back to professional detachment. "Regarding his exposure history, twelve days ago, Mr. Chang boarded a flight from LAX to O'Hare. At first, I couldn't find any link to the cases in Southern California. However, when Dr. Lee sent over the passenger lists from his flight, one of the names jumped out at me. He sat directly next to a Kathy Beckett."

"Cameron Beckett!" Nat snapped his fingers. "They have to be related."

"Exactly. Sisters, in fact. Per the flight manifests, Kathy visited Los Angeles, presumably to see Cameron, right around the time we believe Cameron first acquired the virus," Rory said. "And before you ask, I sent a message to Adam in New York regarding the status of Kathy Beckett. He said he was going to look into it."

"This gives us something to work with. Namaste House came up in many of my histories. At least three-fourths of the cases here are employees," Mallory said. Hearing Cameron's name again triggered a memory. *Cameron was Alfie's ex-girlfriend. Alfie...*

"Same," Tanvi added. "Namaste House was the only common denominator I could find."

"We need to isolate all contacts, starting with the initial case—family members, co-workers, anyone and everyone they interacted with," Mallory said.

"Agreed," Rory said. "At least ninety Namaste House employees have shown up at the Northwestern ER. I have another twelve cases that are family members of the employees. I think we should issue a home quarantine for anyone who's set foot in their Chicago office within the last ten days—even those not showing symptoms—and all those living in the same households with those who are sick."

"That sounds like a good plan. Do you have help?" Mallory asked.

"Yep. The Northwestern staff has been pretty easy to work with. The Cook County Department of Public Health has also agreed to send a few people over tonight." Rory blew out a breath. "Given the number of cases here, Dr. Lee has requested Sergeant Major Mitchell of the National Guard to work with me directly. He'll be sending his people to implement the home quarantines. They'll also be in charge of bringing food and other supplies to the quarantined households."

"Who is following up on the other plane passengers?" Tanvi asked.

"Dr. Lee and others in Atlanta," Rory answered.

"Good. For our part, we can issue a home quarantine for all contacts of the other eighteen to twenty cases." Mallory paused. "Maybe there still is a chance to contain this."

"Maybe," Tanvi said. The word hung in the air.

"At this point, I guess it depends on how California and New York are going," Rory said.

"The only thing we can do is pray," Nat added, changing the subject. "Okay, so Rory has one hundred and two cases. I have no cases so far at U of C. What about you, Mallory and Tanvi?"

Mallory said, "At Cook County, there are twelve probable cases."

"Five at Rush," Tanvi said. "I'm waiting on lymphocyte counts for two more."

"All right, we have around one hundred and twenty-one potential cases, not including the smaller hospitals and urgent care centers. I'll check with Cook County Public Health to get their numbers. When I finish up here, I'll update Dr. Lee and then head to Northwestern to help Rory," Nat said.

"That's it…Alfie," Mallory said suddenly.

"Alfie Hughes?" Nat asked. "Cameron Beckett's ex-boyfriend? What about him?"

"I knew that name sounded familiar," Mallory said. "That was the name of one of the paramedics who transported a patient to UC Irvine from the FEMA camp. I remember checking his gear and going over isolation procedures with him. Somehow, he must have been exposed, and then inadvertently infected the others."

"So, that's how the virus left the camp," Tanvi said.

"Seems so," Mallory replied. "Let's schedule another conference call for three tomorrow."

After the call ended, Mallory opened her door, pausing briefly outside Park's room. She planned to head back to the ER to fill in her contact gaps. She would also need to re-interview each patient in isolation to see if they had a connection to Namaste House. She could then send the list on to Dr. Greene's team in Atlanta. They could work with the National Guard and get a head start on imposing the home quarantines.

Let him sleep. At least one of us will be refreshed and coherent tomorrow.

She felt nearly sick with exhaustion by the time she made it back to the call room at around three-thirty in the morning. There was one last thing to do before she could close her eyes for the night.

She sat back in the worn chair and rummaged for a piece of paper in the recycle bin. Starting with the cluster of FEMA cases at the top right corner of the paper, she made a source diagram, using arrows to map out the cases that followed. Once complete, she spent a few precious minutes staring at it, her mind working and re-working the course of events that had led them to this point.

Finally, finding she could no longer concentrate, she set her alarm for seven-thirty and collapsed onto the twin bed. She didn't remember falling asleep.

∿∿

The next morning, Park was showered, dressed, and sitting at a small desk, sipping a steaming cup of coffee when Mallory peeked out of her room.

"Oh, you're up," Mallory said groggily, clearing her throat. "Give me ten minutes." She shut the door.

"Okay, then," Park mumbled to the closed door. "Good morning to you too."

True to her word, Mallory was ready nine minutes later. Park, covered from head to toe in white overall-style isolation gear, passed her a coffee.

"I'm not sure how you take it, but you seemed like you could use a cup."

"I'll drink anything that has caffeine in it. Thanks, Park." Mallory turned to him, awarding him a smile.

They walked side-by-side, Mallory sipping her coffee. She paused a moment to put on her PPE.

"Any news from your end?" Mallory asked as she stepped into her suit.

"I received an email update this morning from my Staff Sergeant. The quarantine line has been expanded to encompass all of northern Illinois." Park leaned against the wall, waiting for Mallory to finish dressing. "Apparently, individuals on foot breached the more remote suburban areas overnight. The Staff Sergeant extended the line, taking advantage of natural barriers like the Mississippi River and Lake Michigan, and then focusing more manpower on the north and south."

Mallory paused to consider this. "It makes sense," she conceded. "Could you zip this for me?" She turned her back to Park. "Did they catch the people who breached the line?"

"They believe so. Apparently, to keep the area contained, they were forced to use rubber bullets. The email was pretty short on details."

"Thanks for sharing with me," Mallory said. They resumed walking.

"You'd have heard anyway," he said, shrugging as he pulled out keys procured from Hospital Maintenance in order to lock the doors to their temporary private corridor.

They walked the rest of the way in silence, each lost in thought.

The rest of the day, Park stayed close to Mallory as she worked. Two new cases had come in in the early morning hours. The ER staff followed protocol and immediately placed the patients in isolation. The isolation procedures, though necessary, made every patient interaction take three times longer than normal. Mallory continued tirelessly for hours, until

Park finally suggested they take a break. Mallory reluctantly agreed.

"I need to find a bathroom and then we can grab some food and eat in the call room," Mallory said. Park followed as she went in search for a bathroom.

It's strange to think about such mundane things as finding a bathroom when people are sick and dying.

They located a room near the ER entrance, hidden half-way around a corner and at the end of a brightly lit, deserted hallway.

Park knocked loudly on the door and pushed it open a few inches.

"Anyone in here?" he called. Silence.

"Ok, you can wait out here," Mallory said. "Could you unzip me please?" She turned around.

"Thanks. I'll be right back," Mallory said, hurrying in without a backward glance. Her mind was several steps ahead, planning. A conference call for all medical officers was scheduled for three that afternoon. She set a reminder on her phone in case she lost track of time.

The bathroom was compact, identical to every other hospital restroom she had ever seen. It reminded Mallory of an office bathroom, devoid of all character. Like the county hospital itself, it was new, functional, and unapologetically institutional. The air was heavy with the scent of industrial soap and the faint, barely detectable smell of ammonia. Cold air blasted from a vent in the ceiling, filling the small space with arctic air.

Mallory entered a stall, sliding the lock in place. She heard shuffling and the sound of a toilet flushing.

Someone is in here.

The woman blew her nose loudly and, without warning, broke into loud, heaving sobs.

"Miss? Are you okay?" Mallory asked. She quickly squirted her hands with sanitizer and began sealing up her protective gown and mask.

Though she raised her hand to knock on the stall, she froze when she heard it—a wet cough… and moaning.

"Help me," said a small, fearful voice, the words floating beneath the stall door.

"All right, let me get some help. I'll be right back." Just as she was turning to have Park zip her up, the stall door flew open with a bang.

"Please don't leave me!" The young woman's face was anguished, pleading as she looked at Mallory. She appeared to be in her twenties, heavyset, with the ends of her hair dyed a bright blue. Her whole body, from head to toe, was the shade of an over-ripe tomato, as if she had experienced a severe sunburn. Mucus streamed from her nose and her cheeks were wet with tears.

She's erythrodermic—

Before she could finish her thought, the woman's movements became agitated, frantic. She wobbled toward Mallory, looking as if she would collapse to the floor at any moment. "Am I going to die? My sister died."

"Miss, I need you to calm down. Please, sit down so you don't hurt yourself. I promise I'll be right back," Mallory said, acutely aware of the open gap at the back of her gown. She turned again for the door, but the woman suddenly fell forward, grabbing desperately at Mallory to keep from falling. She could smell the woman's hot, fetid breath.

The next few seconds felt surreal. Disbelief clouded Mallory's mind even as the woman's girth pressed into her.

Mallory struggled to hold the woman up, staggering under her weight. As if sensing Mallory's unstable footing, the woman panicked, her arms shooting out and grabbing onto Mallory as if to keep from drowning.

Mallory managed to lower the woman to the floor, taking care her head didn't bump the tiled floor. Straightening up, she was breathing hard from the exertion.

"You need to stay here. For your own safety, don't try to get up," Mallory instructed firmly.

Only then did she realize her mask was askew and her gown nearly torn off. She automatically replaced her mask and spun around. She collided solidly with Park, nearly losing her footing for a second time.

Do life-changing moments always feel this way? Is there an automatic, innate sense that nothing will ever again be the same?

"What happened?" Park demanded, a note of worry in his voice as he took in her disheveled appearance.

Tears flooded her eyes. With enormous effort, she pushed away the fear and eerie sense of disbelief.

Focus. Concentrate.

"I may have been exposed to the virus. I need you to get help for this woman. Make sure everyone who enters and those transporting her are in protective gear. Then have the staff seal off this bathroom for disinfection."

As she talked, she could see his eyes narrow behind his visor.

"What can I do to help you?" he asked.

"I need to decontaminate. You can't help me with that. Please, get help for her," Mallory said, gesturing to the woman, now moaning on the ground.

Park hesitated for a long moment, then abruptly turned and left the bathroom.

Mallory crouched next to the woman. "Help is on the way. You said your sister died. I'm very sorry to hear this. Did this just happen? Was she sick?"

Barely conscious, the woman was unable to answer Mallory's questions. Mallory waited with her, applying hand sanitizer liberally to all the surfaces exposed by her displaced gown.

When a stretcher was unceremoniously pushed into the room, she stood and left, asking one of the nurses to find an address for the patient's sister. From there, she went directly to the call room, carefully sealing her clothes in a red biohazard bag. She rinsed her nasal passages with a sinus irrigator. It probably wouldn't help, but it wouldn't hurt. There was nothing else she could do about her mucosal membranes, the most likely port of viral entry. She showered, scrubbing her skin with anti-microbial soap until it shone pink and raw. She dressed in scrubs and then pulled out clean biohazard gear, making sure her mask was sealed before leaving the room.

As she knew he would be, Park was waiting for her, leaning against the wall.

"I'm sorry," he said. "I should have cleared the bathroom. It's my fault."

"It's not your fault. I was the one to tell you to wait outside. No one could have foreseen this." She wanted to reassure him further, but she was too emotionally drained. "We need to find that poor woman's sister. I think she may have died from the virus."

He zipped her coveralls and the two walked back toward the hospital, this time to find an empty isolation room for Mallory.

∿∿∿

"Kathy Beckett's CT scan demonstrated lesions consistent with parasitic Toxoplasmosis," Robert said. "I believe she had a cat; she must have picked up the oocyst form from the litter box. It was fascinating, really. The neurologic deficits found during the physical exam matched perfectly with the imaging. Witnesses who are, regrettably, now infected say she was acting erratically and, sure enough, her amygdala had nearly been obliterated. A textbook case—"

"Sounds interesting," Nat said apologetically. "Sorry to interrupt, but we really have limited time here, Robert." Nat was a stickler for keeping conferences and meetings on schedule. In this situation, especially as Robert, who was known to be quite enthusiastic and verbose when talking about interesting cases, Mallory had to agree. She felt the seconds ticking by and, like a physical presence, pressing down on her.

"Oh, I'm sorry," Robert said, sounding slightly miffed. "Of course."

Mallory remembered the first time she met Robert, one of the medical officers currently stationed with Adam in New York. He had introduced himself as Robert and, before she could reply with her name, he broke into a windy speech about how his name must never be shortened. He, very emphatically, stated he wouldn't respond to a nickname like Bob or Rob. Fighting to suppress a smile, she solemnly reassured him she wouldn't make that mistake.

It was well accepted that Robert had difficulty responding appropriately to social cues. She suspected he might have Asperger syndrome and, because of this, she'd always been protective of him.

"Thanks, Robert. You were a huge help in tracking down Ms. Beckett, who, I'm sad to say, has now passed away from the virus," Adam said.

"What's your situation there, Adam? How many known cases?" Nat persisted.

"We have twenty-three identified cases, all at New York-Presbyterian. All twenty-three seem to have been in contact with Ms. Beckett at some point and, by sheer luck, hadn't left Manhattan since their exposure. We are in the process of isolating all contacts. Manhattan remains under quarantine, but Director Quinn has lifted it for the other four boroughs," Adam said.

"I'm afraid the situation is much worse in California," Freya, from Dr. Powell's team, said. The fatigue in her voice was immediately evident.

Mallory looked around her small isolation room, taking in the bare white walls, and the tiny, faux-oak closet with plain silver handles. She shivered. The room's starkness reminded her of a psychiatric ward.

She had informed Dr. Lee about her potential exposure but hadn't yet told the other medical officers. Dr. Lee had kindly offered to make arrangements to bring her back to Atlanta for isolation. For a fraction of a second, she was tempted to agree, but then thought of all the work here she still had to do. How much time would be lost handing things over to someone else? Plus, the cost of traveling in isolation via an air ambulance would be enormous.

More than anything, she didn't want to be a distraction to her colleagues. After the conference call, she would be forced to tell them all. If new cases came into Cook County, she wouldn't be able to examine and interview them, though she could continue working from her room, making phone calls, researching, and coordinating home quarantines with the National Guard.

At least until I get too sick to work.

If. If I get sick. I need to stay optimistic.

"We have all of southern and central California under quarantine, including San Francisco, with the line ending just south of Sacramento. As far as how many cases we have…" There was a pause, then the sound of a mouse clicking. "As of right now, there are a total of 3,148 confirmed cases. We have CBCs pending on about four hundred more suspected cases."

Mallory sucked in a breath, nearly dropping her phone.

"Shit," Tanvi said breathlessly.

"Yep. Pretty much," Freya replied glumly.

There was an explosion of questions. Mallory felt stunned as the sense of unreality crept in and pushed its way back over her. She reached out a hand, touching the white sheet on her bed to ground herself.

"All right, all right everyone," Nat said in a firm voice. "One at a time."

"Do we know what the r naught is?" Mallory surprised herself by speaking. One part of her mind was on her fate, the fate of the country, the fate of her family. The other, slightly larger part, was focused, determined, razor-sharp. "I know we've talked about this before. Given the small number of cases, we estimated the r naught to be similar to adenovirus, which is two. Now that we have a larger number of cases, has anyone on your team looked into this?"

"I can speak to this, Freya," a male voice added, his tone businesslike and earnest. "Derrick here. I've done some preliminary calculations and it seems that the r naught is around five, much higher than we initially predicted." He cleared his throat.

Derrick was a medical officer but also their *de facto* statistician. His chair squeaked and Mallory imagined him leaning back, his comfort level increasing as he talked about his beloved numbers. "I'm sure everyone on this call is familiar with the concept but, as a refresher, r naught is the average number of people infected by *one* person with the disease. For reference, Ebola is around one to two while SARS can be as high as five. Our goal, through intervention, is to decrease it to less than one. Statistically...well, it's going to be an uphill battle."

Involuntarily, Mallory's mind flew to those closest to her—her family and friends. Marcus' face floated into consciousness. She knew she had feelings for him, and they weren't going to just disappear overnight, but she knew she would never get back together with him, especially now that he had scared her. Regardless, she wasn't planning on telling her family or friends that she was in isolation. She couldn't stand the thought of worrying them unnecessarily.

But now...this virus is much more contagious than we initially thought.

The probability of my infection has just gone up significantly. Why is it more contagious than primary adenovirus? Did it mutate?

She realized someone else was speaking and forced herself to listen. She didn't want to miss any important information.

"I'll take the first flight to California." Nat said, then explained. "Obviously, commercial flights are not an option, but the Army is still using planes to transport people and equipment."

"I'm in," Tanvi said. "Things are under control here at Rush. I can fly from Chicago with you, Nat."

Several other medical officers from New York and Atlanta also offered to come. Dr. Powell's team accepted gratefully.

"Conference call, same time tomorrow?" Rory asked.

There were murmurs of assent.

"Nat, Tanvi, Rory—will you stay on with me for a minute?" Mallory asked, willing her voice not to break.

Chapter 55
Mashriq Specialty Cuisine, Chicago
Day +44

Barakah couldn't stop his leg from bouncing, though if he concentrated—really thought about it—he could. But the moment his mind focused on something else, there it was again, bouncing of its own accord, as if he were some grotesque marionette unable to control his limbs.

The restaurant was nearly empty, which wasn't surprising considering it was just past midnight. Barakah couldn't believe the place was even open, given the situation in the city.

The scent of cumin-spiced falafel was heavy in the air. It enveloped him, yet he derived no comfort from the familiar and overpowering smells. In fact, they turned his stomach.

He thought briefly of his family in their tiny apartment in Malmö. It would be morning there. Breakfast time. Was his mom preparing a similar meal four thousand miles away? Were they worried about him? He hadn't spoken to anyone from his family since the day he left.

A small corner TV was tuned to a news station. Mercifully, the sound was low and he was able to keep his back to the screen. He shivered as a blast of cold air raised goosepimples on his bare arms. He shifted slightly, angling his chair so he wasn't directly below the vent.

Two men, who appeared to be brothers, had been chatting animatedly in Arabic at the table next to them. Barakah watched as they left the restaurant, still talking and gesturing. He felt a welcome puff of warm, humid air as the door closed.

Barakah's stomach clenched as he realized he could now clearly hear the TV. He couldn't help but listen as the newscaster spoke grimly about the viral crisis in Southern California. The death toll from the infection had risen to just over four thousand.

The anchor went on to describe how the virus had been officially confirmed north of the quarantine zone in Central California. It was now in Sacramento and Lake Tahoe.

"The CDC is working on determining how the virus breached the quarantine line." The anchorwoman looked straight at the camera, her face somber. "In related news, the Dow Jones is down a record-breaking 2,377 points..."

Out of the corner of his eye, Barakah saw the Imam's face pale. He swallowed noisily once, twice. He avoided looking at Barakah, keeping his gaze fixed on the screen. He picked up his phone, murmuring quietly. After a few moments, he sighed and hung up.

"Sidra will be here in fifteen minutes." Imam Khatib set his phone carefully on the table, adjusting it until it was perfectly aligned next to his untouched plate. Neither of them had been able to eat.

The Imam sat, staring at the condensation obscuring the windows.

They waited in silence.

Under the table, Barakah's leg continued to bounce.

Chapter 56
Pineview Apartments, 3B, Malmö, Sweden
Day +44

Ada moved her chair closer to the painting. She examined the canvas carefully, pulling smoke deeply into her lungs. The red-orange chips of paint under her ragged nails blazed the same shade as the tip of her cigarette. She exhaled slowly, tilting her head to the side. Her blunt haircut, with its ruler-straight fringe, brushed her shoulders. Streaks of light through the dirty window caught her sharp cheekbones, made more angular by her recent weight loss. Her new hair, dyed the color of midnight, matched the paint-splattered tank-top she had worn for days. She couldn't be bothered to put on a bra, shower, or otherwise dress properly—not, at least, while in the throes of creativity.

She studied the canvas, which was a swirl of angry, dark colors seamlessly infused with bright reds, yellows, and oranges. Ada closed her eyes, taking in the oil paints' intoxicating scent.

The painting was unlike anything she'd created before—unlike anything she had done prior to what she privately referred to as "the incident." It was completely unrecognizable as hers, the aesthetic of a deeper, darker, wholly different person.

She had changed in other ways, too. Not just in her appearance and art, but in something more fundamental. Her previous general optimism had been replaced by something bitter, murky.

Of course, there had been an official inquest into Erik's death. Although she was cleared of wrongdoing, the details surrounding her relationship with Erik were forced into the open. The press eagerly latched onto all of the sordid details. And, just like that, her leverage was gone.

Because of provisions in the contract inserted by the crafty Paragon law-yers, there was no large check coming her way. She no longer needed to leave Malmö, although she hadn't decided if staying was still a good thing.

She swore she would never set foot in her dingy flat again, but her landlord refused to let her out of her lease. Only after threatening legal action did he allow her to move to another flat in the same building. Not surprisingly, it was even smaller and more outdated than her previous one.

Ada continued to stare at the painting. At last, she approached the canvas, wielding her nails like broken talons. She scratched and dug through the tacky paint until she was satisfied. She stepped back from the canvas, the ghost of a smile on her lips. A single eye, carved in strikingly realistic detail, stared back at her.

I'll call it Ett Monsters Öga—Eye of a Monster.

Chapter 57
Mashriq Specialty Cuisine, Chicago
Day +44

Sidra pushed open the door of the restaurant and paused, scanning the room. Her gaze locked on the Imam. She hurried over to them, a tall woman in a suit following close behind. The woman looked to be in her mid-thirties. She held her back straight, her bearing professional. Glossy black hair was pulled into a bun at the nape of her neck.

A tight smile briefly touched Imam Khatib's drawn face when he saw them. He stood to embrace Sidra. "Thanks for coming, both of you."

"Barakah, this is Sidra. She's the social worker who's been helping you," the Imam said, nodding at his cousin.

"Nice to meet you," Barakah said awkwardly, his eyes on the floor.

Imam Khatib moved to the woman in the suit, kissing her on both cheeks. "This is my friend, Kali. She's a lawyer. She's here to help…facilitate things."

Kali gave a polite, reserved nod toward Barakah.

"Let's sit," the Imam said. He passed cups around the table. "Here, have some tea. It's going to be a long night."

Once they were settled, Imam Khatib turned to Barakah. "Why don't you tell Sidra and Kali exactly what you told me? Don't leave anything out."

Barakah began his story as they sipped cups of cold hibiscus tea. A few minutes into the narration, the tea was forgotten. As she listened, Sidra's face blanched, the color slowly leeching away. Kali was able to maintain an air of neutrality, except when Barakah first mentioned the virus. Barakah noticed her jaw drop and eyes widen for a few seconds.

After he was done, Kali and Sidra both sat perfectly still, stunned into silence.

After a moment, Imam Khatib spoke, his resonant voice low and serious. "Could you take him on pro bono, Kali? I know your firm requires a certain amount of volunteer work each year. He has no money and no family in America."

She hesitated. "To be honest, I'm not sure. Bioterrorism? I mean, this is way beyond anything in my experience."

"We really don't have any other options," Sidra said. "We need to get this to the police as fast as possible."

Imam Khatib added, "It will generate publicity for you and your firm. This is beyond national—it will be a story told around the world, so to speak."

Kali looked thoughtful. "He definitely needs a lawyer, someone to make sure his rights aren't violated." She nodded slowly. "Okay. I'll do my best."

Sidra grabbed her phone to set up a meeting at the Wentworth Second District Police Station. She had worked with a detective from there, Ben Marshall, on a previous child custody case.

"He's fair," she said, her voice tired. "He also works nights."

Sidra spent several frustrating minutes being transferred from person to person, but she was ultimately able to negotiate a meeting with Detective Marshall. She slipped her phone in her purse and stood abruptly. "I'll drive."

On the way to the station, Sidra pushed the speed limit, cutting turns and speeding through yellow lights.

She apologized when she noticed Imam Khatib clutching his arm rest, but she didn't slow down. Kali peppered Barakah with rapid-fire questions. Barakah marveled at Kali's ability to type into her laptop as they slid helplessly on the leather seats. He kept his eyes fixed on the horizon as he answered, trying to quell his rising nausea.

They arrived at the station in record time. As they walked toward the entrance, Barakah lifted his eyes to the dark sky.

Allah, please guide me. Am I doing the right thing?

The interior wasn't what Barakah expected. It reminded him of pretty much any office, nondescript and without character. There was no trace of the gritty, raw atmosphere depicted on American television. Mostly empty yet brightly lit cubicles lined the walls and covered the bland gray carpet.

They waited in the lobby for nearly twenty minutes. Barakah gave up any pretense of trying to keep his knee from bouncing, despite the not-so subtle looks of annoyance from Kali. Finally, Detective Marshall appeared, and they followed him to an interview room. He wore pleated khaki pants with a slightly wrinkled button-down shirt. Barakah's racing mind was struggling to process his surroundings. He was using most of his energy on trying to keep himself from throwing up.

Once the five of them had squeezed into an interview room, and Barakah told his story for the third time in quick succession, things moved rapidly. Barakah had barely finished before Detective Marshall jumped up and left the room to make calls.

After ten minutes, a stout female officer bent her head inside the door.

"Do you want something to drink?" she asked, not unkindly. "A sandwich?"

"Yes, please. A Coke, if you have it," Barakah answered.

By the time she returned, Barakah had laid his head on his arms. He was fast asleep.

Chapter 58
Stroger Cook County Medical Center, Chicago
Day +45

What is that?

Mallory's eyes flew open. The prior day's events rushed back into consciousness. For a moment, she didn't want to move, a depressing sense of futility rooting her to the spot.

Tap. Tap. Tap. Mallory pushed herself onto her elbow. Park looked expectantly through her observation window, pointing to his phone.

She unplugged her phone from its charger and lifted it to her ear.

"Hmm?" she said, falling back onto her bed and closing her eyes.

"Wow, you really aren't a morning person, are you?" Park said by way of greeting.

"Nope."

"It's a good thing I brought you fresh coffee then." She lifted her head, gazing at him through one open eye.

He pointed. "When you are ready, it's waiting on your breakfast tray."

"Oh, thanks, Park. Sorry, I was up late last night doing research. You don't have to...you know, do things like that. You aren't at fault for what happened and, really, I'm not your responsibility anymore." She cringed as the words came out, recognizing too late how they might have sounded.

Maybe she *was* more than a little cranky from lack of sleep. She had stayed up working, poring over articles on adenovirus, immunosuppression, and infection, while intermittently watching the news.

Within the quarantine zones, rioting and looting had occurred in record numbers. In Chicago, general violence had increased astronomically due to a significantly decreased police presence. 911 calls were averaging more than a ninety-minute response time. The police, firemen, and para-medics weren't showing up for their shifts, choosing to stay home and protect their families. The National Guard was stretched thin, their main priority being quarantine enforcement. Garbage was piling up in the streets and fires were burning out of control.

In southern California, the deteriorating situation was the subject of constant TV coverage. Aerial views of the overflowing hospitals and riot-ing were played over and over. When Mallory finally did shut off her light, she couldn't shut down her mind.

To her relief, Park took it all in stride. "I know I don't have to. It just so happens I like your company. And, for the record, you're still very much my responsibility."

"How do you figure?" Mallory asked, swinging her feet to the floor.

"Well, as I've said before, you and your work are important. Hospitals don't install locks on patient doors, so that means you'll be seeing a lot of this ugly mug in the coming days, especially with everything going on out there." He gestured outside. "Now, how about we get to work?"

"We?" Still clutching her phone to her ear, she raised an eyebrow.

"Yes, ma'am. You don't think I'm just going to sit out here on my a…, um, butt all day, do you? I'll be bored out of my mind."

"Well, we can't have that, now can we?" she said, rolling her eyes. She couldn't stop a small smile forming on her lips. "Give me fifteen minutes."

∿∿

"You found her?" Mallory asked, impressed. "The sister?"

"Yep. The fifth house on our list," Park replied through the phone. He pulled a chair to the observation window, positioning himself so he could see her while they talked.

Yesterday, after the conference call, Mallory asked Park if he could find a small table she could use for her computer. Park returned fifteen minutes later, looking slightly sheepish. He dressed in protective gear and then painstakingly coaxed a solid, pockmarked wooden desk into her room. It looked like an old teachers' desk. *Where did Park find this? A school?* She smiled to herself. *He knows how to get things done.*

She set up her temporary workspace and spent more than an hour making phone calls, trying desperately to locate the sister of the woman who had collapsed in the hospital bathroom. The woman, whose name she learned was Allison Whittaker, was intubated and in isolation in the ICU. She hadn't regained consciousness.

Mallory was able to locate several Whittakers in the area. She called each number with the same result—no one picked up. When she realized she wasn't getting anywhere, she reluctantly asked Rory for help. She knew he had his hands full at Northwestern and, with Nat and Tanvi leaving for California, their Chicago team was down to two.

Armed with a list of addresses from Mallory, Park volunteered to escort Rory in the Humvee. They weren't even sure Allison's sister had the same last name. There wasn't a wedding ring on Allison's finger, but it was possible her sister was married.

Mallory spent the rest of the afternoon making phone calls and tracing contacts of contacts. She hadn't heard anything more about Allison's sister until now.

"Was she alive?" Mallory asked, knowing the answer but asking anyway.

Park's voice turned serious. "No. Dead when we got there. Her name was Danielle Whittaker, according to her ID. Luckily, her blinds were open and I could see her on the living room floor. Otherwise, I don't know when she would have been found. I had to break down the door." He suppressed a shudder. "The image of her body ... it's not something I'm going to forget anytime soon."

"Unfortunately, it may not get any easier," Mallory said softly.

"Anyway, three people from the Cook County Department of Public Health came and helped Rory remove the contaminated body and seal off the residence. It took a few hours. Rory interviewed the neighbors, to see if they knew anything or had seen anyone visiting—that sort of thing."

"Did they see anything?" Mallory asked.

"No, it seems the two sisters were the only ones living there—renting apparently. They didn't interact with the neighbors much. But, get this: The youngest sister, Danielle, was a cleaner at Namaste House. We found a pay stub in a pile of mail on the kitchen counter."

"Look at you—quite the detective. Good work." Mallory tapped a finger to her chin. "I wonder why she didn't come up on our initial list."

"Rory wondered the same thing and called Namaste House's HR. The woman he spoke with was not happy about being under home quarantine. She told him so in no uncertain terms. Rory worked his charm, calming her down until, reluctantly, she agreed to help us." Park gave her a crooked grin. "She had remote access and was able to easily access employee information. It seems Danielle was new—like this was her first week. No one thought to mention her, I guess. Or, maybe her name hadn't yet made it onto the official employee roster." He shrugged.

Mallory felt the buzz of a text message, the phone hot against her ear.

"Hold on a sec, Park." She glanced at the screen. It was from Rory.

Park noticed the change in her body language. She could hear a faraway, tinny voice asking, "What's wrong? Mallory, what does it say?"

She slowly pressed the phone back to her ear. "The virus. It's in Las Vegas, Sacramento, Lake Tahoe, Vancouver, and," she swallowed hard, "Atlanta."

"Let me know if there is anything I can do," Park said.

"Thanks, Park." Mallory clicked off and immediately called Kate, who picked up on the first ring.

"Kate, where are you?" Mallory asked.

"Mom and Dad's. You told me to stay here. What's going on?" Kate replied, picking up on Mallory's serious tone.

"Good." Mallory breathed out a short exhalation of relief. Kate could be stubborn; Mallory wasn't sure she would stay put with their parents. "The virus is in Atlanta." She waited a beat, letting this sink in. "Do you have a pen and paper? I need you to write this down. You, Mom, and Dad need to get some supplies together and head to the basement."

Their parents' basement was small and only partially finished but, most importantly, had just two small windows, limiting places of entry.

"Take down the blackout drapes from Mom and Dad's bedroom and nail them over each of the basement windows. Seal the edges with duct tape. If Dad has plywood or something more solid, use that too. Fill all the bowls and buckets you can find with water. Bring the food from the pantry down with you." Mallory closed her eyes, concentrating. "You'll also need candles, matches, a can opener, a radio, batteries, phone chargers, toiletries, and lots of hand sanitizer. Stacks of books for entertainment, too. There should already be a first-aid kit down there, but double check just in case."

"It's that bad?" Kate asked, sounding surprised.

"If it isn't now, it soon will be."

There was a long moment of silence. "Okay."

"Gather everything you need to sustain the three of you for at least a month, but be quick about it. Things have gone downhill surprisingly fast in the other quarantine zones." Mallory thought of the smoke filling the air in Chicago when she arrived. "Double check to make sure all the doors and windows are locked. Leave a few lights on upstairs. Once you have everything set, double bolt the basement door. Place masking tape around the seams so no light can get through. Nail wood across it for reinforcement."

She could hear worried murmurs from her parents in the background, asking what was wrong. Kate paused to tell them Mallory was fine and that she would update them in a minute.

"Don't worry, Mal. We've got this. What about you? Are you okay?"

"Yes, I'm fine," she lied. "All of the CDC medical officers have National Guard soldiers assigned to them for protection. I'm safe."

"Thanks, Mal. I wish we could all be together, but I know you have essential work to do." Kate's voice held a slight, barely audible tremble. "Well, we'd better get to it then."

"Call me once you're safely locked downstairs?"

"Of course."

"One last thing: Do not, under any circumstances, let anyone enter the basement. I mean it. Use deadly force if necessary. They could be infected or up to no good. There will be looting. The police don't have enough manpower to keep everyone safe. If someone breaks into the main part of the house, let them take whatever they want, as long as they don't try to come downstairs. Keep completely silent and, remember, do not open the basement door for anyone, no matter what."

"We won't. I promise." It sounded like Kate was trying to hold back tears. "Love you, Mal."

"Love you, too."

Mallory made sure the call was disconnected, then covered her face with her hands and wept.

ᴧᴧ

The tone of the conference call that afternoon was somber and subdued. The tentative optimism from their previous conversations had vanished.

No new cases in Chicago or New York, and the rate of new cases in California seemed to be stabilizing. More importantly, all new cases in California had been within the extended quarantine line around Sacramento and Lake Tahoe. These small victories were overshadowed by the news about Las Vegas, Atlanta, and Canadian Vancouver. Three medical officers from Dr. Greene's team were sent to Las Vegas, while the World Health Organization dispatched a rapid response team to Vancouver.

"Has anyone heard anything further regarding vaccine development?" Mallory asked.

The farther the virus spreads, the more we need to shift focus from containment to cure, or at least prevention.

"Dr. Lee gave me an update this morning," Rory said. "The good news is the lab is actually really close. They have something that seems to be around eighty-five percent effective in animals. Yesterday, they vaccinated the first wave of human volunteers, mostly CDC employees. The real problem is manufacture and distribution. They're estimating it will take around six weeks to get out the first batch."

Mallory's mind raced. *Six weeks? That's too long. The virus could be all over the country in much less time than that.*

"There has to be another way. We need every lab in the country helping. Surely no one would object. This could potentially infect tens of millions, probably even more," Mallory said.

"It's not just antibody development; it's also the logistics of everything," Adam explained. "There are only so many available sterile medical supplies out there. I know Dr. Bakshi and others are working with the pharmaceutical companies for donations of vials, needles, etc. Any way you look at it, it's going to take time."

"Time we don't have."

Mallory wasn't sure which of the medical officers said this, but it echoed her thoughts.

"Are any of the existing antivirals effective?" Nat asked.

"None, according to Dr. Bakshi. Just as with influenza or herpes, antivirals aren't curative. They can shorten the duration of symptoms, but by then it's too late. The lymphocytes have already dropped and, as we know, it's the secondary infections that kill the patient," Rory said.

Mallory listened as several of the medical officers made plans to fly with the National Guard to Las Vegas or back to Atlanta.

That should be me. I should be on my way to help. It's beyond frustrating being stuck in this room in Chicago...It's suffocating. It's like I'm trapped in a nightmare.

Her phone beeped. She grabbed it, thinking it was Kate or her parents. Instead, it was Special Agent Coleman.

"Sorry it took so long to get back. I can't disclose details, but it looks like you were right. We have reason to believe this is a bioterrorist attack, with the FEMA camp as ground zero. Homeland Security is working on the case. If you learn anything that could help us, please don't hesitate to reach out. And stay safe."

After thanking him and letting him know she would keep him updated, she sent a short, encrypted email message to the team leaders and medical officers, letting them know that bioterrorism had been confirmed.

Mallory spent the next several hours at her desk, working remotely with several of the other teams, tracing contacts. She talked with her parents and Kate, who reassured her they had followed her instructions and were securely locked in the basement.

Rory checked in with her several times, monitoring for symptoms and giving encouragement. As if she could forget, he reminded her to take her temperature at least twice a day.

Park remained stationed outside her door, assisting when he could. Mallory appreciated his help and was even more grateful for his company.

She glanced at the digital clock. It was a little past eleven. She yawned and stretched, her back slightly stiff. She needed some sleep.

A small, slightly crooked dry-erase board hung across from her bed. It was used by nurses to communicate with patients, listing their medical plan for the day. Someone had drawn a cheerful flower in the corner. Its leafy vines snaked and curled along the top and side. The first thing she had done was erase the incongruous image, turning the board into a make-shift calendar.

Using a red marker, she drew a thick slash through day number one. She had completed her first full day in isolation. Thirteen more to go.

A part of her wanted to stay in bed and ignore the world around her, but she knew if she fell into that particular hole, she might never climb back out. She wouldn't—couldn't— allow herself to succumb to the hor-ror of her situation.

Sighing, she waved goodnight to Park and slipped into bed, the obliv-ion of sleep overtaking her within minutes.

∿

She wasn't sure what woke her.

She flipped over to face the observation window, ears straining for any unusual sounds. She couldn't see Park's cot from her bed, but she knew he was there.

Hearing nothing further, she closed her eyes. She felt her body relax;

her mind blissfully empty for the moment. She was drifting into sleep when she heard a faint squeak, like a gym shoe on a polished floor.

It's probably a nurse or LPN walking by. Maybe a janitor. This is a hospital, after all. There's always someone around.

In reality, Mallory was at the end of a dead-end hallway. The patient rooms surrounding her were empty, ready for additional isolation cases that, luckily so far, hadn't yet materialized. Except for the daily meal delivery and Park, she was there by herself.

Still, a feeling of unease settled over her. She was acutely aware of her surroundings, the rough hospital sheet draped loosely over her, the faint musical *ting* from the faucet. Her muscles tensed.

She snapped open her eyes. Her mind didn't believe, or couldn't comprehend, what she saw.

Am I hallucinating?

Goosebumps prickled her flesh.

I have it—adenovirus B7x. It's an opportunistic infection altering my brain functioning.

Her mind whirred with possibilities as her body felt the sharp, cold shock of adrenaline pouring into her bloodstream.

Could it be an infectious lesion? Is it my optic nerve, inflamed by herpes simplex? An infectious mass compressing my temporal lobe? Maybe Aspergillus or another type of fungal ball? Any number of brain lesions can cause visual hallucinations.

She stayed perfectly still because Marcus was there, standing outside her room. He was unmoving, staring at her through the observation window.

What if I'm not hallucinating? What if this is real?

She sprang into action. As she scrambled out of bed, her toe caught on the metal safety railing and she almost fell. She landed heavily on one foot, hopping a few steps to get her balance. Breathing hard, she pushed her hair out of her face and looked toward the window.

He was gone, if he was ever there in the first place.

She rushed to the window and pressed her cheek against the cool glass, stretching to peer down the hallway. It was silent and dimly lit. She could just make out a door under a red exit sign slamming shut.

She tapped on the window to wake Park, then backed up, never taking her eyes off the window, and grabbed her phone. Her hands were shaking when she lifted it to her ear.

"What's going on?" he asked. "Are you okay?" He sounded breathless, as if he had been running, not awoken from a sound sleep.

A second later, his face appeared at the window. His hair was tousled and his face creased with sleep, but his eyes were calculating and alert.

Mallory's stricken gaze met Park's. "I'm okay but...I may have seen my ex-boyfriend, Marcus, standing at the window. I'm not sure."

"Did you see which way he went?" Park's voice was measured but with an undercurrent of urgency.

"I think I saw the stairwell door closing. He may have gone that way."

"What does he look like?"

"Medium height. Um, dark hair, wavy, on the longer side. Brown eyes. It looked like he was wearing a navy-blue sweater, or maybe black."

Park sprinted toward the stairwell.

Mallory sank onto the edge of her bed, trying to make sense of what had happened.

What would I do if a patient reported visual hallucinations?

She took a deep breath, taking stock of her situation. *Okay, I don't have a headache or nausea indicative of increased intracranial pressure.*

She took her temperature, blood pressure, and pulse, then tested what she could of her strength, light touch, reflexes, and proprioception.

My vitals are normal. There are no obvious neurologic deficits.

She used the flashlight function on her phone to check her eyes in the bathroom mirror. Her pupils were equal and reacted appropriately to light.

Cranial nerves appear intact. A brain lesion can't be ruled out without imaging, but my examination is reassuring. Also, I haven't had a sore throat or any signs of a viral URI.

She felt the tension in her shoulders lessen.

I think Marcus was here. He looked...different somehow—thinner, as if he had lost weight. But how could he possibly know where I am? He couldn't have followed me. I would have noticed him on the flight to Chicago.

Park appeared back at the window, shaking his head. He raised his phone to his ear and Mallory did the same.

"I couldn't find anyone matching that description. I must have missed him," Park said. "All right, start from the beginning. Tell me everything."

Mallory did. She told Park about his cheating and their subsequent breakup. She recounted the confrontation in the parking garage and her sense that something was seriously off about him.

"I thought I heard something and then...I had this strange sense that someone was watching me. I opened my eyes and, at first, I thought I was hallucinating, but the more I think about it, the more I believe he really was there." She shook her head in confusion. "But why? It just doesn't make sense. How could he know I was here, in this particular hospital room? Why would be come all this way and knowingly enter a quarantine zone?"

Park considered this, then asked, "Who knows you're here?"

"Just CDC colleagues. Also my sister and my parents. I don't think I told anyone my room number. Wait!" Mallory sucked in a breath, her hand flying to her forehead. "I think I know."

Park waited as Mallory tapped at her phone. After a moment, she pressed it back to her ear.

"I can't believe it. It didn't even cross my mind to disable it." She shook her head in disbelief.

"What?" Park asked.

"The Find My Friends app. This whole time, he has known *exactly* where I was." She shuddered. "I completely forgot I even had it."

"It's not like you haven't had other things on your mind. Did you turn it off?" Park asked.

"I just did," Mallory said. "And I deleted the app."

I can't believe I let him talk me into activating it in the first place. He convinced me it would be safer to know where I was given some of the rough areas I worked in.

"So, we know how he found you, but why did he come? What does he want from you?"

"I don't know," Mallory said softly.

"I hate to state the obvious, but this is not normal behavior. It's stalking." Park said.

Mallory nodded.

There was no other explanation for it, but she was having a hard time reconciling his behavior with the Marcus she knew—the person who made her laugh, whose touch she'd once craved.

She bit her bottom lip and closed her eyes, determined not to cry. She thought of their first Christmas together. It was late afternoon and her parents and Kate were scheduled to arrive any minute. The air was redolent with the smell of evergreen, a scent that she invariably associated with holidays and time spent with family.

The doorbell rang. Marcus hurried over, opening the door with enthusiasm.

There, holding a fruit cake wrapped in layers of plastic, was Mallory's middle-aged neighbor, Mrs. Wesley. Just as Mallory was about to greet her, Marcus threw his arms open and gave her a hug, all the while warmly wishing her a "Merry Christmas!" Mrs. Wesley's surprised expression was priceless.

When the door closed, Mallory dissolved into laugher. "You thought that was my mom!"

"Hey, they have the exact same hair. How was I to know? I've only met her that one time," he said, spreading his arms, palms up.

Tears poured down her cheeks as she continued to laugh helplessly. After a moment, Marcus joined in. When she accidentally snorted, they laughed so hard she thought she was going to wet her pants.

In hindsight, there may have been a few incidents that should have given her pause, like his insistence on the Find My Friends app.

When Marcus was four years old, his mother left his father for another man. Because she had a history of drug and alcohol abuse, his father was awarded primary custody of Marcus and his older brother. Although his mother had been sober for the last eight years, his relationship with her never recovered. Mallory had asked him about his childhood but, he had never given any indication that those memories still bothered him. He told Mallory he had come to accept that he would never have a close relationship with his mom.

To Mallory, he was the epitome of confidence. He had had a difficult childhood but, despite the odds, managed to excel in school and earn a scholarship to Cornell.

Did he hide his true self from me? Or did our break-up trigger some form of mental illness?

"We need to call the police and file a report, though, given the state of the city, I don't think we can expect much help right now," Park said, speaking quietly, as if to himself. "More importantly, we need to be extra vigilant. We need someone awake and alert at your door twenty-four hours a day."

"Park," Mallory said.

"I'll talk to my Staff Sergeant. I'm sure he can spare someone to be here while I get a few hours of shut-eye."

"Park," Mallory said, raising her voice slightly.

"What?" he asked, surprised.

"I think I should text him—see what he wants. Maybe if I tell him I was potentially exposed to the virus, it'll scare him off."

"I don't think that's a good idea. Wouldn't that be like rewarding bad behavior? It might just encourage him."

Mallory looked at him thoughtfully, frowning in concentration.

"All right. Well, promise me you won't make any decisions right now. It's the middle of the night. At least sleep on it," he said reasonably.

"I think I can do that," Mallory replied, giving him a small smile.

"Good," he said, nodding. "Now, you should get some sleep. I'll stay awake and keep watch, just in case."

"Park." She paused, waiting for him to meet her eyes through the glass. "Thank you."

"Don't mention it," he said, grinning.

Mallory couldn't help but notice his straight white teeth and appealing dimples. She had to admit it: He had a nice smile.

Chapter 59
Stroger Cook County Medical Center, Chicago
Day +46

M allory awoke the next morning feeling as if she had barely slept. Her limbs felt heavy, and she seemed sluggish. In her room, which was mostly dark, dull light was just beginning to seep in. She clicked on the TV, turning the volume low in case Park had fallen asleep, then felt her heart sink.

Martial law, not seen in America since the Civil War, had been declared in all five of the country's quarantine zones. The newscaster also described, in detail, a mandatory curfew, requiring all civilians to be indoors by six in the evening. Offenders would face immediate imprisonment.

Mallory clicked the volume up a few notches and leaned forward.

The screen was centered on a haggard-looking anchor, her airbrushed makeup unable to hide the worry lines framing her eyes.

When she spoke, her voice was strangely devoid of inflection, almost robotic. "...National Guard efforts are focused on enforcing the quarantine lines, though it's the large surface areas that are posing a significant challenge. Take a look."

An American topographical map filled the screen. Thick red lines indicated the quarantine zones.

"As you can see, the sheer number of square miles surrounding Chicago, New York, Atlanta, Southern California, and Las Vegas—and as of last night, Sacramento and Lake Tahoe—is staggering. According to National Guard chief General Salazar, maintaining these lines has required more manpower than initially predicted, leaving the U.S. with a substantial shortage of soldiers to fully enforce order within the quarantine zones.

"In many of these areas, most police, paramedics, and firefighters are reportedly not coming to work, choosing instead to protect their own families. Nearly all emergency calls are going unanswered.

"In a historic move, the President has ordered the mobilization of alternate military branches for domestic purposes, including the Army, Marines, and Air Force, in a desperate effort to lend support to local and state police."

The camera panned to a middle-aged male anchor in a slightly rumpled navy suit. His gaze was somewhere off-screen, as if he were thinking about something else.

After a long moment, he turned and looked at the camera, his voice only marginally more animated than his colleague's. Clearly, neither was happy to be there. "Thanks, Tamsin. Numbers provided by Commonwealth Edison show that approximately thirteen percent of Chicago residents are currently without power, and this percentage is increasing daily. The outages are due to fire damage and, with a drastically reduced staff, ComEd is unable to make the necessary repairs. There are no estimates as to when residents can expect power restored."

The anchor, his expression grim, continued. "What you are about to see is raw footage from the CNS news helicopter. This will be immediately followed by videos e-mailed to us from viewers around the Chicagoland area. Some may contain disturbing images and, as always with coverage of this crisis, viewer discretion is advised."

The first was of a raging industrial fire, the video shot from several thousand feet above. The enormous factory building was completely engulfed by thick black smoke. To Mallory, the fire somehow looked evil, alive. Once these images were exhausted, at least twenty blazes in different parts of the city were shown in quick succession.

The next set of videos had shaky, grainy images that gave them an amateur quality. All of the videos showed a variety of people fighting, shooting, and rioting. Mallory was shocked to see bodies lying crumpled in the street. Gone were the typical flashing red and blue lights and yellow crime-scene tape.

The anchor cleared his throat, straightening slightly in his chair. "As you may be aware, the CNS Chicago branch, located in the heart of the city, falls within the quarantine zone. Despite this, we are continuing to provide the public with the most up-to-date information available.

"Coming up, we have the official CDC recommendations on what you need to know about adenovirus B7x and how to avoid it. Grab a pen and paper because you'll want to write this down. These important guidelines will continue to be shown twice each hour."

Mallory threw back her covers and hurried to her computer, scanning news websites for coverage of Atlanta.

It was much the same as Chicago, although possibly not quite as bad. Excluding Southern California, where thousands were infected and dying, it seemed that the violence and disorder were posing much more of a threat to individual safety than the virus itself.

At least for now.

She fought the urge to text her immediate family, but knew everybody would still be asleep.

She began to pace in her room, running her fingers through her hair, a cry of frustration threatening to erupt. She bit down on her bottom lip, attempting to suppress the urge.

Her phone vibrated. She picked it up, not bothering to look at the screen.

"Mallory? Are you okay?" It was Park, his voice full of concern. "You seem...stressed." In one hand, he held a well-thumbed book. She couldn't make out the title.

Mallory realized she might well be looking a little unhinged, pacing in her room like a caged animal, her hair a mess of tangles.

She forced herself to close her eyes for a moment and say a brief, silent prayer.

"Yes, I'm fine. Just feeling helpless, stuck in here." She gestured half-heartedly around the room. "Not to mention the cabin fever. I never thought I'd miss fresh air this much. These windows don't even open."

"I know what might help," he said. "After breakfast, let's do some PT: push-ups, planks, burpees. Exercise will make us both feel better."

"That sounds good to me." She attempted a smile. "How are you, Park? Did you get some more sleep?"

"Nope. I wanted to keep watch. But one of my buddies is going to cover for a few hours tonight so I can do a little catch-up."

Mallory walked to the window. The sky was overcast. The weak dawn light and low clouds made the scene appear washed of all color. Most of the view was blocked by the original outpatient building. Only a small stretch of sidewalk and street was visible. She could see an empty blue bike rack and a plastic bag blowing in the wind.

"It's getting bad out there," she said, still gazing out the window.

"Yeah, it is," he acknowledged.

"Where's your family, Park?"

"South Carolina. My parents still live in the same rural house I grew up in," he said.

"I thought I detected a hint of a southern accent," Mallory said. "What about siblings?"

"Naw." He spread his arms and grinned, giving her an exaggerated wink. "Just me."

He dropped his hands, turning serious. "My parents are doing just fine, though. In fact, middle-of-nowhere South Carolina sounds like a pretty good place to be right now."

"Good point," Mallory agreed. "What book are you reading?" she asked, nodding to his hand.

He looked down. "Oh, *The Maze Runner*. It's not my usual thing, but it's actually pretty good. One of the nurses took pity on me and let me borrow it."

"Nice," Mallory replied. "Give me a few minutes to change. A workout might be just what the doctor ordered."

Mallory found that the exercise cleared her mind. Park was in excellent shape and she enjoyed the challenge of keeping up with him. During her workout, she was relieved to get a text from her mom letting her know that all was well.

After a quick shower, she settled in at her desk and called Rory.

"How you feeling?" he asked quickly.

"I'm good," she reassured him. "I have no symptoms, and my temperature remains normal."

"That's great news," he said, relieved.

"So, what's the plan for today? How can I help?" Mallory asked.

"We've managed to locate all of the primary contacts from the Northwestern cases. So far, so good. Could I forward you the list of secondary contacts?"

"Sure. Send it over." She stretched her slightly sore muscles. "The conference is still on for three today, right?"

"Yep, as far as I know," Rory replied.

"Anything new with your cases?" Mallory asked.

"Unfortunately, no. The first wave of patients to arrive at the ER have all succumbed to secondary infections. Just as in the FEMA camp—the infection is invariably fatal."

They talked for a couple more minutes, agreeing to touch base in a few hours.

Mallory sat for a moment, contemplating what Rory had said.

An infection is effectively a death sentence.

This is so vastly different from other viruses—a fatality rate of one hundred percent is unheard of. Ebola, without supportive care, has a fatality rate of fifty to ninety percent. Though this is considered comparatively high, ten to fifty out of every one hundred people survive.

For most viruses, a certain percentage of the population will either be able to mount an effective immune response or depend upon pre-existing protective antibodies—antibodies that have arisen from a prior exposure or vaccination.

Antibodies are secreted by plasma cells, plasmablasts, or memory B cells, which all arise from a type of B lymphocyte. The complete lack of lymphocytes precludes any type of antibody response.

There is only one way to stop adenovirus B7x—prevent the initial infection.

Chapter 60
Stroger Cook County Medical Center, Chicago
Day +46

Mallory's phone emitted a short, low buzz. In the semi-darkness, she groped for it blindly. It was a text from Park: "U awake?"

Instead of texting back, she called him.

"I thought your friend was supposed to relieve you," she said.

"He'll be here a bit later."

"Oh, good," she said, yawning. She leaned her back against the metal bed rails, drawing her knees toward her chest. "I'm exhausted but I can't fall asleep."

"I saw you tossing and turning," Park replied, suppressing his own yawn. "What's up?"

"Don't be mad, but I sent a text to Marcus today," she said quickly, cringing in anticipation of his response.

Park was silent a long moment. "What did he have to say?"

As if he had asked for an explanation, she continued, "I knew you would talk me out of it, so I just did it." She drew in a breath. "It didn't go well."

"What happened?" he asked with no hint of judgment.

Mallory pulled the white hospital sheet over her knees and stuffed a pillow behind her back.

"He's angry that I didn't give him a chance to talk. I think he believes that if he can just explain, everything will be fine—that I'll forgive him."

"Forgive him for what?" Park asked, then added quickly, "I mean, you don't have to tell me. It's none of my business."

"He cheated on me," Mallory said, her voice flat. "For me, that's a deal breaker."

"I'm sorry you had to go through that, Mallory," Park said softly.

She shrugged, unexpectedly struggling to keep her composure. She took a deep breath and continued, "Anyway, I unblocked him and sent him a text, asking him if he's in Chicago. He immediately sent me this flurry of texts, something like thirty, before I even replied to his first one." She shook her head.

"Did he admit to being here?" Park asked.

"No. He ignored my question."

"What else did he say?"

"Mostly, he just said we were meant to be together. At times, he seemed contrite. In other texts, he was angry, blaming me for what happened." Mallory switched the phone to her other ear, resting her chin on her knees. "In the end, I just came right out and told him I may have been exposed to the virus. I warned him that I'm in quarantine, and if he came here again, he would risk exposure."

"And?" Park prompted.

"Radio silence," she said, her face grim.

"Hmm. Well, maybe he'll leave you alone now," Park said, his voice lacking conviction.

"Maybe," Mallory said. "There's nothing we can do about it now. Let's talk about something else." She straightened her legs and leaned forward, lightly stretching her hamstrings. "I'm a little sore from our work-out this morning."

"Ahh, I wondered if you'd be able to handle it. I'll go easier on you next time," Park teased.

"I said *a little* sore. Trust me, I can handle anything you throw at me," she said, a smile in her voice.

They talked easily for the next twenty minutes, comparing stories of their stints in the military. After a while, Mallory's eyelids began to grow heavy. She laid her head down, pulling the sheets up to her chin.

She listened as Park recounted stories from basic training at Fort Jackson.

"It was the toughest ten weeks of my life. I wouldn't give back that time for anything, though," he said.

"I wouldn't either," Mallory said in a sleepy voice. "Thanks for staying up to chat."

"Anytime," Park said, stifling another yawn. "Get some sleep, Hayes."

"Night, Park."

As Mallory lay on the cusp of slumber, she thought back to her own basic training at Fort Benning in Georgia. Although no longer with the Army, she appreciated the skills and mental fortitude acquired during her time with the military. It prepared her well for the intense years of medical training.

She groaned inwardly. *I have never been as sick as I was in boot camp.* The crowded, uncomfortably close quarters and intense physical strain created a rich environment for infection.

In the haze of near sleep, her mind flashed to her first anxious days at Fort Benning. She hadn't known what to expect, and the high stress seared the experience into her memory.

On their first day after arrival, the new recruits were instructed to report to the medical bay. Mallory's nose wrinkled unconsciously as she remembered the smell of bleach that couldn't quite cover the smell of nervous sweat permeating the air.

The recruits were lined up and unceremoniously stuck with multiple needles, all the while given only the briefest of explanations. She recalled a small, flimsy paper cup of lukewarm water and a handful of pills pushed into her hands.

That was prior to medical school and well before I became familiar with vaccinations. What did they give us?

Thoughts of the FEMA camp medical center floated in and out of consciousness. Maybe it was the sight of Army BDUs in a medical setting, or maybe all Army medical centers looked the same, but the FEMA center strongly reminded her of Fort Benning's medical bay. In her relaxed state, she marveled again that none of the Army personnel at the FEMA camp caught adenovirus B7x. It was a miracle, especially because the isolation precautions were set in place *after* many of them had already cared for infected patients.

She felt an unexpected surge of emotion as she thought of Mindy. Prior to getting sick, her eyes had been full of life, reflecting both energy and vitality. After falling ill, Mindy and her personality seemed to diminish. She remembered her small body, lying pitifully on a cot, unresponsive to those around her. Mindy wasn't Army. She was a selfless community volunteer who had died in the line of fire.

Mallory eyes flew open. She sat up, her heart pounding.

Maybe the Army soldiers' survival wasn't a miracle after all.

In a flash, Mallory was at her computer, her fingers flying over the keys. She pulled up PubMed and began searching. After just a few minutes, she pushed back from her desk, tugging her fingers through her hair, thinking hard.

That's it. This might be the only way to stop adenovirus B7x in its tracks.

There was a slight, nearly imperceptible tremor in her fingers as she called Rory. Placing the phone on speaker, she began a brief email to Dr. Lee. She had just attached the article from PubMed when the screen blinked off.

She sat there, uncomprehending. In the back of her mind, she detected Rory's familiar voice coming from the phone on her desk—it was actually from voicemail.

The primal part of her brain recognized another sound—an urgent, insistent warning sound.

"Mallory!"

She flinched.

A shadow stood by her window, gesturing frantically to her. It was a person, backlit by a weak, flashing red light.

"Park?" she said, confused.

The smell of smoke tickled her nostrils. Finally, her brain seemed to comprehend what was going on around her. She grabbed her buzzing phone and pressed it to her ear.

"The power's out and there's a fire in the building. We need to get out. Now." Park's voice was calm but insistent. The fire alarm continued to sound an uncomfortably loud, shrill warning.

Mallory was already pulling on her protective gear. "You get out. I'm right behind you."

"Not without you. Come on!" he urged, now shouting through the glass. Mallory dropped her phone on the bed, needing the use of both hands.

"I can't risk exposing others. You go!" she yelled back.

"No."

"Then you'd better suit up. And you'll need to zip me."

With a fluid, practiced motion, Mallory first pulled on sterile gloves, then spent the next several long moments donning the rest of her PPE gear.

Immediately on opening the door, she was attacked by an acrid cloud of gray smoke, which was quickly filling the hall. Without speaking, Park zipped her, and they ran toward the dimly lit exit.

As they neared it, the smoke became so dense in spots that Mallory could barely make out Park's form in front of her. They dropped to a crouch.

Park leaned over and yelled, "Stay here! I'm going to check the stairwell!"

He vanished into the thick smoke. It surrounded him, swallowing him whole. In an almost detached way, Mallory noticed her heart rate ratchet up and her breathing come fast and shallow. She could barely see through the cloud of hot condensation on the inside of her visor. She coughed, swiveling her head desperately from side-to-side. She couldn't breathe. She saw only a faint, pulsating red glow in an endless sea of swirling smoke.

The sound of the alarm had become nearly unbearable. It blared angrily from somewhere directly above her, adding to her disorientation. She couldn't move, the claustrophobia from the smoke having paralyzed her. She felt hot tears on her cheeks as she sank to the ground.

Suddenly, Park was again at her side, his hand gently squeezing her shoulder. He spoke into her ear, his voice firm, "Breathe, Mallory. Take a deep breath. That's it."

He looked intently at her through his visor. "You're doing great. Keep taking those deep breaths. It's going to be all right."

Mallory nodded, coughed again, and stood. She was light-headed and her legs felt weak and shaky. Park latched his hand onto her arm, pulling her in the opposite direction. He shouted over his shoulder as they moved.

"That stairwell door was blisteringly hot; I think that's where the fire originated. There should be another exit this way."

They came to a set of double doors. Gray-white smoke slid from beneath it, swelling around their feet before rising. Park touched one of the doors with the back of his gloved hand. He jerked it back, sucking in his breath.

A look of concern briefly creased his features. "We need to find another way out."

They ducked into the nearest patient room, closing the door behind them. Nearly identical to Mallory's, it was empty and dark.

Mallory ran to the window, feeling along the sash with gloved hands. No latch. The window was fixed, non-operable.

She looked down through the glass. Three floors below them lay a sidewalk and a metal trash can, bolted to the concrete. Mallory scanned their surroundings for flashing lights, for any sign of help. The area looked deserted.

Park searched the room, looking for something with which to break the glass. His eyes settled on a plastic and metal chair. It looked to be around fifteen pounds, the heaviest moveable object they had.

"Stand back!" Park yelled.

Grunting, he swung the chair hard toward the window. The impact produced a spiderweb of cracks in the glass, but it didn't break.

Smoke had begun to seep in, twisting and curling beneath the door.

Park, his shirt damp with sweat, picked up the chair, throwing it again. Finally, on the third try, the tempered glass collapsed, rippling like a sheet toward the ground.

"Help me with the mattress," Mallory said, dragging it off the gurney. Park took it from her and hefted it up to the sill.

"Try to drop it straight down," Mallory instructed. "Keep it close to the building."

She didn't wait to see where it landed but rushed to the bed and ripped off the bedding. Using a double fisherman's knot her uncle had taught her, she tied the ends together. She didn't have anything with which to cut the fabric, so the length was limited to a sheet, mattress cover, and tightly

PARTICLES IN THE AIR

woven white blanket.

She tied one end to the bed's metal railing. They unlocked the wheels and pushed it under the window, dropping their makeshift rope over the side, then peered down.

Her heart sank. The rope was only about ten feet long, leaving a drop of around twenty feet. She looked behind her toward the door, wondering if she had time to run to another room for more sheets. Thick gray smoke flowed into the room, pushing its way in around the door seams. She could hear a muffled crackle from the hallway. The fire was close.

Park spoke quickly. "You go first. Get as far down the rope as you can. Push yourself about a foot to the right until you're over the mattress. Then let go."

Park helped her over the windowsill and held her arms until she had a solid grip. She painstakingly lowered herself, her arms quivering from the exertion. Sweat poured into her eyes and soaked her back. Her nitrile gloves squeaked, the fluid pooling in the impermeable plastic.

"Park, if something happens to me, you have to make sure Rory contacts the Army. They have a stockpile of adenoviral vaccines they give to recruits at basic training." Mallory was breathing hard, her words coming out in short gasps. "There are over one hundred thousand new recruits each year. If the vaccine is used strategically, we can contain this. You have to tell him."

As she spoke, she used her toes to inch along the brick until she was centered over the mattress.

"Nothing is going to happen to you," Park said firmly, almost angrily.

"Just promise me you'll tell Rory."

"I promise," Park said. "Now focus."

Her arms had begun to vibrate and jerk, the muscle fibers firing in rapid succession under the strain.

"Try to distribute your weight evenly! Land on your feet with your knees bent a little!" Park called.

She looked down, took a final deep breath, and let go.

T he fall was over in seconds. Mallory landed with a bone-jarring
thump. She felt her right foot connect with the mattress, and actually heard the snap before she felt it. A split second later, the
pain washed over her, taking her breath away.

The force of the fall caused her to half bounce, half roll off the mattress onto the concrete. She lay there for a few seconds, her mind unable
to comprehend anything but the pain.

Park.

She looked up. Park was already climbing down. His eyes followed
the progress of his hands, concentrating. He yelled without looking down,
"Mallory, talk to me! Are you hurt?"

Mallory could barely summon the breath to speak.

"I'm okay," she managed, "but I've twisted my ankle."

She forced herself into a sitting position. Because of her fall, the mattress had slid farther from the rope.

"Don't drop yet, Park," she called up to him.

Gritting her teeth against the pain, she awkwardly maneuvered the
mattress inch-by-inch.

Park didn't complain about her slow progress. He hung from the rope,
completely still. Gray smoke poured out of the open window above him.
Despite this, his face appeared neutral, composed.

"Good to go!" Mallory finally gasped. She checked her mask, pinch-
ing the metal nose piece to ensure there was a good seal.

Park glanced down once more and then let go. He landed squarely on the mattress, using the momentum of the fall to propel himself into a head-first safety roll. He ended on his feet and, without stopping, rushed toward Mallory.

He knelt beside her, reaching to examine her ankle.

"No, no. Don't touch me. I might be contagious," she said urgently, pointing to his torn nitrile gloves.

In fact, after learning that military recruits like herself received the adenovirus vaccination during basic training, Mallory thought there was a good chance she wasn't infected. However, vaccinations weren't one hundred percent effective, and didn't necessarily last for years, so she wasn't taking any chances.

Mallory probed her swollen ankle gingerly. The skin around the ankle was morphing into a deep purple and blue. There were no obvious bone deformities. If it was a fracture, it was a closed one.

"I'll be right back," Park said.

He jogged across the grassy courtyard, disappearing into the main doors of the hospital. The emergency room and surrounding hospital buildings seemed unaffected by the fire, but Mallory could feel heat radiating from the building next to her. A huge column of smoke disappeared into the air above.

I hope everyone is able to get out. The fire seems localized to the empty section we were in, at least for now. But where are the fire trucks? Surely, someone is coming. A huge hospital like this would be a priority.

The previously deserted sidewalks were now filled with dozens of people, indistinct figures bathed in moonlight. Many of them clutched cell phones, their apprehensive faces illuminated in the glow of their screens. Medical staff pushing patients in wheelchairs and in medical beds flowed from the blackened entrance, like creatures from a dark cave.

Park emerged less than a minute later, brandishing two pairs of clean gloves and a bottle of alcohol-based hand sanitizer. He spoke into his phone as he jogged toward her. As he neared Mallory, he ended the call, slipping the phone into his gown.

"Is it broken?"

"Either broken or sprained. Only an x-ray can tell for sure," she said grimly.

"There's an Army unit close by. They're on their way. ETA about eight minutes."

After pulling on gloves, he gently helped Mallory stand up. She winced but managed to balance herself on her left foot. Draping his arm around her shoulder, he led her around the hospital to the corner of Ogden Avenue and Harrison Street.

Park texted their location and lowered Mallory onto a bench to wait. After just a few minutes, a camouflaged Humvee screeched to a halt in front of them. With the help of Park, Mallory hobbled over, still unable to fully bear weight on her ankle.

As soon as Park shut the door, the Humvee got moving. Mallory looked behind her, relieved to finally see a lone fire truck, its horn blaring and strobe lights reflecting off the dark buildings, pull up in front of the hospital.

"Where to, sir?" a soldier sitting in the passenger seat asked. He held an assault rifle loosely in his hands.

Before Park could answer, Mallory spoke, "Northwestern Hospital." She clicked her seatbelt into place. "Do you know how to get there?"

Mallory was desperate to talk to Rory. She also knew her ankle need- ed medical attention; it was hard to concentrate on anything beyond the pain pulsating up her leg.

"Yes, ma'am. Born and raised in Chicago."

"Perfect. Thank you." Mallory closed her eyes and leaned back, finding it difficult to say more than a few words at a time.

Park turned to Mallory. "How far away is Northwestern? Are you going to be okay until we get there?" He snapped his fingers. "Wait. There should be a first-aid kit in here with ibuprofen in it." He leaned forward but Mallory stopped him.

"No need. I can't take off my mask." Mallory shifted her weight, looking for a comfortable position and somewhere, anywhere, to elevate her leg. She settled on the gunner's platform next to her.

"Without traffic, it's ten to fifteen minutes," she said between breaths, "and I'll be fine." Even through the fog of pain, she realized the absurdity of her statement about traffic. The streets of Chicago were completely deserted and dark. Even the Humvee had its headlights off.

Smart. Headlights could make us an easy target.

In downtown Chicago, even in the morning's early hours, there were always taxis looking for fares and Uber drivers idling as they waited for bar patrons.

Now, there were none.

The scene chilled her to her core. It looked like the end of the world. She saw ripped, overflowing bags of garbage, piled ten feet high in some areas. Red eyes winked at her in the scant light. A few of the garbage bags moved, the plastic rippling with rats or feral cats.

At least in this part of the city, people are following the rules of martial law and abiding by the curfew.

Mallory felt the pockets of her PPE suit, searching for her phone. Swearing under her breath, she realized she had left it at the hospital. If only she had grabbed it then. Without it, she felt strangely lost and even more disconnected.

"Park, you have Rory's number, right? Could you text him and let him know we're coming?"

"On it," he said, pulling out his phone.

As they neared the hospital, Mallory was relieved to see that the medical campus had power. As she exited the vehicle, Mallory explained how to disinfect the interior of the Humvee using a diluted aerosolized bleach solution. The two soldiers listened closely, obviously taking her instructions seriously.

After entering the doors of Northwestern Memorial, Mallory nearly burst into tears when she saw Rory, his hair mussed and scrubs wrinkled from sleep, hurriedly pushing a wheelchair toward them. She got into it gratefully. Rory and Park nodded to each other in greeting.

"Rory, I need to talk to you," she said, steeling her emotions.

Rory was already pushing her chair, charging toward the ER. "We need to get you pain medication and an x-ray."

"No, please wait," Mallory said earnestly, twisting to look at him. "This is more important. We need to call Dr. Lee—right away."

Rory slowed to a stop.

"What do you mean?" he asked, confused.

Mallory looked around, spotting a group of upholstered chairs. "Let's go over there. I'll explain everything."

Park and Rory quickly settled into chairs and turned toward her expectantly. Mallory saw Rory's eyes catch sight of her swollen and discolored ankle. He winced.

"Rory," she said, her voice slightly muffled by her mask. "In the FEMA camp, do you remember noticing that none of the Army medical personnel caught the virus?"

"Yes," he said, nodding. "I remember."

"Well, I think it was because, according to multiple articles I found, all Army recruits are immunized for adenovirus during basic training. Not only that, but they are immunized with serotypes 4 and 7, which by amazing luck or divine intervention, matches the serotype of adenovirus B7x—serotype 7."

Mallory leaned forward, excited and speaking quickly, her ankle a throbbing ache pushed to the back of her mind. "I can't believe I didn't realize it sooner. The Army has over a hundred thousand new recruits a year. They must have a huge supply of the vaccine.

"The best thing is, it's already proven safe and effective in humans. There's no need for testing. No need to wait months for mass production, either. It's available *right* now."

Rory looked stunned for a moment, uncomprehending. Then his face broke into a wide smile. "We can give it to select communities and groups, focusing on specific geographic locations to keep the virus from spreading. As more and more doses are manufactured over the coming weeks and months, everyone could eventually get it. It's all about the timing."

"Exactly. We have to be very strategic. We need to encircle the virus, contain it. We start with those at high risk, like health care providers and those living slightly outside the quarantine zones. Then, as more vaccine is produced, we give it to those within the zones, then the major cities, and so on.

"We also have a ready-made vaccine formula with prior research and production techniques—this will greatly speed up mass production. And, unlike most vaccines, this one is oral. There is no need to have trained medical personnel to administer shots. It also cuts down on the amount of supplies needed. Instead of syringes and alcohol wipes, you just take a pill with water.

"It's not a guarantee, but it could work. At the very least...it gives us hope. Well, it gives *me* hope. Maybe it will for the rest of the country too," Mallory said.

"You're brilliant, Mallory!" Rory said rather dramatically. "All right, here's the plan. Park, could you take Mallory to the ER? She's as white as a ghost. I've assigned an isolation room for her. The desk will let you know which one."

He turned toward Mallory. "The technicians are due to your room any minute for a portable x-ray." He stood up briskly, brushing his hands together. "I'll call Dr. Lee and the rest of the team—wake them up. We have work to do."

Mallory couldn't ignore the pain any longer. She barely managed a nod in response to Rory's words. The sharp pulsations of pain rushed over her. It was as if, after passing along her new-found knowledge to responsible others, her mind could finally and fully recognize the depth of her pain.

As directed, Park wheeled her to her assigned room. He was quiet, thoughtful.

As they approached her door, he asked, "You've taken the vaccine during basic training, right? I must have too."

"I can't say for sure but, yes, I think it's likely we both received it."

Park didn't say anything but squeezed her shoulder.

Mallory was first given pain medication. As her pain began to ebb, her muscles relaxed and her eyelids drooped—they felt too heavy to keep open. Through her lashes, she saw the familiar silhouette of Park outside her door, reading a book. Her eyes closed, and she faded into a deep, dreamless sleep.

Chapter 62
Northwestern Medical Center, Chicago
Day +47

When Mallory's eyes fluttered open, she was surprised to see an unfamiliar figure at the end of her bed.

"Ah, Sleeping Beauty awakes." The man was in full protective gear, hovering near her right ankle. He was short, with unruly gray hair sticking haphazardly out from his cap. He looked to be over sixty and maintained a wiry, compact frame. His words were adorned with a thick Eastern European accent.

She raised a questioning eyebrow, trying to push herself up in bed.

"Sorry, I couldn't resist. I'm Dr. Stojanovic, Orthopedics. Do you want the good news or the bad news first?"

"Umm, bad?" Mallory raised the head of the bed, trying to push away her disorientation. She glanced toward her door, hoping to catch sight of Park or Rory.

"You've sustained a pilon fracture. It seems you fell from a pretty good height. Which means, in a nutshell, you'll likely need surgery. But…" He raised his hand. "It depends how displaced the bones are. We need a CT scan to determine that."

"What's the good news?"

"The good news is that you have me," he said, giving her a wink. "The other orthopedic doctors on staff here? Ha!" he huffed. "Cowards. No one wanted to take your case because you're in isolation. They didn't want to risk exposure."

Mallory blinked at him, unsure what to say. She really couldn't blame them. "Well, thanks for being willing to help me. If it's any consolation, I think the chances are low that I'm infected. To be safe, we should wait until my isolation course is over before any surgical procedures."

"Hmm, let's see what the CT scan shows first. Then we'll talk again." He waggled a finger at her, as if admonishing a child. "In the meantime, no weight on your ankle."

"Got it," she replied.

With a final wink, he left the room as suddenly as he'd appeared.

Mallory was still processing the news about her ankle when another PPE-clad figure appeared at her door.

"May I come in?" Park asked.

"Of course. Come in. Sit down," Mallory said. "Any word from Rory?"

"I haven't gotten many details, but he said things are moving along nicely. They already have thousands of crates of the vaccine—in pill form—en route to the areas surrounding the quarantine zones. You were right—it's estimated the Army has nearly a quarter of a million doses just sitting there, ready to go."

Mallory briefly closed her eyes, relief flooding her body.

"The CDC also has gotten word of the vaccine out to the major media outlets. Hopefully, that'll quell some of the panic."

"I hope so," Mallory agreed.

"There's something I don't understand," Park said. "How is it the Army docs at the FEMA camp didn't realize the potential of the adenovirus vaccines they had?"

"I wondered the same thing," Mallory said. "According to the articles I found on Google, the Army actually stopped giving new recruits the adenovirus vaccine from 1999-2011. Dr. Walsh, a man in his forties, was the doctor in charge of the FEMA camp medical center. Given his age, he probably went through Basic Training during the twelve-year window of time when, for whatever reason, the vaccine wasn't given.

"I think it's likely he never received the vaccine and was completely unaware of its existence." Mallory shrugged. "Plus, the Army isn't the best at communicating things on an individual level. I certainly don't remember what vaccinations were given to me at boot camp."

"Yeah, that makes sense," Park said. "The only thing I remember was getting stuck multiple times. I don't recall swallowing any pills." He scratched his head. "Are you going to contact Fort Benning to check your vaccination record?" Park asked.

"Yes, but it won't really change anything. I still have to remain in isolation here. And, with my ankle, I won't be going anywhere for a while. What about you? Did you call Fort Jackson?"

"Yep, while you were sleeping. I received it."

"That's great news." Mallory smiled. "Do you know if Rory was able to get a hold of Kate? He should have her number."

"Yep. He let her know you're okay. They're still hunkered down in the basement but doing fine."

Mallory felt her shoulders relax slightly. At least for now, her family was safe.

"Park," Mallory said, her voice catching. "Thanks for saving me back there. The smoke, the darkness—well, I'm severely claustrophobic. If you hadn't been there...I don't know what would have happened."

"Anyone would have done the same." He waved off her words. "You were amazing, thinking on your feet, tying the sheets to make a ladder and using the mattress."

"I'm not sure about that, but thank you. Did everyone make it out okay?"

"According to the news, no deaths reported so far. The few firefighters who responded were apparently able to contain it to the section of the building we were in."

Mallory nodded.

Park cleared his throat. "Speaking of the fire…"

His serious tone made Mallory's muscles tense involuntarily.

"What about it?" she asked. She shifted in the bed. The dull, persistent ache in her ankle made it difficult to get comfortable.

"In my mind, it's too much of a coincidence that there were two separate fires blocking the only two exits from your hallway."

Mallory's blood ran cold. "You think it was set deliberately?"

Last night felt like a half-remembered nightmare, blurry and unreal. She hadn't had time to process, let alone question, the events surrounding the fire. Her mind had been consumed with relaying the information she had learned about the vaccine.

"Yes," he said quietly, letting his words sink in.

Either she, or Park, had been targeted. There was only one person she knew of who might want to harm her.

"Marcus?" she asked, feeling numb.

"I don't have any proof but, as I said, I don't believe in coincidences. The only reason I'm even bringing it up right now is because I want you to be careful." He leaned forward in his chair. "Either I, or one of my Guard buddies, will be outside your door at all times."

Mallory's stomach twisted and bile rose in her throat. She swallowed it down, her chest burning.

This is too much. Someone I once loved tried to burn me alive? How could I have misjudged him that terribly?

Her ankle throbbed in earnest. The pain medication was definitely wearing off. She pushed a button on her patient-controlled analgesia.

"I need to rest," Mallory said quietly.

Park looked surprised at the abrupt change in subject but recovered quickly. He rose to his feet. "Of course. Let me know if you need anything."

Mallory rolled over and pulled up her blanket, temporarily blocking out the world.

Mallory's CT showed significant bone displacement, meaning it was a bad injury that required complicated surgery and a minimum six-month recovery time. Dr. Stojanovic wanted to take her to the OR immediately but Mallory refused. She was determined to wait until her quarantine was over.

The next ten days passed by in a haze of medication, boredom, and restless nights—excluding late afternoons.

Starting at noon each day, Mallory braced herself against the pain and held off on taking her medications, determined to remain lucid for the daily three o'clock conference calls.

Tanvi and Nat remained in California, strategically seeing to the vaccine administration to health care workers and at-risk groups. They amassed a large team and continued to painstakingly trace contacts of contacts, liberally vaccinating those in proximity. Rory, and the other teams spread across the country, used a similar approach by administering the vaccine to secondary and tertiary contacts.

Since initiation of the vaccination efforts, no new cases were reported beyond the quarantine lines. The number of new cases within the zones decreased dramatically and eventually dwindled to the single digits. On the twelfth day of Mallory's isolation, the number of new infection cases had dropped to zero. For those within the zones, the countdown to the end of the quarantine had begun.

Medical labs across the United States were called upon for help. Overnight, scientists had a proven formulation, which allowed immediate synthesis of the vaccine in large amounts. Instead of six weeks, the CDC announced that the first batch of newly manufactured oral vaccinations would be ready in two weeks.

Mallory followed the news closely. She noticed a subtle shift in public sentiment occur. Desperation gradually turned to optimism and, as the threat of the virus lessened, evolved into outrage at the individuals responsible. This unquenchable thirst for retribution, expressed by every American interviewed, bridged socioeconomic status, race, and political affiliation. For the first time in years, the country was united in a common goal.

When news broke of a possible terrorist link to Malmö, Sweden, tens of thousands of soldiers were deployed to the area, and hundreds of investigators and journalists flooded the city. Unconfirmed rumors, spread on social media, described covert terrorist cells embedded in the legal immigrant population of Malmö.

Mallory's family remained in self-imposed isolation, waiting for the quarantine to be lifted. Five days after the virus hit Atlanta, the Hayes residence lost power. Each morning, they would alternately turn on one of their three phones and check in with Mallory.

On the last hour of the last day of her quarantine, Rory, Park and the floor nurses surprised Mallory with balloons, flowers, and a cake sporting fourteen candles—one for each day of her isolation. When she blew them out, her tiny, overflowing room filled with cheers and applause. She felt her spirits lift a little.

Park had promised to wheel her outside for a walk around the hospital grounds before Dr. Stojanovic rushed her to surgery.

It's going to feel amazing to breathe clean, fresh air again.

She looked over at Park, who was talking animatedly with Dr. Stojanovic. As Mallory watched, the doctor broke into booming laughter—loud and uninhibited. Park grinned back at him.

Park's dimpled smile sent off a fluttering in her chest, like a split-second of a free-fall. She couldn't deny it—she was attracted to him, and not just because he was good-looking.

It's his quiet, unassuming confidence. It's also something else—something I can't quite define.

After what happened with Marcus, she couldn't imagine dating again. A large part of her felt as if she would be content to remain single forever. Life would be simpler. She would be able to dedicate all her time to work.

As if sensing Mallory's gaze, Park looked over, still smiling. His face softened at the sight of her.

Well...forever is a long time.

She knew she wouldn't be ready for a relationship anytime soon, but maybe, just maybe, Park would be patient enough to wait for her.

Epilogue

The first person Detective Ben Marshall called when he left Barakah's interview room was an old college buddy, Tommy Dubois, a consulting analyst for the FBI. He relayed the main points of Barakah's story. Once Tommy was convinced it wasn't a prank, he thanked Ben and quickly ended the call.

Tommy scrambled to his creaky roll-top desk. Pushing papers and receipts aside, he frantically searched for the phone number of an acquaintance at Homeland Security. After a few minutes, he found it tucked under a stack of utility bills. He puffed out a relieved breath and dialed.

A team of five agents arrived at the Second District Station within forty minutes of Detective Marshall's initial call.

Barakah was immediately whisked off to parts unknown.

In the days that followed, Imam Khatib fought hard to see Barakah, threatening to leak his story to the public. When it was clear the Imam wasn't going to back down, the FBI decided to disclose certain details of Barakah's situation in an effort to appease him. The Imam agreed to keep the information confidential under threat of prosecution. After weeks of uncertainty, he eventually learned, on a superficial level, what became of his young charge.

Barakah was officially classified as a confidential informant. He was now safe and protected, living with a foster family in a semi-rural setting. In four years, at the age of eighteen, he would be given a new identity—a new life in the country he almost played a part in crippling.

For his own safety, his involvement in the outbreak wouldn't be released to the public. Only a select few agents would know where he was taken. Most Americans wouldn't even know he existed.

∿∿

Barakah told the authorities everything he could recall about Sameer, Fakir, and the mosque where it all began. This information led them to Fatima, who was interrogated relentlessly by FBI and Swedish investigators. After forty-eight long hours, she succumbed to the intense pressure and led the police to Erik's abandoned condominium and the rented lab space they had used.

Over time, forensic scientists were able to piece together the steps taken to engineer the virus.

When investigators learned of Erik's death, they immediately interviewed Ada. She was more than eager to tell her story, to let the world know about the pure evil that was Dr. Erik Lindgren.

She hired a savvy PR manager and gave a series of back-to-back television interviews. Seemingly overnight, Ada Ekstrom became a household name. Her painting, *Eye of a Monster,* sold for nineteen million kroner.

∿∿

Two days after the fire at Cook County Hospital, Marcus' body was found floating among plastic bottles and other bits of debris in the Chicago River. He had no identification and was initially listed as John Doe #371.

City officials didn't have the investigative manpower to perform crime scene analysis for the thousands of bodies found in Chicago during the time of the quarantine. The absence of obvious injury made his case a low priority. His body remained in the cold chamber of the morgue for several months before it came up for autopsy.

The medical examiner's report cited significant water saturation in the pulmonary tissues. Investigators noted his shirt had caught on a rusting steel post, four hundred yards downstream of the Michigan Avenue DuSable Bridge. The cause of death was listed as hypoxemia due to aspiration and ruled a suicide.

John Doe #371 was formally identified by name five months after his death, when a private investigator hired by Marcus' older brother, Jack, tracked him to Chicago.

The investigator, after coming up empty on hospital listings and accident reports, made a visit to the Chicago ME's office. He viewed hundreds of John Doe autopsy photographs before he matched #371 to a family picture of Marcus.

∿∿∿

The Cook County Hospital fire was deemed an act of arson after large amounts of accelerant were found at the scene. Who the arsonist is remains undetermined by authorities.

∿∿∿

A somewhat agitated Sameer rolled over in bed, kicking off the Egyptian cotton sheets. He couldn't sleep. His mind was full, whirring with excitement at the events of the last several weeks.

Fakir's snores reverberated from the room next door, making sleep even more elusive. Sameer pulled his pillow over his head, trying to drown out the noise. It was no use; he wasn't going back to sleep tonight. Sighing, he reached for his phone: 4:12 AM.

His bare feet slapped the cool travertine tiles as he made his way to the en suite bathroom for water. Just as the glass was about to touch his lips, he froze.

The sound of a faint groan floated through the large house.

What was that? A door opening?

Sameer stood completely still, his senses on high alert. He carefully set down his glass and gripped the marble countertop, straining to hear.

Other than the distant waves of the Mediterranean Sea and the ongoing snoring from Fakir's room, silence dominated the Moroccan-style private residence.

The house was owned by one of seven oil sheiks who had funded the viral release. Sameer and Fakir had become celebrated heroes in their small circle of devout Muslims. Although Sameer was secretly disappointed the virus didn't result in a higher number of infidel deaths, he was outwardly satisfied. He knew he'd earned a place in Paradise for his work in the war against the Great Satan.

The vacation retreat, used for mere weeks a year by its owner, provided an unlikely hiding place. Sameer couldn't help but luxuriate in the central courtyard with its reflective pool enclosed by three stories of open-air balconies. The house was perched high on the Algerian coastline in the town of Tipaza, isolated from Western intelligence.

When he heard no further sound, Sameer relaxed and picked up his glass. As he gulped, he heard a *thwump* from the direction of Fakir's room. The snoring ceased abruptly, cut off mid-exhalation.

Was that...a silencer?

Sameer instinctively dropped into a crouch and scooted until he was flush with the wall. He rotated his head to peer into the master bedroom.

Hidden among the shadows, the Navy Seals moved in a fluid, seamless motion. They separated like water, flanking each side of the hallway, their night-vision goggles giving them the appearance of giant, creeping insects.

Sameer saw nothing in the near-complete darkness. Still clutching the glass, he half-crawled, half-walked like a spider in the direction of his night stand.

How could they have found us? It's not possible. But if I can just make it to my gun—

Thwump.

Acknowledgments

A huge thank-you to my amazing family: Josh, Brennan, and Claire Podjasek, Chris Petschke, Dr. Adam Petschke, Angie Petschke, Nate Petschke, Rachael Petschke, June Podjasek, Joe Podjasek, Lindsey Podjasek, Jason Podjasek, Justin Podjasek and Dr. Melody Hrubes.

Likewise to my co-workers and friends: Dr. Valeria Simon, Melissa Vick, Carolyne Koffenberger, Bruce Bortz, Dr. Rama Jager, Dr. Shefali Samant, Kristie Ruchala, Dr. Sujan Patel, Dr. Gerald Volcheck, Dr. James Li, Dr. Miguel Park, Dr. John Hagan, Dr. Young Juhn, Dr. Joseph Butterfield, Dr. Martha Hartz, Dr. Avni Joshi, Dr. Anupama Ravi, Dr. Matthew Rank, Dr. Hirohito Kita, Mary McDonnell, Kimberly Erikson, Alejandra (Aly) Martinez, and Kathleen Wallish.

About The Author

Jenna Podjasek, MD, is an allergist/immunologist who trained at Mayo Clinic in Rochester, Minnesota.

She lives with her husband, two children, and numerous pets in the suburbs of Chicago, Illinois.

Particles in the Air is her first novel.

Follow Dr. Podjasek on Twitter @JennaPodjasek or visit her at JennaPodjasek.com.